Time Rider
WILDERTREK

JACK-KING.com

Time Rider - Wildertrek / Jack King
1st Edition Paperback: September 2014
ISBN 13: 978-1-940676-06-7

Editor: Amy Nedrow
Interior Design: Susan Veach
Cover Design: Richard Turylo

Upcoming books by Jack King:
Time Rider - Red Attack
Quest for the Middle Kingdom - Tribulation

Readers may contact Jack King at:
www.Jack-King.com

Printed in the United States of America

Published by Charles River Press, LLC
www.CharlesRiverPress.com

Dedication

To everyone, everywhere, for whom history is a living, breathing adventure into the past.

Acknowledgements

To those who gave me encouragement in the writing of my first novel, huge thanks; an itch finally scratched after more than a decade of procrastination.

CONTENTS

Chapter One
ANOTHER BAD DAY

As he passed by in the crowded hallway, the tall blond headed teen spotted his prey. He sped up, leaned in to the left and slammed his shoulder roughly into the back of the unsuspecting student, bouncing the other boy's forehead off the metal wall.

There was a clanging smack. The boy's books fell to the floor.

"Oops. Sorry about that."

The big kid grinned evilly and his lanky buddy guffawed stupidly at the smaller boy. "Honest, Cockrell, I didn't see you standing there." He threw his arms outward in a teasing query. "What? Are you trying to make it with your locker now? Why don't you get a real date?"

Brent Hasselbunt stuck his touting face closer in. The other boy's eyes were watering from the nasty blow. He turned to face the bully, holding his aching head between his hands. Brent shoved the boy in the chest. "Answer me, Cockrell. You're trying to hump your locker?"

The boy moved his feet and put up his hands in a martial arts posture. Brent just laughed and backed out of reach. "Catch you later, COCK-rell," emphasizing the first syllable.

Big Brent shot the kid one last scathing look. Then he and his pal, Mike Nelson, a starting tight end on the school football team, hurried off to second period class, still laughing.

On either side of him, little Sammie Johnson and Bobby Oldham looked at each other and shook their heads. Bobby mouthed the words to Sammie, "TJ's dead meat," before turning to go.

Bending over, TJ Cockrell put his hands on his knees and winced. He closed his eyes with the pain. His stomach was nauseous, and he felt really, really bad all over. Weak-kneed, he wobbled his way toward the next class.

"Tege, Tege! Hold up!" Down the hall, his two pals caught up with him. They hadn't seen the episode with Brent, but they could tell by TJ's grimace that something was going down.

"Brent slammed my face into the locker," he explained.

"Man, what a wuss he is. I bet if he ever had to fight a bigger dude, he'd be a real coward. Bullies always are," David sagely said.

As TJ's two best friends, David Beam and Robert

Whitlock showed appropriate concern as they shuffled along between classes. "Ouch, my head is *really* throbbing now," he moaned and gingerly massaged his forehead with his fingertips.

TJ's horrible headache had started when he saw his English test score in first period. Getting his head busted against the locker wall only made it that much worse.

Bad days last forever, and this was no exception. As the school day dragged on, his only got worse when Melissa Carter and her gang of the popular girls and lookers-on made fun of him during lunch. Her loud, exaggerated southern drawl could be heard over most of the normal din of the cafeteria.

"Oh my gawd, TJ," she laughed, with hands on hips in front of the growing crowd. "You can't make a decent grade. Somebody told me you actually failed the English test. That test was so easy." She had only gotten a C+ on the same exam.

Amy Bradbury chimed in, "TJ, you're not good enough to make any sports team here: basketball, football, baseball, track, or anything." She shook her pretty head for emphasis and checked off a litany of organizations. "Math club, chess club, band, orchestra, Spanish club, computer club, Honor Society, newspaper…hey, you don't fit in anywhere. You do such crappy work on everything in school. TJ, you put out so much junk that maybe you would fit in with Mr. Hobbs, the janitor."

"Yeah, and you can't get a date to save your life," cruelly added Jessica Smith. She glanced over at the two boys standing behind TJ. "To top it off, you don't have any cool friends."

The girls snickered together. Melissa smirked and shot one last zinger at the deflated-looking figure slumped in front of her. "What can you do, TJ? Really? You're just bush league. Your dad is famous and he's smart. But, boy, you're just hopeless."

Melissa laughed again and strolled away, surrounded by her clique of beautiful people. TJ's two totally uncool friends, David and Robert, stood by him in awkward silence with food trays in their hands.

"Gosh, that was embarrassing," muttered David, as the three boys watched the three girls and their friends leave the cafeteria. "They're all so Hollywood. Like they're so much better than everyone else."

"You think?" said TJ, frowning and rubbing his temple. He could taste bile coming up from his stomach.

Ever since Mom and Dad divorced, my life has become nothing but failure and rejection, he thought, bitterly. Little pains punctuated every now and then with big pains. Watching Melissa and her posse glide away into their coolness of being, his head pounded even more.

TJ knew of other kids whose parents were divorced. But their family circumstances were not nearly as strained as his. It had been World War III at his house, during and after the *event*. It felt like his mom and dad were now mortal enemies, with him and his sister caught in the middle as helpless pawns in a brutal game of power chess.

Robert said his father was gone three weeks out of every month as a national sales director. Robert's father drank too much and his parents quarreled a lot when the dad was home. But at least his family stayed together. Of the three friends, David's situation was by far the happiest. His parents seemed to get along very well, did everything as a family, and even went to church every Sunday.

For TJ, the afternoon turned out to be just as lousy as the morning.

After the last period, TJ had to go back to his English class to do yet another remedial extra credit assignment. "You know what to do," Ms. Primm snapped at him when he slouched into the room. "You have your textbook with you?"

"Yes," he replied.

"Well, get busy then."

The teacher's drab clothes, heavy black horn-rimmed glasses, and sour disposition made Ms. Primm a real favorite with all the students.

"Yeah, well, you're ugly, mean, and nobody likes you either. Not a good combination," he said under his breath, taking care to sit down in a last row seat. Getting as far away as possible from the teacher didn't help him. Ms. Primm gave TJ eagle-eye looks from her cluttered desk as she caught up on her paperwork. Her constant staring made him feel all the more a failure.

TJ tried to ignore her continued glances as he muddled through the boring assignment as best he could.

"Okay, I'm done," he announced an hour later. It seemed like three hours.

The teacher glared up at him. "Young man, you have got to start paying attention in class, taking better notes, and studying harder for your tests."

"Yes, ma'am," he meekly replied, handing in his work.

Finally free, he walked down the long hallway, his head down, stomach burning, temples throbbing, hands thrust deep in his pockets. TJ turned left, and went out the door to wait beside the big gymnasium.

Standing outside, he could faintly hear the coach's loud, gruff voice coming from inside the building. It made him sadder still to hear Coach because he had desperately wanted to make the basketball team.

Wistfully, he stood close to the wall and listened carefully to pick up every word. "Son, if you don't start hustling, everybody on this team, including you, is gonna be doing fifteen extra minutes. You better start movin' your lazy butt! You got that?" Inside the gym, Coach Lemmons, his beefy face contorted with rage, was yelling at David Beam.

"I want you to hustle! Every minute, every play,

every drill! One hundred ten percent! No letup. That means all of you! If you don't *put out* in practice, you won't be able to *put out* at game time. The better conditioned you are *now*, the better you'll play when it *really counts.*" The burly coach clapped his hands sharply as he spoke to emphasize his points.

The rest of the squad glared at the offender as they halted for a few precious moments and caught their collective breath. Sweat dripped off every part of their bodies in the over-heated gym.

TJ learned firsthand that Coach's power dribbling sprints were legendary killers when he tried out for the team.

You stood at one end of a basketball court. You dribbled at break-neck speed to the nearest foul line and returned to the baseline, then dribbled to half court and returned again, then dribbled to the farthest foul line and returned, then dribbled the entire length of the court, and returned to the baseline from which you started.

You got to do it, over and over, until you felt as if your lungs would burst, or you'd cramp up, or you'd puke your guts out in the shower afterwards.

The Coach's fury fell on any player who dawdled during any of his demanding drills.

Finally, the torture was over; basketball practice was done. The exhausted squad limped into the shower room. Soon, team members began trickling out of the gym.

Outside, TJ stood waiting for Robert and David to emerge. Unfortunately for him, the motley trio of big bad Brent, who was one of the starting forwards, and his two sidekicks, Stephen Monroe, the starting point guard, and gangly Johnny Utley, the starting center, stumbled out first.

There seemed to be no end to TJ's horrible day.

Brent's eyes lit up with mischief as soon as he spotted TJ. "Hey, looka here," he nudged Stephen in the side and cackled.

"Not again," TJ said with a voice of resignation.

Wasn't this morning enough for you, Brent? He watched with foreboding as the three players approached him. Now, his head pounded like tsunami waves on a naked shoreline. His stomach heaved and he felt like he was going to throw up any minute.

"Dang. Whatta we got here? Look, it's the Ninja Master!" Brent shouted out.

"Hey, Cockrell, you done making out with your locker? You can do mine if you want. We'll watch."

The bully made a beeline for TJ, while his pals crowded around on either side and whooped with glee. Brent turned and looked to the left and the right with an exaggerated motion. "That's too bad, son. Just too bad. I guess Robert and David aren't here to protect you this time, are they?" he jeered.

"Show us your moves, Mr. Black Belt!" he taunted TJ.

Brent reached out to shove TJ. The smaller boy instinctively blocked the blow. "Oh, you're so slick, Cockrell, with your little martial arts crap." Brent retaliated with his other hand when his first was blocked. He went into a fake martial arts pose. TJ instinctively crouched into a proper stance. Brent began circling around him, waiting for an opening.

"Come on. Come on, show us what you got." said Brent, his face drawn into a sneer.

"Dude, you think you're tough, huh?" Brent lashed out now with his long arms, attempting to humiliate his foe by irritating cuffs to the face. TJ knocked away the thrusting hands, finding it very difficult to maneuver with his heavy winter coat on. He knew he'd have to take it off to properly fight, but he couldn't exactly ask Brent to stop while he unburdened himself. Besides, ever since his parents' divorce, his confidence in all areas of life had plummeted. He wasn't sure he could beat Brent in a real fight.

He felt a thrill of fear as the big bully paced around him, continuing his barrage of slaps. Breathing hard in the cold air, TJ managed to parry each of the strikes until finally one of Brent's long dirty fingernails caught his cheek and drew blood. Seeing the scratch, the bully intensified his attack.

Brent faked another move, and TJ, frustrated, countered with a desperate roundhouse kick that almost connected. Big Brent ducked his head back just in time. Instinctively, he reached out and grabbed at TJ's tennis shoe as it whizzed a fraction of an inch by his chin. The larger boy barely caught it, but held on and yanked as hard as he could.

TJ's leg twisted along with his body. He lost his balance and tumbled to the ground, landing rough on his side. He felt blood dripping down his face.

Brent and his buddies howled with derision. Robert and David came out of the gym with some other players. "Hey! What's going on?" Robert saw the crumpled figure of his friend and rushed to the scene, as David, Martin King and Troy Carson followed behind.

"Brent, you butt-hole, leave him alone. Give it a rest, why don't you?" Robert knelt down by TJ's side. "Why don't you pick on somebody your own size?" Robert glared up at his towering teammate.

"Aw, Robert, you're as lame as he is," Brent sniggered. "You're nothing but a big sissy, too. Just like your pal lying on the ground." Brent shoved Robert playfully in the side of his head, and punched the air above Robert with a mock one-two combination. He slapped his two tagalongs on the back. With witnesses standing around, Brent decided not to press his advantage.

He sneered at TJ one last time and said, "Let's get

out of here. 'Till next time, Cockrell." The three players strutted away, their harsh laugher echoing off the grey-brick gym walls in the deepening winter afternoon.

Robert stared at the backs of the departing boys.

"Brent is such a punk. He tries to bully a lot of the smaller second team players, too, when coach isn't looking. One of these days somebody bigger or tougher or meaner--"

"Yeah, he hassles me during practice all the time." Martin said darkly.

David added, "My dad went to school with his dad all the way through high school and said he was the exact same way."

"Tege, are you okay? You know you've got some blood on your face?" Robert leaned forward, inspecting his friend's cut.

TJ wiped it off with the back of hand. "He only scratched me. Like a girl."

David and Troy helped TJ up. David said, "Tege, it's my bad. We would have gotten out quicker but coach wanted to chew me out some more." His handsome face frowned. "Robert's right. Brent's a total jerk. He even picks on me a little bit in practice." David shook his head. "Look, forget about him."

David repeated, "I'm really sorry this happened."

"Are you sure you're not hurt?" Robert asked.

"No. I'm fine. Just another great day in the

wonderful life of Mr. Cool," he said. TJ stood and dusted off his clothes. He wiped his face one last time as the little red spot began drying up.

Minutes later, David's mom drove up. Mrs. Beam always took Robert, TJ, and her son home after basketball practice. The three boys said bye to Martin and Troy.

As they got into the car and Mrs. Beam drove away, TJ rubbed at the sore spot on his cheek and mentally tallied all of the bad things crammed into one day. *Could things get any worse? Another failing test grade. Dad will love that. It's not that I didn't try, my mind just went blank. It's hard to learn anything because Ms. Primm is so frigging boring. And then Melissa Carter and her gang of witches have to go and humiliate me at lunch in front of practically the whole student body. She's not a nice girl. Yeah, she's pretty, but she's so vain and she's just mean. And that punk Brent twice in one day. Oh, crap! I've got that stupid history exam tomorrow. My favorite subject.*

TJ hated class, hated studying, hated tests, and hated how lonely he was. He was barely passing in most of his classes, listless and unmotivated. Robert and David were his only close friends. Bullies such as Brent made school even more miserable for him. When he didn't make the basketball team, he was really bummed out. He loved almost all sports and round-ball in particular. He was a loser with the girls at an age when many boys were getting their first real girlfriends and dating.

And then there was his mom and dad getting divorced. Six months later, his grief was still raw.

Some days, it seemed like an acid cloud of hopelessness hovered over him, paralyzing him as soon as he woke up. Despair embedded in the very marrow of his bones, a black barrier that prevented anything good from happening, any meager success, any light at the end of the proverbial tunnel. On really bad days, like today, his inner strength was exhausted, leaving him mind-numbingly weak.

"My life totally sucks," TJ muttered under his breath.

He glared out of the car window, drumming his fingers on the door handle, his headache pounding away. He kept blinking his eyes with the pain. Meanwhile, David and Robert babbled on about how tough practice was, and about the upcoming game Friday night with Madison, their primary district rival. "Yeah, they won over Richardson by 16 points. They're going to be hard to beat," exclaimed Robert.

Lost in his own dark thoughts, TJ didn't hear them.

He was still in a royal funk when Mrs. Beam pulled up to his house. As they sped away, he stood in front of the door for the longest time, still seething over his day. Finally, he went inside.

TJ slammed the heavy door shut. He wished he could smash the innocent door to bits. *I want to break something, anything.* He let out a gigantic sigh of frustration and scowled.

TJ listened for the annoying beep of the alarm keypad by the garage door. If it were on, he would have to race to the back to turn the darn noise off. Everything and everybody got under his skin, these days.

He heard no beep. That meant Dora must still be there.

TJ wearily took off his winter coat and hung it up in the entry hall closet. He trudged into the spacious living room and stood staring blankly at the kitchen area.

"Dora!" he yelled out. "Dora, are you here?"

"TJ?" A warm, grandmotherly voice came from the back of the kitchen. Dora stepped out. She smiled broadly at the boy as she put on her scarf and gloves.

"I'm running a little late today."

Dora smiled again at the dejected-looking boy in front of her. "I made you a peanut butter and jelly sandwich. It's on the table. You can pour yourself a glass of milk."

She peered at his face. "Did you know you have a red spot on your cheek, honey?"

"Yeah, I know. It's nothing."

Dora was a stout, late middle-aged woman, with liberal streaks of gray in her thinning brownish hair. She had five grandkids. One of them, a boy, was just a couple of years younger than TJ. Her husband, Charley, had died two years ago. As a recent widow, she had become a housekeeper to stay busy and earn extra money.

"I'm running a little late today, sugar," she repeated. "Tell your father to leave all the dirty clothes in a pile by the washer the next time I come."

She gave TJ another compassionate look. "Did you have an okay day at school?"

TJ just nodded his head.

"You sure you're all right?" She remained unconvinced.

Dora reached out and turned his head to the side so she could examine the red spot. It didn't escape her attention either that the boy had a grimace on his face.

"I'm fine," the boy said.

"Are you sure?"

"I have a bad headache, that's all," he partially lied, "nothing else."

"Well, there's aspirin up in the medicine cabinet in the hallway bathroom. You be sure to take a couple of tablets with your milk, okay?"

"Sure."

She smiled kindly at the boy again. "Well, I've got to go."

The old lady looked at him with concern. For the hundredth time she said, "I know things will get better. I know it's been hard on you since, you know."

"Well, bye, sweetie."

"Bye," he muttered.

After she left, the big house echoed with the stillness.

The day had turned out to be one of his worst days ever. TJ felt strangely disembodied. He couldn't think straight, couldn't think what to do next. His aching head didn't help.

Finally, he went to the kitchen phone and dialed his dad's office number. "Dad always wants to know the minute I get home," he complained. The voice recorder came on.

"Dad, TJ. I'm here. I'll get busy studying and doing my homework tonight. I promise. See you when you get home," he said.

That terrible aching loneliness in his stomach that came and went flared up once more.

The hardest part of his world was his broken family. TJ missed his mom and sister Natalie, more than he let on. The feeling of helplessness and loss settled deep within. Outwardly, he tried to put on a composed front, but some days his insides were jelly.

Weeknights were the toughest.

Dora came in two or three times a week to clean the house and left before TJ got home from school. And since Robert and David both made the Highland Hill basketball team and had practice nearly every afternoon, TJ was alone at school until their practice was over. At least until theater started up again for him. He had tried out for the b-ball team too but had just missed the cut.

For the last six months, every school night was the same dreary routine. His dad would came home from the university tired, distracted, but putting on a smile while feigning interest in TJ's school activities, as he started dinner.

"What do you want to eat tonight?" Dad would always ask. "How was your day?" TJ always lied. His days stunk, and the last thing he needed was his dad trying to cheer him up.

His father could easily have afforded to go out every night, or pay Dora extra to prepare and refrigerate meals for them to microwave later. However, Dad was a decent cook. It helped to relieve his stress. Plus, he valued the personal time with TJ.

The phone rang. It was his father. He said, "TJ, I'm going to be late, maybe an hour and a half, maybe two. Can you hold off eating until I get home? Remember, I was going to make homemade spaghetti with meatballs tonight. It's your favorite!"

TJ responded, "I'm all right, Dad. I can wait until you get home."

"Okay, son. I'll see you between seven-thirty and eight." He paused and added, "I love you."

As animated as his Dad could be in lecturing a class

of upper level college students, he tended to be restrained in family communication.

TJ hesitated in his reply. Not until Mom and Nat were gone away in the aftermath of divorce did his Dad start saying he loved his son like that. TJ's voice constricted. It felt plain weird saying it to his father. Besides, the Cockrells had never been very good at expressing love and affection. After an uncomfortable pause, TJ finally mumbled the words, "I love you, too," just to satisfy his Dad.

TJ hung up the phone. And he hung down his head.

Chapter Two
THE PROFESSOR'S SON

TJ wished his father would stop trying so hard. He knew his dad felt guilty about the divorce and wanted to make it up to his son. *He's overcompensating again*, was a refrain that ran through TJ's mind far too often.

Mere silence was better than their strained attempts at dinner conversation. His father wouldn't give it a rest at their last meal. "Dad, I don't mean to be rude or anything, but I really don't want to hear about what happened at the university today."

"Well, we can talk about your day at school then," his father persisted.

"And I really don't want to talk about things at school." TJ stopped picking at his food and looked up at his father's hopeful face. "Please."

Being left alone on the weekends was better than their forced father-son outings that, despite his dad's best intentions, usually resulted in frustrating or even humiliating situations for TJ.

Jack King

Only last Friday night, his father had insisted on accompanying TJ to the away basketball game, a contest in which Highland Hill had to overcome a mighty deficit to win at the buzzer. His father had royally embarrassed him by trying to act cool in front of TJ's friends during and after the game. "Tege, that game was *The Bomb*! The way we came back to tag the other team was way harsh." No, his Dad wasn't his buddy and didn't know how to be, and his use of jargon from his teenage years made his attempts almost intolerable.

"Sheesh, it was pathetic." TJ shook his head and groaned at the memory.

There was nothing to talk about over dinner anyway, he thought, *because nothing exciting ever happens at our school that's worth repeating.* But then, he caught himself, and remembered a few episodes. *Hey, how about the time Ms. Vanessa, the elderly chief cook, caught her apron, and then some of the food in the serving trays, on fire? The old bat tried to use the fire extinguisher but couldn't make it work, so she grabbed what she thought was boiling water off one of the stoves. It turned out to be hot grease that splattered everywhere and spread the fire.*

Two fire trucks had pulled into the parking lot, and five burly firemen stormed into the cafeteria as the fire swept across the buffet station from the grease-soaked fish sticks to the neighboring apple crisp to Amy White's sleeve and Dan Thomas' shirt-front.

"Move out of the way! Give us room!" the lead fireman had shouted.

Or, he thought again. *How about the time Ms. Primm got food poisoning from the tuna salad she brought from home?*

Ms. Primm had rushed into the teacher's lounge to retrieve her coat to go home. As she flung open the door, her stricken face blanched even whiter and her eyes bulged in sudden shock.

"What the--Joe? Eve? What the devil's going on in here? Stop it! Stop it, I say. Get out of there. Right now!" she shouted hoarsely, just before she lost her lunch right in front of them. A little vomit actually splattered right on Mrs. Miller's exposed backside, TJ had heard.

What grouchy Ms. Primm saw was Mr. Longley, the track coach, passionately entangled with Mrs. Miller, the Spanish teacher, and the winter coats inside the big closet in the lounge. As the spinster Ms. Primm had no private life of her own, she was the biggest tattletale in the school and soon everybody knew including the insanely jealous, quick-tempered, redheaded Mrs. Longley who beat the lanky coach black and blue for his indiscretion.

That caused a bit of juicy gossip. The boy smirked.

No, few things at school captured TJ's attention.

The one subject TJ cared about was drama. Everything else was boring, or confusing, or both. Mr.

Jack King

Mackey, the Highland Hill teacher, always kept the drama class and after-school theater productions lively with his creative flair and willingness to try new things.

"A whole new realm is open to you in theater," he would say. "Be whatever you want, whatever you dream, whatever you imagine."

"Let yourself go! Always dream *big!*" Mr. Mackey would boom out encouragement in that large compelling voice of his.

Mr. Mackey had done off-Broadway theater, and had even been an understudy once on a major Broadway play in his mid-twenties.

The man was an unstoppable fountain of positive energy. He believed in his kids and they knew it. Several of his star students had gone on to professional careers in acting after graduating from college; one girl had actually made it to Hollywood and gotten bit speaking roles in several moderately successful chick flicks.

Whatever. At least Mr. Mackey and drama class makes me feel a little better about myself and my life. Theater is about the only thing in school I'm good at, he brooded.

But it would be another week until they had tryouts for their last play of the year. And rehearsal wouldn't start until after Spring Break.

TJ walked into the kitchen and sat down at the table. He picked up one sandwich half and started munching on it, then unenthusiastically worked his way through the second piece. He had no real appetite. "Darn it. I forgot to pour myself some milk or take the aspirin." He grabbed a glass out of the cabinet.

Finishing his snack, TJ went back into the living room. He flopped down on the plush, darkly beige and tapestry-patterned couch. Out of sheer habit, he grabbed the TV remote off the end table and hit the button.

The anchorman's face was serious as he read from the teleprompter and his notes, "Good evening and welcome to Channel 11 six o'clock news. At the top of the hour, the police report that late last night, another deadly home intrusion attack occurred in the 4700 block of Forest Lane. This is the fourth such incident of violent breaking and entering happening in north and northwest Knoxville suburbs within the last three weeks."

TJ scowled at the TV. He rubbed his forehead as he watched.

The anchorman continued, "The authorities have dubbed the robbers the Al-Qaida Burglars, because seemingly they kill without mercy.

"This latest home robbery resulted in the death of a man, aged 46, and severe injuries to the man's son, aged 20. The victims were each shot twice. The son was also stabbed multiple times after attempting to fight off the intruders. He remains in critical condition at Presbyterian West Hospital. Investigators say the robbers took jewelry, cash, silverware, a TV, smaller electronic items, computers, and other easily carried valuables. Police are placing extra patrols throughout the northern areas of the city, and caution all residents to--"

TJ abruptly turned the set off. *That's the last thing I want to hear. More negative stuff.* Things were bad enough for him.

After staring dully at the rich mahogany-paneled walls of the living room, TJ blew a raspberry in frustration and forced himself to get up.

The phone rang again. It was Natalie. Sometimes she called TJ at the end of his school day before their mom came home from work. "Hey, Tege. This is your sweet little sister who loves her big brother *very* much."

"I know. Me, too." He grinned a little bit in spite of himself. "Gosh, it's good to hear your voice. I've had a terrible day, Nat." He sighed. "And of course, I can't tell Dad. You know how he always over-reacts and tries to give me old-folk advice. He doesn't have a clue what it's like at school."

"So tell me what happened, Tege."

He screwed up his face. "Let's see. In first period, I found out I failed my English test. I missed passing by one stupid point, can you believe it? Because of that, I had to go back and do extra-credit work after school with dear Ms. Primm. Before second period started, that jerk-ass Brent smashed my head into the locker. Claims it was an accident. *Sure* it was. And, oh, you've heard me mention

Melissa Carter, Amy Bradbury, and Jessica Smith before, right?"

"Yeah, and also Mark Bolger told me his big brother said they were the biggest skanks in Highland Hill."

"Well, they each took turns insulting me in front of the packed cafeteria at lunch. It was really humiliating. Then, after doing the extra-credit for Primm, I had to wait for David and Robert outside the gym, and who comes out first but Brent and two of his punk friends. We almost got into it for real. He scratched my face and made me fall down hard. I know he's not going to stop until I fight him."

TJ could hear the concern in Natalie's reply. "Tege, stay away from him. Don't get pushed into a fight. He's so much bigger than you. He's an ape. Please be careful."

"Right, like I enjoy getting pounded. So far, it's just been shoving and slapping, but Nat, I'm afraid I can't keep avoiding him. He's aching to start something, and I don't know if I can beat him. He's quick for his size and he can hit hard."

There was a pause at the other end of the line. "Tege, I think Mom just got home. I better jump off. Send me an email tonight. And watch yourself, okay?"

"I will. Bye."

"Bye."

Instead of lifting his spirits, Natalie's phone call renewed TJ's inner ache. Thoroughly dejected now, he dragged his feet over the lush tan carpet to the other side of the room and climbed the stairs to the bedroom level. His room was the second on the right.

Reaching inside, TJ flipped on the light.

He went past his carefully made-up bed to the cluttered wooden desk and dropped his textbooks by the computer. He turned it on and also powered up the Xbox 360 console lying next to it.

"Let me see. Do I want to play a couple games of *Gears of War* before I start studying?" he pondered.

"No, not tonight," he decided. "I've *got* to get busy. I *have* to pass that test tomorrow, no matter what it takes."

Once he started playing, he knew he would spend hours, right up until he heard the door to the garage open and close, announcing Dad was home. He had that history exam tomorrow, and a five page history paper due next week. He was not close to being prepared for the test. And he didn't have a clue what topic he was going to write for the essay.

"Dad's going to be disappointed, major league, if I screw up another history test or louse up that paper," he scolded himself.

Of all the school subjects that he cared little about, history was perhaps the least interesting. Perplexing, because his father was an award-winning historian, but TJ, his son, thought it was incredibly unexciting and useless.

However, he wasn't ready to start studying. Not just yet.

TJ went out of the doorway and down the hall to Natalie's old room. He stepped inside and switched on the light there.

He stared into the room.

Except for clothes and a few other personal items demanded by Mom in the divorce settlement, his sister's bedroom, with its jade-green textured walls and top border of pink ribbons and roses, looked exactly the way it did seven months ago.

He studied the ivory-colored antique twin beds occupying one side, the antique off-white dresser, and the light-blue bookshelf filled with an assortment of snow shaker souvenirs from Mom and Dad's many business and academic trips.

"Nat loved getting those shakers," TJ fondly recalled, as he stared at the little bubble-shaped city.

He also saw the two sturdy Koa wood chests of drawers from Hawaii, the still carefully arranged work desk, the tiny table lamps, and the cloistered remnant of Nat's collection of American Girls and accessories maintained in pristine innocence on the floor next to the closet.

Dad had insisted on keeping half of the doll collection along with all the snow shakers. They reminded him of Nat. Even more so, now that he only got to see his daughter once a month, at the most.

Mom had accepted a new job when the divorce was finalized, and she had moved to Atlanta with Natalie.

"You're going to make new friends. Atlanta is a really neat place to live. You'll have your own TV, computer, games. Whatever you want," she had bribed Natalie to cheer her up.

Prior to the divorce, Mom had wanted to redo Nat's room, including new furnishings. Afterwards, she just didn't take any of the existing furniture, and so the room kept most of its old contents.

"We're just going to start all over with everything," she had told Natalie. "You get to pick your new bed and all of the new furniture for your room. In whatever colors you want. Everything new," she enthused.

TJ walked over and opened the closet door.

He must have glanced inside a gazillion times since Natalie was gone. He saw the same three dingy basketballs on the closet floor--one blue, one green, one orange--that he had won as game prizes for Natalie by making free throws at the smallish, rigged midway basketball hoops at the previous three state fairs. The green one was almost flat.

He remembered how tightly Nat had hugged him each time he had presented her a prize from the fair.

"Cheap ass basketballs," he smirked. And yet

Natalie was always happy with any gift he gave her, no matter how inexpensive. She loved her big brother.

Next to the basketballs stood the old, brown rocking bear with its head torn, stuffing bulging out like exposed brains. "Hello, Mr. Bear," he said. Mom and Dad had specially ordered the bear from the Charlotte, NC Neiman Marcus for Nat's third Christmas.

He picked at the bear head stuffing as he stood there.

TJ shut the closet and closed his eyes tight. He felt the pressure of the past six months building up like a teapot ready to explode. Finally, he blinked open and peered at his reflection in the full-length mirror. His light brown hair was unkempt from the strong winter wind outside. His brown eyes looked morosely back at his own image: skinny, average height or slightly above for fourteen years of age, he knew he was surprisingly strong despite his lack of visible muscle.

Natalie, on the other hand, had beautiful brunette hair and the dazzling emerald-green eyes of her mother. His sister was very pretty and very self-assured for a girl nine years old, about to be ten.

Unlike many brothers and sisters, he and Natalie had become close friends from the very instant she could walk and talk. Wise beyond her years, she had a grown-up's way of speaking and considering things. And she carefully analyzed things before she spoke, just as her mom did.

But she also had a lot of Grandma Cockrell in her. Grandma C was a real people person: a genuine encourager, a great listener, and a gifted homespun psychologist. She knew when something was wrong and always found a way to make dark situations look brighter. And she doted on every one of her grandkids.

In countless situations, he had said to his sister, "Nat, can we talk?" And she had always listened with that composed, reassuring demeanor of hers. "Tege, is anything wrong?" she would ask.

Nat was there for him whenever he needed the confidential advice of a friend who wouldn't squeal or repeat secrets. Robert and David were his buddies, but Robert's got a big mouth, and David's a big joker--a mischievous prankster who never misses the chance to one-up both of his pals.

No, Nat was the only one he could trust with his secrets. Plus, she was smarter. Smarter in many ways than he, and he had enough sense to know it.

And now she was gone. The ache started up again as he gazed around her room.

"Damn it!" he screamed at the top of his lungs into the empty space.

He knew he shouldn't swear, but the pain was awful. He wanted to scream again. Tears welled up in his eyes as he moaned, "Natalie, I miss you so much. I wish we were still together as a family even if Mom and Dad didn't get along."

The telephone rang again. TJ wiped his eyes with his sleeve and stepped out of Nat's room to answer the hallway phone mounted on the wall.

"H-Hullo?" His voice was thick with the emotion of his outburst, but he didn't care to hide it.

It was Dad. "Tege," he hesitated. "You don't sound good. Are you getting sick?" TJ didn't respond and his father continued. "Tege, this is very important. One of my graduate assistants told me there was another robbery and shooting in the north side of town, not that far from where we live. She said this attack happened after midnight, like the other ones."

The professor hesitated. "I'm sorry I can't get home any earlier tonight. However, I should be there before eight. Listen, if you hear anything suspicious outside the house, anything at all, you call 911.

"Okay? Promise me!"

"Sure, Dad, sure. I promise." There was a long pause. "And I'm not sick."

"That's good." There was another pause. "I know you'll be fine. And I know you'll be safe. I'll see you later. Love you." Click.

The phone call had distracted him. TJ stood in the hall, uncertain. Now, he was definitely not in the mood to begin studying right away. He stumbled away from his room and down the hall in the direction of his dad's bedroom.

His brow knitted as he thought about his mom and dad's breakup.

He knew the trouble between his parents had gotten worse, much worse, after his dad came out with his two best-selling history books. Dad had been given tenure, a promotion to full professor, a huge raise, and some type of Historical Association Award for Scholarly Distinction, TJ remembered. That was three years ago.

Before that, his Mom had worked as a CPA and had been promoted several times at a large accounting firm. His mom was very good at her job. At the same time, his dad had worked hard, too. But he had remained an underpaid, under-published, unappreciated assistant professor of nineteenth-century American History at the prestigious University of the South in Knoxville.

His dad had been lucky to get on staff as a lowly junior professor twelve years ago. He was a mediocre historian until four and a half years ago. Then he produced his amazing book, *Pickett's Charge at Gettysburg*, followed by the equally brilliant *Hornet's Nest at Shiloh* three and a half years ago, for which Professor Cockrell received a Pulitzer Prize nomination. Even TJ understood that the Pulitzer was something special.

What transpired after the Pulitzer nomination was almost as incredible as the books themselves.

Mr. Cockrell had gone on a whirlwind lecture tour to some of the leading universities, was chosen to speak at eminent academic events, and was given a fantastic raise, promotion and award, all in the span of six months following the publication of his last book.

His Department Chair had told him at the time, "Vern, I know you'll continue to make the department proud. Frankly, I'm amazed, but genuinely pleased, at how much you've progressed as a serious historian. We've got our eye on you!"

Something miraculous had happened to Vern Cockrell. Something had transformed him from merely average, to widely acclaimed, professorial rock star status, virtually overnight.

Both kids knew that Vern and Anne Cockrell had fought for years, no matter how much the parents tried to hide their increasing arguments. In truth, mostly Mrs. Cockrell had fought. Vern Cockrell usually listened with resentment and silence. Once Mr. Cockrell began making a much better salary and could afford a generous settlement, including alimony and child support, Anne Cockrell, decided it was time to go.

Dad repeated to TJ afterwards most of what happened.

His mom had marched into his dad's study eleven

and half months ago with a grim, determined expression on her otherwise very pretty face.

"I'm not sure I love you anymore, Vern," she declared as she stood in front of him. After further reflection, she stated emphatically, "No, make that I'm *sure* I don't love you anymore."

"You're a nice guy, a good father, a smart person. You've never been unreasonable or unkind, I suppose. But we've grown too far *apart*." She emphasized the last word with finality.

She looked down at him with an almost clinical attitude or like an accountant analyzing financial numbers in company books.

"I've tried to make a go of it. I really have. I've tried to keep the feeling alive." She folded her arms. "But I can't pretend anymore. And I can't go on like this."

She took an impatient breath. "Vern, we've both been unhappy, I know I have, for most of the last six or seven years, perhaps longer."

Her husband sighed dejectedly. "Maybe we could go to marriage counseling." In his heart, he knew it was a lost cause.

She ignored his comment and shrugged.

"Vern, it's too late for that. Years, too late." She shook her pretty head and continued.

"Let's face it. We don't get along anymore," she said, indifferently. "Except for the kids, there's nothing between us now. No passion. No romance. No fun. Our marriage has become a total grind."

She had made up her mind. "Let's call it quits and move on with our separate lives. Agreed?" Anne waited for him to respond. "Look, I don't want to continue to be this unhappy."

She continued to look down at him as he stared, defeated, off into space. She said, "Life's too short. I'm still relatively young and I want to enjoy myself and my relationships."

Professor Cockrell had sat there in his chair, dazed with a wounded puppy dog expression on his face.

Anne had demanded an immediate divorce, no compromise, no counseling, no reconciliation. She simply wanted out, regardless of the cost or family pain. The legal proceedings and wrangling had taken less than five months to the bittersweet conclusion. And that was that.

Now, TJ and his father were left alone, together.

Chapter Three
A LONG KEPT SECRET

For the first three months after his mother and sister moved to Atlanta, TJ had run up big landline phone, cell and text messaging charges, contacting Nat over the tiniest incidents and needs. His dad had allowed TJ leeway, until the outrageous long distance phone and wireless bills forced him to put a stop to it.

"Tege, I know you miss Nat and want to talk to her. I miss her, too. But you *must* cut down on your phone calls and texting," his father had demanded. With his big promotion and raises of the past few years, the professor was not hurting for money even after a costly divorce, but he was still very frugal.

Thereafter, TJ was restricted to emails and instant messages, which he did almost every night, until recently. His little sister looked forward to their chats and was almost always available for him to unload his day.

Lately though, chatting with Nat was not enough to unburden him. Too much crap had been stacking up in his life. *I feel like I'm trapped with no escape and no real hope.*

TJ entered his Dad's bedroom. His father had a big formal workroom in the converted den downstairs, but TJ preferred the compactness of his Dad's smaller study area sequestered in the left wing of the master bedroom.

TJ went to the small office desk, rolled away the cushioned leather barrel-back, and sat down. He leaned into the softness of the chair. TJ slid his hand over the gleaming desktop, touching the smooth cool surface of the elegant veneer finish. "Good old desk," he said.

He'd always liked the feel of it, even as a little boy.

Dad kept the left hand drawer of this particular desk locked at all times. And he had done so ever since he began work on his two acclaimed books. He had the lone key; even TJ's mother had not been allowed to open it.

About four years ago, there was one really weird situation having to do with things locked up in his parents' bedroom, TJ recalled. His mom had used a few days of vacation and taken Natalie to visit Grandpa and Grandma Cockrell. After school and basketball practice was over, TJ had gone to David's for supper and didn't get home until nearly nine o'clock. He didn't see his father anywhere downstairs, so he looked upstairs.

He found the door to his parents' master bedroom locked, which he thought odd because Mom wasn't there. *It's never locked unless Mom is home*, he remembered.

Despite TJ's sporadic door knocking and calling his name over the next hour, his father didn't answer or come out of the room. After watching TV a bit, TJ began to be a little bit worried.

Maybe he's not asleep. Maybe something is actually wrong with him, he thought. The car was in the garage, so Dad had to be somewhere in the house.

"Dad, what are you *doing* in there? Are you okay?" He spoke into the door.

"Dad. Dad. *Dad!* Can you hear me?" Now he was yelling.

"*Wake up!*" At this point, he actually pounded on the door. "If you don't come out soon, I'm calling someone," he fumed and worried at the same time.

He couldn't concentrate on watching his favorite shows until he knew his father was all right.

Fifteen minutes later, TJ had his finger on the wall phone in the upstairs hallway, ready to dial 911, when Mr. Cockrell finally opened the bedroom door and stumbled out into the long hallway.

His dad had seemed strangely dazed and distracted. His eyes were glazed and had a faraway look in them. He turned to TJ, and mumbled, "I'm here, son. I'm back. I'm not hurt." He ran both hands through his hair and took a deep breath. "Everything's fine now."

His words made absolutely no sense to TJ.

TJ had monitored his father for the rest of the evening.

Now, TJ peered down at the desk. His mouth opened in total surprise. "I don't believe it. After all these years."

The left drawer was not only unlocked, it was slightly ajar; making it obvious even to the undiscerning eye it was unsecured. TJ was drawn like a magnet to open it further. His curiosity burned within him.

What's inside that Dad keeps locked up?

He had asked himself that dozens of times through the years. Something of immense importance, he was sure. Dad didn't bother to hide his credit cards, miscellaneous cash, or other obvious valuables from his son. He trusted TJ to leave his things alone.

Yet the left-hand drawer of the small desk in his father's bedroom was especially different and intriguing. Its mystique had gradually built up through the years until it had become the mother of all secrets in his estimation.

Dad had, until tonight, kept its secret and its accompanying key safe from prying eyes and hands, even from Mom's.

TJ remembered exactly when all this secrecy started. When he was younger, in the months leading up to Christmas, he used to sneak into Mom and Dad's bedroom to prowl for bought, but still unwrapped, presents. When the opportunity arose, he would always tell his younger sister, "Come on, Nat. Mom and Dad are both out of the house. Let's go see if we can find what they got us for Christmas." He didn't care that he was destroying his sister's belief in Santa Claus.

The last holiday he did this was early November of the Christmas Nat got her first set of pink roller skates. Natalie was four and half years old then. For the first time ever, the desk was locked tight that night when he pulled on it looking for smaller hidden gifts.

"Darn it, it's locked up," he had whispered to little Nat who was standing close by his side, wide-eyed, watching her big brother yank again and again on the little drawer.

It had stayed shut the next four occasions he invaded the master bedroom in his continued search for concealed Christmas treasure.

He stopped snooping for presents the year after that. Nevertheless, out of sheer curiosity, he had continued to periodically pull on the little desk drawer to see if it was locked, whenever the mood hit him.

The desk had remained locked since then. Until now.

TJ eyed the left hand drawer with apprehension and desire.

He was both nervous and excited. *I shouldn't open it.* His dad had been able to trust him as he had gotten older, and especially now that it was just the two of them at home.

"Perhaps there's nothing inside now," he reasoned. "Perhaps Dad has already removed its secret, and that's why it unlocked."

TJ struggled with himself. *I really should return to my room and study for my history test.* He barely had a passing grade in the class and the semester wasn't even half over. His last exam was a disaster, and he wasn't remotely ready for tomorrow.

History had always been a particular problem for TJ, all the dates, facts, names, events, battles, and places. Everything jumbled in his mind, much like the hodge-podge of colors that ran together in Nat's old kindergarten drawings.

His dad, on the other hand, loved history. The professor liked studying, writing, and teaching about it.

Vern Cockrell had even persuaded his young wife, Anne, to allow him to name their firstborn son after two noted Confederate generals. "We'll call his first name Thomas after Thomas Jonathan "Stonewall" Jackson. And his middle name will be James after James Ewell Brown "Jeb" Stuart," he had said, enthusiastically.

In deference to his father, TJ had read a small, self-assigned section from each of the professor's two bestselling publications. TJ had found the narratives surprisingly entertaining and memorable. For some reason, the facts from his dad's books seemed far easier to retain than the boring stuff found in his history textbook.

"Dad, your books are awesome. I really mean it. They're pretty simple to follow along, too. I totally understood the parts I read," he had liberally praised his father. "Did you know you're a very good writer?" he had teased.

"Thank you very much, son. That means a lot coming from you," his father had replied.

TJ had selected, read, and reported to his dad on a couple of chapters from each work early last fall, as part of his ongoing attempts to cheer his father up in the months after the painful divorce.

TJ glanced down once more at the partly open drawer.

"What would be the harm in peeking," he asked aloud. "After all, I'm not stealing anything. And I didn't force it open."

Maybe what was in there was no longer so valuable to Dad.

"There had to be a reason why, after all this time, it was unlocked today," TJ spoke to himself. "I'll just take a quick look. If there's anything still in there, I can put it back when I'm done, push the drawer the way it was, and get started on studying," he rationalized. "Dad will never know anything."

He wavered briefly. Then he made up his mind.

His hand was shaking as he reached down. He slowly pulled the drawer open and cautiously peered inside as if there were a ticking bomb hidden within.

"Dang it."

After years of curiosity, this was a disappointment. A stack of old paper clippings of various sizes lay in the drawer. TJ could tell the clippings must have been taken from different books, magazines, and newspapers of various kinds.

He gently lifted up the fragile stack. Underneath was a green book with a blank front cover. There was nothing written on it.

TJ's mouth formed a round circle of puzzlement and his eyebrows rose up.

It was baffling, a mystery to TJ, but now that he had finally opened the desk he might as well check everything out. Turning his full attention to the stack, TJ pulled out the topmost clipping and began to read it.

"An historical tour de force, stunning in its gruesome but realistic depiction of the savageries of war. The scenes of battle, bloodshed and hand-to-hand fighting are equally disturbing and compelling. This is one of the best Civil War novels of the last three decades."

New York Times

He gently picked up the next slightly yellowed clipping:

"A morbidly fascinating chronicle, as gripping as anything ever written about battle conditions in the annals of the Civil War. It's as if the author were an omnipresent participant in the day-to-day conflict."
The Chattanooga Times

TJ picked up another and read:

"Beautifully written. Exposes the brutality of war and the human suffering of the Civil War soldier as never before. I highly recommend *Hornet's Nest at Shiloh* to every serious student of the Civil War era."
Publishers Weekly

He read one more:

"*Pickett's Charge at Gettysburg* is vivid storytelling. One hears the cacophony of constant musket fire, the unnerving whine of artillery balls, the cries of agony as brave men on both sides are hit and fall. One literally feels the white heat of the battlefield. A truly superb history."
The Charlotte Observer

TJ counted through the stack. There were close to 30 clippings. He set them aside, then signed and frowned. "So this is it? Dad's big secret? Gosh, what a letdown."

Over the last five years, he had remained so fascinated with that locked desk in the master bedroom, only to find it contained nothing more than press clippings and a small, untitled book.

Nevertheless, reading some of the reviews made TJ even more painfully aware. Now that Mom and Nat were gone, all his Dad had left was his job and his son. History was so important to him. *Dad has done really well since his last two books*, TJ thought proudly. He knew it would mean a lot to his father if he began liking and excelling at history, too.

"I *can* do it. I can get good in history, too!" TJ exclaimed with fierce determination.

"It will make Dad happy if I start doing better in history," he reasoned. "I *am* going to make a decent grade on that Tennessee history test tomorrow, even if it kills me."

For curiosity's sake, he would allow himself one peek inside the green book. Then, TJ promised himself, he would put everything exactly the way it was, go to his room, and really study hard for the test.

TJ placed the pile of clippings on top of the desk, being careful to keep the stacking order intact, and reached in to lift up the book. Except for the sea green color, there was nothing else on its cover: no type, no writing, no artwork, and no photographs. Nothing. He thought it very curious.

At first contact with the book, a gentle tingling sensation flowed from TJ's hand throughout his whole body, like a soft electrical shock.

"What's going on?" TJ cried out. He tried to let go of it, but he couldn't put it down.

TJ stared down at the book in complete amazement. The green cover was now filled with changing panoramic scenes of people, things, places, buildings, forests, and mountainsides. It was a virtual kaleidoscope of moving pictures, none of which he recognized or understood.

He didn't know what was happening. It was as if he were in a trance and falling asleep at the same time. His mind clouded into a dream-like, misty state. From a distance, he dimly watched his hand--he had no control over it--turn the once blank cover over.

Against his will, TJ opened the green book. He felt himself going deeper, deeper, into the fog.

He awoke, with a start.

Chapter Four
ON THE TRAIL TO HOLSTON

TJ found himself standing in the middle of what appeared to be an old logging trail or a very primitive hiking path.

Huge gnarled limbs from trees of various sorts overhung the trail's meager clearing on the ground, forming a tangled, massive, but incomplete canopy overhead. Patches of late winter afternoon sun filtered through the many openings in the ceiling above, casting weak shafts of light upon the shadowed ground.

TJ twisted around in all directions, turning full circle repeatedly, trying to find something, anything, that was familiar or recognizable. "What is this? Where the heck am I?" he whispered. Shock, fear, and curiosity all coursed through his body.

He was in a vast, foreboding wilderness. The terrain undulated in ravines, hills, broken knob country, and narrow valleys. He could hear the gentle sound of creek water flowing somewhere nearby.

As far as his eye could see, TJ was surrounded by an immense forest of trees of all sizes. Numerous plants and other vegetation, underbrush, and thickets intermingled among clusters of trunks. In places, trees were crowded together, in other areas, less so. But everywhere he looked, he saw only an interminable green and brown sea of trees and foliage.

There was no indication of civilization close by: no cars, no buildings, no people, and no signs. Nothing at all. He screwed up his courage, and yelled at the top of his lungs, "Is anybody there? Hello! Can anybody hear me?"

"Hello. Hello. *Hello*!" He shouted the last word as loud as he possibly could. "Is anyone *there*?"

His eyes scanned the surroundings for any sign of movement. His ears strained for any sound of voice. There was no answer.

At first, TJ didn't have a clue what most of the trees were, but as he looked around, an image of the green book floated in and out of his mind's eye. Unexpectedly, the names of the trees began weirdly popping into his brain; this was stuff he certainly didn't know ten minutes ago. Now he understood he was encompassed by an army of hardwoods: oak, maple, silverbell, and cherry. Here and there TJ recognized an occasional hemlock, and saw a fair amount of pine, spruce, and southern balsam or Frazier fir scattered throughout. Also present was the yellow poplar commonly called the tulip tree, ranging from short saplings up to full-grown specimens 150 to 200 feet tall.

He shook his head to clear his confusion. "How the heck do I know all that?"

The sudden and unwanted intrusion of foreign information into his thoughts unnerved him every bit as much as the great forest, which he viewed as forbidding and perhaps even dangerous.

Squinting hard, TJ strained to see more of the path forward and backward. The trail was so crude and so undeveloped, he finished his speculation out loud, "Either it's been an awfully long time since anybody was here and it's gotten seriously overgrown. Or maybe they never got the road finished."

He doubted even the rugged logging trucks could make it through in its present condition. The road was too rough, and the trees were crowded too close to the edge of the trail, for any vehicles to travel on it. "Yeah, well, maybe military tanks could get through," he speculated.

TJ had no clue where he was, or how he came to be where he was. By all rights, he should be frightened out of his wits, but he was too much in shock to be scared yet.

"How can I instantly go from my dad's bedroom to a totally unknown place in some woods?" he asked, still twisting around to view all directions.

As he stood there, shifting weight from one foot to the other, a passing breeze cut into his thoughts. The outside temperature finally got his attention. "Br-r-r-r, it is cold out here." he said. His teeth began to chatter. TJ stomped his feet to try to warm up. Wherever he was, it must still be winter. Even with little wind blowing, he shivered in the pale afternoon sunlight.

Although it wasn't snowing now, a light snow covered the ground. "It must be at least 3 or 4 degrees below freezing," he said. Why hadn't he kept his heavy coat on when he got home? TJ stomped his feet some more. He pulled on his shirt for more warmth, and folded his arms together.

The fabric felt funny. TJ looked down at his sleeves and yelled with frantic alarm. "Oh, no!" he shouted. His school clothes were missing. "What do I have on?"

It was the weird tree thing all over again. Facts flew into his mind, and TJ found he knew exactly what he was wearing now. It was a crudely made, hand sewn, deerskin hunting shirt and deerskin trousers. The shirt fitted loosely and hung to his thighs. It had no buttons, and was held in place by a leather belt. Instead of a collar, it had a cape trimmed with fringe.

He tugged on his strange new shirt, and reached down to feel the crudeness of the trousers. Beneath shirt and trousers, instead of nice store-bought underwear, TJ knew he wore rough underclothes of linsey-woolsey fabric. Two history tests ago, he had missed a question about linsey-woolsey, but now he understood. It's a homemade material that is part linen and part wool. "Whoa, does it ever itch," he exclaimed, scratching for some relief.

TJ looked all the way down. He yelped, "And my brand-new basketball shoes are gone, darn it!" TJ thought angrily, *I only got them a week ago.*

On his feet instead were pioneer shoepacks, which he shouldn't have recognized, but did. They resembled moccasins, covered his ankles, and had deer hair stuffed between his foot and shoe soles. He had to admit, though. The shoepacks were amazingly warm in the cold and the deer hair felt soft as a pillow on the soles of his feet.

He also had a type of wallet, or pouch, slung around his shoulder with a leather strap. TJ jerked on the pouch. It jangled a bit whenever he moved.

He stared up at the overhanging canopy above, as if searching for answers. "That's just great. Somehow, someway, I know what clothes I have on and what the types of trees are, but what use is that? How does that help me?"

He was cold, confused, lost, and getting more scared by the minute. One good thing, though, was that his headache was gone. Just another unexplainable fact in this bizarre episode, but his head felt perfectly fine.

Off in the distance, he heard a harsh, piercing wail.

"What's that?" He spun around in the direction of the noise.

It was a loud, shrill scream sounding half human, though unmistakably feral. The cry had to belong to a big beast. But what? Now, TJ was fully frightened. City boy though he was, he knew it was *some sort* of ferocious creature. Questions panicked his mind. "Oh my God, what exactly is that thing?"

He tried to remember all the larger wild animals he knew of in the U.S.: mountain lions, cougars, pumas, wolves, bears, wolverines, boars, and moose. "Is it headed this way? How close to the trail is it?" he agonized. He listened intently, trying to determine how far away the animal was. All he heard was the rustling of the trees and the faint blowing of the wind. *Panther* floated into his mind. The beast's cries rang out again, and this time the terrifying sounds were coming closer.

TJ stood rooted in horror, afraid to run, afraid to stay, as the cries neared. Even in the cold, drops of sweat began to trickle down his forehead. He literally held his breath. A minute passed, and a big, brownish cat with a body the size of a large Doberman slunk onto the trail twenty yards away. Its claws looked massive and deadly. The cat's eyes were gleaming and evil-looking amidst the deepening gloom of the overhanging trees.

I'm a goner, his paralyzed mind thought. He hoped he didn't pee himself in his fright.

Every nerve in TJ's body was on edge. His face was hot and flushed. Beads of sweat cascaded down both sides of his head. He watched as the panther took a few tentative steps toward him. Snarling viciously, the beast approached to within seven feet of its prey.

Not knowing what else to do, TJ slowly took the pouch from around his neck and held the strap of it in his right hand, intending to use it as a leather mace against the animal's assault.

The big cat growled several times, yet came no closer. It glared at him and beyond him, then turned and leaped back into the shadow of the trees.

Utterly amazed and grateful, the boy stared into the spot where the panther disappeared. Agonizing seconds passed, but the animal didn't return. TJ couldn't think of a single reason why a known predator and meat eater would simply leave him without attacking.

He put his hand on his chest and waited for his heart to stop racing. Finally, he composed himself.

Yet again, he asked himself in desperation, "Where the heck am I? How far away is civilization? And where are all the people?" He scratched the back of his head in puzzlement.

"Somebody, *anybody*," he cried out in a hoarse whisper.

Hearing another sound close by in the thicket, TJ whirled around, his anguished face contorted with fresh panic. "What now?"

"Oh, crap. Oh, double crap." He blanched at the sight.

A large bull elk moved in the timber. It still had its heavy, gray-colored, winter coat. TJ noted its thick neck mane and, more ominously, its four-foot-long antlers. The bull surveyed TJ with distrust. It gave out a low guttural grunt and postured threateningly.

TJ stood stock-still, not daring to breathe or move.

The elk snorted loudly and took three steps toward the boy. Shaking its massive head, it continued to look at him. TJ kept his eyes riveted to the animal and remained perfectly still. Eventually, the big bull must have decided TJ wasn't an enemy after all. It snorted one last time and moved slowly, majestically away into the deep thicket.

TJ stayed motionless, allowing himself to settle down yet again. For the second time, he waited for his heart to stop racing and his frightened mind to begin working again.

"I can't stay here with the wild animals. It'll soon be nighttime," he told himself. His face screwed up in concentration. "This old road, or whatever it is, has got to lead to a gas station, or town, or someplace where I can find people and get some help."

He peered at the darkening path in both directions not sure which way to go. Uncertain, he finally decided to continue forward, putting more distance between him and the big cat and the massive bull elk. From the angle of the fading afternoon sun that he could see in the openings overhead, TJ guessed he would be traveling roughly north. He gave a big sigh of indecision then headed up the trail.

TJ began walking faster now, away from the two beasts. His ears were tuned to catch the slightest forest noise on either side. As he strode along the path, TJ picked up the sounds of many different birds up in the trees. Without conscious effort, his mind filled with the names of them. Among those species he heard were woodpeckers hammering against their trees of prey, the bobwhite quail with its distinctly cheerful *"Ah-bob-white,"* and the singing of mockingbirds and robins. Other birds he heard were bluebirds, meadowlarks, cardinals, towhees, Carolina chickadees, whip-poor-wills, and flickers. The forest was teeming with birdlife. He spotted a screech owl sitting in the upper branches of a towering pine. Peering overhead to gauge time by the sun, he detected a brown hawk soaring high in the sky.

After hiking at a quicker pace, TJ felt much warmer even with the sub-freezing weather. Unexpectedly, he heard sounds of movement and voices from around the next bend in the twisting trail. "Yea! Some people. At last." TJ almost choked with relief.

A few seconds later, two men came strolling into view--one older, one younger. He stiffened. TJ's sixth sense told him these were dangerous types. They looked mean and raggedly poor. Their appearance reminded him of convicts. Something told him he should have nothing to do with the men, but hurry along on his journey.

"'Lo," he nervously said as the two men got closer. They both smelled really bad, like they had rolled around in a garbage dump that day, putrid sweat mixed with rotten food odors he couldn't identify. He had to concentrate not to gag as they approached.

They stared the boy up and down as they went by. The older of the two, who had a scruffy, patchy beard and a balding forehead with graying, scraggly hair down below his shoulders, spoke first. "Has ya got any tobacco on ya, young sprout?"

"No, sir." TJ looked at them, but kept walking past as he answered.

The younger and taller of the two, who looked even dirtier and stank worse, if possible, called out in a whipsaw voice, "How 'bout some vittles then, boy? Whut's in ya pouch, we wonders?"

"I don't have any food or anything else of value," TJ gave them as wide a berth as he could on the narrow path. He continued down the trail, his head half-turned so he could still see them out of the corner of his eyes as he scurried by.

The younger man's tone was mockingly sinister, "Whut's ya hurry? Whut ya doin' traveling with no food or drink on ya, *boy*? Hey, stop a while, little hoss. No need to put on airs." The man's attitude reminded TJ of big Brent.

TJ saw the two men put their heads together, whispering, and glancing furtively at him. Evil plans, it seemed to TJ. He kept looking back over his shoulder, watching the two rough-hewed individuals nervously, all the while hastening his stride to get well beyond them. Although the two ruffians continued to glower at him as TJ rushed around the approaching bend, they did not attack him.

Over the next hundred yards or so of trail, several times he stopped, turned, and faced the path he had just trod, to make sure they hadn't doubled back after him.

For the third time that late afternoon, he had gotten scared out of his wits. "I've got to calm down, got to keep a cool head," he admonished himself.

Gradually, TJ's breathing and pulse returned to normal. He saw no pursuit by the two men, and heard no more fierce animal cries from the forest. He relaxed and focused on covering ground to get to wherever his destination was.

"Wow." TJ spotted a red fox with its white underbelly, flashing across the path at the trail's bend ten yards up ahead. He sped on. More minutes passed. The heavily wooded path took TJ up and down a continuing succession of lazy hills and mini-knobs. At one point, a noisy streamlet forded the trail. TJ saw a number of snowshoe hares, their white fur semi-hidden against the snow patches, as they scurried over the ground. "Hey, there're a couple of raccoons. And there's a possum."

He remembered his Dad used to squirrel hunt as a boy growing up in the Pennsylvania backwoods. TJ began to search for squirrel in the treetops on either side of the path, and soon lost count of how many he saw. "There's so much wild game out here!" he exclaimed.

He had gone hunting with his father once for deer and twice for squirrel. And they had never seen such an abundance of wildlife. He recalled that his friend David loved to go hunting.

"David would totally flip out, being here." Then he glumly thought, *Yeah, if I only knew where HERE is.* The word, *Holston*, briefly flickered in his head.

As he traveled, TJ fancied he heard the echoes of human voices far off. However, the sounds were so slight, so indistinct, he decided it must the whipping winter wind or unknown animal cries he was hearing. At one point, he did discern voices in the woods, perhaps less than a few hundred yards away.

TJ stopped. Should he head out into the forest, following the sound of the voices? Or should he continue on this rustic path, trusting it to eventually lead him to civilization, some town called Holston, or whatever? The episode with the two criminal-looking men had made him leery.

I don't know who I'm going to meet in this place. I got to be careful.

TJ stood huddled against the wind, trying to make up his mind. "I better stay on the trail and try to find a place up ahead." It would be nightfall in a couple of hours. He knew he could easily get lost trying to locate the people behind the voices. Besides, maybe they were individuals he didn't want to hook up with.

"Just keep going, keep moving forward," TJ steeled himself.

He resumed his fast stride. Time passed, and he didn't see or hear another person or hiker or vehicle. Wherever he was, he must be in a real wilderness area.

As he passed the next sharp bend, the winding path straightened up. TJ could see up the narrow trail, more or less straight, for about fifty yards. Just coming into view at the far end was another party of travelers. It seemed to be a whole family, as far as he could tell. He breathed easier. They didn't seem threatening at all.

The party approached. He saw a buckboard wagon pulled by two ambling mules. In front of the wagon walked a full-bearded man with a rifle braced lazily across his shoulder. On the wagon seat sat a woman with a solemn, age-lined face, and an old man. In the wagon bed TJ counted five children, ranging in age, he supposed, from three to fourteen or fifteen. The oldest was a pretty, black-headed girl, who smiled coyly at him as he came nearer. He wondered if the wagon would be able to get through the narrow path behind him. There were spots were the trees drew so close that there was barely room for the width of the wagon to pass.

"Hello," he said, cautiously.

The man merely nodded. The woman barely looked at him, but the old man suddenly barked, "Youngin', ya best keep a lookout! What are ya doin', traveling with nary a gun?" He sternly glared at the boy, as TJ walked by. The young children stared at TJ, but the black-headed girl smiled yet again.

"Hi," she coyly whispered, as TJ came abreast. She put her arm out over the side of the wagon with her hand dangling for TJ to touch it.

"Hello, there," he looked up into the face of the girl and gave his best impression of a rakish smile in return. Impulsively, he stretched out his hand and let his fingers slide off of hers as the two passed.

He looked back. The girl had put her fingers up to her lips. She kissed and gently bit the tips of them. TJ's face flushed a little at her gesture. He waved to her. She waved back. And the heavy-laden wagon was soon gone around the corner.

As the group receded into the distance behind him, TJ wondered what the old man meant about a gun. *Did he mean this is a very dangerous area, and I better have a weapon to defend myself?* Now, he was even more afraid. He continued walking, with his fear mounting.

Suddenly, TJ's ears perked up.

The faint sound of a horse's unhurried clip-clop echoed behind him. He couldn't mistake the distinctive rhythm. The rider was steadily gaining on him. TJ froze. Should he run into the woods and hide until the unknown party passed by? Should he wait on the trail where he was, hoping this individual was not some bloodthirsty, insane criminal? Could he trust this person would be safe for him and would actually help him?

"After all," TJ said miserably, "I don't know if I'm in the same state, in the same country. I don't know where on earth I am." He waved his arms up and down once as if it were hopeless. *Whatever the source is of all this new information I've been receiving, it isn't giving me a clue to where I am.*

His indecision stretched out. In the meantime, the rider was slowly approaching. TJ struggled to control his feeling of dread. Finally deciding that meeting the person head-on was better than hiding in the woods, he forced himself to turn around and face his fate.

TJ prepped himself. "Okay. Chill out. I know how to *act*. So this time, how about acting as if I know what I'm doing and where I'm going.

"That old man could tell I was scared, and that's why he said what he said," he added. "Just be confident. Just focus," he commanded under his breath. TJ licked his lips as he waited with foreboding. He forced himself to stand still. He had begun shifting his weight off one foot to the other in his anxiety.

A horse and rider moseyed around the last turn in the path behind him. The stranger had a long rifle resting lazily on his massive thighs. Across the front of the saddle were draped leather bags, filled with something heavy. The horse's saddle horn had a very long, stout rope wrapped around it. The rope dragged behind, tied in succession to five plump hogs that were grunting and following like a madcap caravan. TJ stared unbelieving at this curious picture.

As the rider spotted TJ, he reined his mount down to a walk, gawked in mild surprise, and came to a halt ten yards from the boy. He gigged the horse and hogs to within five yards. He stopped again. TJ stood, motionless.

The stranger spoke first. "Lad, where are ya goin' by yourself on such a cold winter's afternoon?" He paused briefly and beamed down on TJ, who was shivering lightly, not from the cold but from his passing fear.

TJ tried to reply. He couldn't. He had stage fright. Even after his pep talk about pretending he was in control of the situation, his brain and tongue had totally blanked out.

The man smiled genially at TJ's silence. He continued, "My name's Samuel Robertson, or Sam, or Mr. Robertson. Call me whut ever suits ya. Who might ya be?" The man looked benignly at TJ and waited. "I mean ya no harm, youngin'."

TJ guessed, from the stranger's sitting height, that he would be over six feet tall. He wore the traditional humble pioneer garb of his day. Nevertheless, he could tell the man's clothes, hand-sewn of course, were of a better quality than his. The stranger had dark middle-length hair, bold blue eyes, and a fair complexion. He was kind spoken and exuded an even-tempered, yet strong personality.

He smiled again, and got down off his horse with his rifle still in hand. "I'm a goin' to Long Island on tha Holston to sell my hogs and corn whiskey. I gotta little homestead down tha Nolichuck in Greene 'bout twenty miles back. I need a new plow for early spring planting. My ol' one's plumb wore out. Tha peddler that used to come around, he up and died a month ago. I wanna be ready when tha weather turns."

He continued, "There's a trading tavern called tha Sloppy Bucket off Long Island. I heard from other travelers thay has tha best quality merchandise. I've bought goods before in Jonesborough, and Greeneville, and from tha blacksmithy in Rogers, but I've never bin satisfied."

Sam good-naturedly contemplated the boy in front of him. "It's another thirteen, fourteen more miles from here, lad. Is that where ya are goin'?" he asked.

Sam paused for TJ to speak. "If so, I reckon there's

room on my horse for two. Ya kin slide on behind me. Jest ya mind tha hogs' tie. We'll go tha rest o' tha way, together." He patiently waited again for TJ to reply.

TJ finally found his voice. "Yeah, sure, Holston. That's where I'm headed to. The next town."

"Well, it'll be much safer for ya, lad, if ya travel with me. There's bin noise, lately, o' robbers and thieves up in this neck o' tha woods."

The boy solemnly considered the offer. After brief hesitation, he decided he could trust this stranger, after all. "My nickname's TJ," he said simply.

"Tee-Jay? That's a funny handle, lad. Are ya part Injun? Cherokee, perhaps? There's a fair number still around these parts. Not all are savage, anymo'."

TJ blinked. The man's statement about savage Indians in the area really threw him for a loop. *Indians?* He replied, "Uh, no sir, Mr. Robertson. My given name is Thomas James."

TJ's brows furrowed. He had always been sensitive about playground nicknames since first grade. He continued speaking under his breath, "But I don't like Thomas or James or Tom or Jim. And I really hate to be called Tommy or Jimbo." The thought suddenly ran through his mind: *Maybe I ought to be careful about my true identity until I can find out where I am and what the heck is going on.*

Amused, Sam watched the boy talking to himself.

"Uh, you can just call me Jeb, Mr. Robertson," he finally said, more loudly, remembering he was named after the famous Confederate general.

"Well, Jeb, sun's a goin' down. We best git. It'll be another hour or so with these hogs trailing behind, slowin' us down. And lad, no need for high manners out here. Ya kin jest call me plain ol' Sam." He winked at TJ and gave him another gentle smile.

Sam Robertson turned to his horse, put his boot in the stirrup and smoothly mounted, the packed whisky satchel still straddling his lap in front of the saddle.

"Here, lad, lemme help ya up." He extended a strong hand to TJ, effortlessly pulling the boy onto the back of the saddle.

Sam lightly kicked his horse. The odd little caravan was on its way to Holston.

Chapter Five
THE SLOPPY BUCKET

The sky was darkening as Sam, TJ, horse, and hogs pulled up to the outskirts of the small, yet thriving outpost on the banks of the Holston across from the Long Island tavern. TJ could make out eight or more buildings in the dusk.

On the first leg of their journey to Holston, they had gone through wildly wooded terrain that teemed with game of every sort. As they traveled further, the ever-present forest gradually thinned on both sides of the trail, and they began to see signs of settlement. Here and there were isolated farms. As they approached their destination, the countryside changed into rising foothills and knobbed retreats.

Toward the east and northeast in the not far distance, TJ saw the Blue Ridge Appalachians peaking through the smoky evening mist. The hazy ramparts were guarded by a rising vanguard of small valleys and steep ridges leading upwards to the mother range itself.

TJ vaguely recognized the Smoky Mountains from vacations his family had taken and from his geography lessons at school. He thought, *At least I'm still in the good old USA, still in my home state of Tennessee.*

But the year certainly was not 2014. *It can't be. That stupid green book must have sent me back into the past.*

This countryside was too unsullied: too undeveloped and free of human spoil. That fact, even more than the crudeness of dress and the absence of modern vehicles, convinced TJ he must be in a much earlier era.

On the trip to Holston, he had attentively listened to the big man. He let Sam ramble on, speaking proudly about his family and his farm carved out of seven acres in the thick woods close to the Nolichucky River in upper Greene country.

"Yup, my homestead's on some right purty land," said Sam. "Soil as fertile as kin be. Crops almost grow themselves. Good timber. And game a'plenty. Not too crowded, yet. Got decent folk for neighbors." Sam smiled with contentment. "Be glad to git home and see my little Ruthie."

He looked over his shoulder and nodded at TJ mounted behind him. "She's my youngest, tha baby. Ruthie is tha darling o' my eye, my little honey pot. She's smart as a whip, sassy, laughs to beat anythang I ever saw. Jest to hear her laugh gits me started," he chuckled to himself at the fond memories.

Intentionally, TJ had managed to keep the topic of conversation off himself, and all about Sam's life. TJ had avoided answering where he was from, what he was doing, or where was his family. Sam hadn't pressed. TJ didn't volunteer.

Since arriving, TJ had searched in vain for anything familiar he could recognize, remember, or make sense of. The name of Holston meant nothing to him; neither did he remember the Nolichucky River from his state geography lessons. Now, seeing the brooding mountains on his right, he got the courage to ask the one question he'd been afraid to ask Sam during their ride.

Sam reined his horse to a lazy stop in front of the wharf. Tied flatboats floated gently on the river current. Before Sam dismounted, TJ hurried to ask him the difficult question. "What year is it?" he said.

Sam partially turned in the saddle and replied, "Why, it's eighteen and two in tha year o' our Lord, Jeb."

TJ blanched and swallowed. "You mean, as in 1802, the year 1802?" He asked Sam in a resigned voice, "What month?"

"It's late February, lad." Sam turned full in the saddle and looked square at TJ. "Winter's gittin' by. Before ya know it, it'll be sprang." He eyed TJ with some concern. "Did ya not know what year?"

Sam continued to gaze quizzically at him. "Well, Jeb, lad, don't ya be worrying. Ol Sam'll take care o' thangs tonight. We kin both figure out whut's whut in tha morning. Now, we need to hop down and git a flatboat. We're gonna have to cross over if we wanna sleep in tha tavern. That'll be a sight better than bunking on tha rocky ground. Not much place to stay on this side o' tha river."

He gave the boy a reassuring smile. "Lemme talk to tha keeper. Ya jest wait here."

They dismounted. Sam clapped his hand on TJ's shoulder and said, "I kin tell there's something a troubling ya, lad. Lemme git thangs sorted out, and we kin chat a bit while we et dinner."

TJ watched him as he ambled over to the dock. He had known Sam Robertson for a few short hours. Intuitively, though, he knew Sam was a big-hearted man--someone he could trust.

But, he thought dismally, *what can I tell Sam? I don't know when, or if, I'm ever going to get back to Dad, back to my own home. Sam would never believe me, anyway. I wouldn't believe it, if I told myself.*

He squeezed his eyes tight with a sudden flash, an inspiration so mind-blowing, so elementary he wondered why it hadn't come to him sooner. *What if Dad has gone into the past, too, just like I have? What if that's the reason he always kept the green book under constant lock and key?*

The mere possibility of it gave him newfound courage. And hope. Out loud, he whispered fiercely, "Well, if Dad did travel back in time, he obviously was able to return to the present. If he did it, I can do it."

The more he considered this awesome revelation, the more he understood it would be best if he didn't attempt to share with Sam anything about his *future*. No, he would make up a story. A story about missing family, about being lost, all alone and willing to work for food and shelter. He would play along until he found the secret to getting home. In the interim, he would have to be as clever, as cautious, and as cunning as he could; in short, one of his best acting performances ever.

He formulated his made-up tale on the spot as he waited for Sam. "Okay. My name is Jeb. And my entire family got wiped out by the Indians," he said, as he kept watch on the flatboat.

"I totally blanked out at the very beginning of the attack. I don't remember much of anything from when I came to, until Sam found me wandering on the trail. I don't even know how I wound up being there. Until Sam told me, I didn't know for sure where I was. I can't recall how to get back to the old home place. I think the Indians may have burned it down, but again, I have no memory. The one thing I know for certain is that I have nothing left to go back to. All of my family is gone."

That was his story. And he was sticking to it.

He rehearsed these facts over and over, while Sam continued his discussion with the flatboat keeper by the dock. He went over his storyline again and again, until he had it firmly planted in his brain. He couldn't slip up; he couldn't reveal his secrets. He couldn't be himself.

Yes, Jeb would be his new name. He was a pioneer boy who had lost his family, lost most of his memory since the attack, and now he needed a new start. He saw Sam had finished his business with the keeper and was coming back.

Sam nodded agreeably as he strode past Jeb to the side of the horse. Lifting the reins over its head, he led the horse and parade of hogs to the waiting flatboat.

He turned his head slightly toward Jeb. "There's a stable next to tha tavern where we kin put up my horse and keep tha hogs safe for tha night. Tha tavern's a might full, but there's room for us if we scurry along."

"Okay," Jeb nodded in reply and followed Sam, his mind now filled with thoughts of his new identity and of successful escape back to the future.

The small parade of people and animals crowded onto the flatboat deck, and the keeper pushed off. Off in the deepening shadows, Jeb could see a huddle of buildings with the silhouetted land and mass of trees disappearing into the darkness on either side, giving the impression the island was very long indeed.

The trip was short. They docked. Sam paid the keeper, who led the animals off to their evening's shelter while the two of them continued on to the Sloppy Bucket. By now, Jeb felt very tired. The dangers of the trail, the shock of learning exactly when and where he was, had brought him to a point of exhaustion.

Sam told the story behind the funny name as they hiked up the snaking path to the entrance. "Tavern was built before tha turn in '99 by William Gibson. He went and had five barrels o' tha finest whiskey shipped by wagon from Bourbon County, Kentuck. Well sir, the first night he got 'em there, two o' tha barrels leaked so bad that good whiskey got spilt over most o' tha barroom floor. Three o' tha guests slipped feet straight up on that Kentuck whiskey.

"Shame, though. Twas a waste o' some o' tha best liquor known to man. Ever since, tha locals in these parts have called it tha Sloppy Bucket."

Jeb glanced up when they reached the tavern front. It was by far the largest man-made structure he had yet seen in this wilderness land. He saw an imposing three-story, five-bay building. It had exterior chimneys, constructed of stone and brick, on its gabled ends. He could see the tavern was set into the slope of a steep hill which, looking back, he saw angled all the way down to the River's edge.

Sam explained the layout of the building. "Tha first level has a right big bar and tap room in tha front where guests kin sit a spell, rest their bones, chew tha fat, and hash thangs out before dinner. In tha back, there's a hall down tha middle with little meeting rooms spread out on either side. Upstairs, tha second floor has tha best dining hall and eating in tha country here 'bouts. Tha third floor has got five or six nice sleeping rooms for paying guests to stay over."

He added, "We'll take one o' tha sleeping rooms, on credit jest for tonight, 'til I sell my hogs and corn whiskey in tha morning."

They entered through the tavern commons on the ground floor level. Besides the barkeep, there appeared to be eleven or twelve other persons in the room. Jeb saw some men standing by the bar or in the open area, and some sitting at the handful of tables against the walls. Most were smoking pipes. There was a slight haze hovering between the low ceiling and the floor. One particularly tall, swarthy fellow with a barrel chest and broad shoulders was engaged in earnest conversation with the barman. The bigger man stopped and nodded curtly as Sam and Jeb came in.

Two drunken travelers in the middle of room were locked in bitter argument. A few others gaped at the two newcomers, then returned to the serious business of heavy drinking. One squinty-eyed, scar-faced, scraggly-looking individual stared intently at Sam and Jeb as they entered. For some strange reason, he kept stealing furtive glances at Jeb's pouch slung around his neck. His attention made Jeb nervous.

One person, Jeb noticed right away, looked to

be only a little older than he. Perhaps fifteen or sixteen, he guessed. Sam led Jeb to the bar next to the giant gentleman who was in deep discussion with the barkeep. Sam patiently listened to their banter, than at the first chance, broke into the flow of conversation to speak to the barkeeper about a place for the night.

When he had procured promise of a room, Sam turned to Jeb and said, "Lad, thay kin water down a whiskey for ya, if ya ain't used to strong drink."

Jeb vaguely nodded his head, his attention focused on the feuding pair of guests who were standing, jaw-to-jaw, in the middle of the room. Whatever they were fighting about, it was becoming more heated by the moment.

"Ya yellow-bellied, rot-gutted polecat, I said I'd whip and outshoot ya three days to Sunday!" the first man snarled, a thickset individual with ham-like hands, bulging gut, and salt-and-pepper beard.

"Tha hell ya will. I'll beat ya so bad, they'll tar and feather ya right out o' tha shooting match," rejoined the second man, who was younger and taller with a wiry frame.

The man with the flecked beard cursed loudly and pulled a wicked looking knife. The younger man grabbed his arm before he could strike, driving a knee to his exposed groin.

"Dern ya, I'll kill ya now!" the heavier man

screamed out. The man dropped his knife as he fell to the floor, dragging down his opponent with him.

Jeb stared fascinated as the two rolled on the floor, kicking and gouging. The older man grunted as a fist connected with his massive gut. He grabbed the younger one by the hair, slamming his head against the floor. One flailing boot connected with the shin of a seated man, bringing him to his feet in an instant rush of anger.

The younger man rolled on top of the older one, who bucked like a wild horse, trying to unseat him. Failing in that, he heaved mightily, rolling to the side and slamming the other to the floor. Fists and feet flailing, each tried to land a knockout blow.

Abruptly, the older man jammed his thumb into the other man's nostril while clamping his teeth on the younger man's left ear. "Yahhhhhh!" The younger man screamed as blood spurted from the lower portion of his ear.

Half crazed with pain, he slammed his fist into the first man's throat. "Take that, and that, and *that!*" he cried, making his foe wheeze for breath.

Gasping for breath himself with the exertion of the fight, the second man now grabbed his enemy by the top of his hair with one hand. He fastened the fingers of his other hand on the man's ear for leverage, then jammed his thumb into the eye socket and cruelly gorged out the left eyeball of his stricken opponent.

The fallen older man lay prone on the floor, acknowledging final defeat with the loss of his eye. The victor glared down with a wild bestial expression, the blood from his bitten ear flowing freely upon his exultant face.

"Yessir! Yessir!" he kept yelling out, defiantly, drunkenly. "Who's tha hoss now?"

The room full of spectators had watched, with complete indifference as the entire engagement erupted and ended, without any attempts to separate the adversaries. A couple of onlookers eventually ambled over and helped the unfortunate loser up and out the door.

The thought ran through Jeb's stunned brain, *Whoa! This sort of thing must happen all the time. Nobody tried to stop them. Nobody seems to care they tried to kill each other.*

The winner shuffled unsteadily to the bar, oblivious to the severity of his own wound.

The barkeep left and returned with a long cloth piece. He soaked it in whiskey and gave to the man as a bandage. "Here, ya kin use this. But stop ya dern bleeding on my floor."

The second man wrapped his still bleeding ear and head. "Hot piss, I knew I cud beat 'im." He stumbled to a far table for further boasting and drinking.

Jeb couldn't believe what he just witnessed. His entire body was petrified in shock and disbelief. Jeb felt his insides burning with a hot sickness. He struggled helplessly against the feeling, then turned and threw up against the side of the bar.

Sam solemnly leaned over the violently retching Jeb, patted him on the shoulder, and said in a calm, comforting voice, "Lad, don't trouble yourself over such darn fools and hotheads. They ain't got tha common sense tha Lord above gave 'em. Men that fight to kill, or bad hurt their fella man, over such trifling matters are jest plain mean or plain stupid. Their fists and their mouths are thrice tha size o' their pea brains."

He leaned further in. "Come on, Jeb. Let's go upstairs and git dinner. You'll feel a whole lot better after some vittles and a night's rest."

He continued to pat Jeb as if to offer reassurance.

The big man who had been talking to the bar hand, turned and casually watched Jeb as the boy continued to vomit up against the bar. As Jeb's heaving subsided, the giant leaned over and said in a low, sympathetic growl, "It's over now, boy. It's all done n' over."

A young voice spoke out, "Not a purty sight, is it, to see grown men act like animals?"

Chapter Six
YOUNG DAVY

The guest who was slightly older than Jeb had strolled over to offer his support. "Ya gonna be all right? Bit rough, that there fight was. Almost as rough to watch it, as to be in it," he said with a hint of humor.

Gradually, Jeb straightened up and regained his composure. Wiping his mouth on his sleeve, he stepped gingerly away from the splattered side of the bar, and took a long breath to still his nerves before he turned around to face the new speaker.

Jeb saw a rawboned young man not fully grown. He was slender, yet athletic-looking, with penetrating eyes, dark brown hair, and a slight, mischievous smile playing on his good-natured face. He was nearly four inches taller than Jeb, approaching six feet in height.

"My name's David, David Crockett."

"Hi, I'm…" He almost slipped up and said TJ. "I'm Jeb." The two shook hands.

"I'm on my way home," said young David. "I bin

off for a few years driving cattle to Virginia and Maryland. My folks have a tavern on tha Knoxville-Abingdon Road down in Jefferson. It's bin quite a spell, since last I seen 'em. Bit homesick to see my sisters and my Ma, I am."

He stared at the spot in the middle of the floor where the combatants had tussled. "They were fighting over who has tha better eye, and here there's gonna be a shooting match tomorrow morning to settle tha argument for everyone." He laughed. 'Instead o' waiting 'til tha morning, one insults tha other 'bout his poor aim. Thay both lose their tempers, and we all seen tha result. Instead o' a better eye, there's a missing eye."

He paused and gave another half-grin. "Guess tha second fella was right. Tha first fella has *no eye* for shooting, if ya git my drift."

He ended the discussion with an effusive boast. "Tha fight jest now don't matter none anyhow, because I'm gonna win tomorrow, no matter who puts their rifle in tha ring. There's one less rascal to tuck his tail, after I git through shooting tha eye out o' tha bull."

He clapped Jeb on the shoulder and said gaily, "Tha fight was nothing, youngin'. Ya jest catch some shuteye tonight. I'll see ya'll in tha morning for tha shootin' at nine-ish." He gave them a sly wink and sauntered out the door.

Jeb gaped with an open mouth at the departing stranger. He shook his head like he had water in his ears, then turned with a stunned expression to Sam and asked, "Is that *the* Davy Crockett?" He glanced from one person to the other.

"You know, the famous frontiersman," he exclaimed excitedly. He caught the questioning looks of Sam and the big man. He stopped talking.

Almost too late, Jeb realized that in 1802, he couldn't possibly know in advance what Davy Crockett was going to become and achieve as an adult. In their minds, this would be the first instance he, or they, had met, or even heard about a David Crockett.

Recovering, Jeb declared, "It's just that he sounds like he's an excellent shot, or something." He watched Sam's amused expression and asked, "Are we, are you, going to stay and watch the shooting contest in the morning?"

The giant fella smirked at Jeb and Sam. "I need to be movin' along, boys. I've got better thangs to do than to jaw 'bout some shooting match." He gulped down his drink, nodded his head to them, and lumbered out the door and into the chilled night air.

Sam nodded in reply as the imposing figure walked by.

Just then, Jeb noticed out of the corner of his eye, the scar-faced man sidling slyly up to the bar right behind him. The thought flashed through Jeb's mind, *He's eavesdropping on us.*

Sam gazed amiably at Jeb. "Lad, lets speak 'bout that shooting match and tha other subjects while we et." He finished the last of his own drink and set the glass down. "I never did git into whut's troubling ya. It'll take us most o' a day gittin' back tomorrow. I'll have to load that new plow on my horse like a pack mule. We'll be traveling on foot tha whole way, and it's a far piece, thirty miles and more. We cain't stay long in tha morning."

Jeb didn't say anything. He knew the time had come for him to tell Sam his carefully rehearsed, sad story over dinner and hope for the best. He contemplated his situation. Here he was, an unwilling captive trapped in the wild and woolly frontier days of Tennessee, without family, friends, guidance, plans, or even money.

Without money? The thought repeated itself as an out loud question: "Wait a minute. What *is* in the leather pouch around my neck?"

With Sam watching intently, Jeb carefully opened the flap on the pouch and peered inside. He gingerly shook the contents out, one-by-one, into his open hand placed tight against his chest. His surprise matched that on Sam's face.

There were seven coins of five different sizes: three gold coins and four coins that seemed to be silver or part silver. He had twenty-seven dollars and seventy-five cents in his left jeans pocket when he came home from school, or what was left of his spending money for the month.

Jack King

Just like his clothes, his modern money had magically transformed into its 1802 equivalent: two Gold Eagles each worth ten dollars, one Gold Half Eagle, two Silver Dollars, one Half Dollar, and one Quarter Dollar.

Looking up at Sam, then down at the pouch, he poured the coins back inside and pulled the top tight. After seeing what happened to his modern clothes and basketball shoes, he should have guessed what was in the pouch before now.

Sam's amazement was greater than Jeb's.

What Jeb held was the equivalent of many months' worth of cash for the typical marginal and hardscrabble Tennessee farmer of the early 19th century. Actual money was difficult to earn and accumulate. Most of the wealth of the average farmer was in his livestock and land. Real cash was hard to come by. The overwhelming majority of the smaller farmers, traders, and even merchants, notably in the Eastern region and mountain parts of the state, bartered raw goods of all forms for finished products, and visa-versa. In his new setting, Jeb was, for the present, a person of some means.

Sam gawked some more, his eyes as big as saucers. He spoke in a hoarse whisper, "How'd ya git that much hard cash on ya, lad?"

Sam's thick eyebrows furrowed together. "Lad, it ain't safe for ya to be carrying that amount o' money in these parts. 'Bout three, four weeks ago, I heard from a passing trader. Thay found tha crew o' a Holston flatboat. Three men were kilt. Gutted jest like fish, with stones piled in their innards to make 'em sink down in tha river. All tha goods on their boat were stolen. Locals blame tha Hansen clan, and a more evil, devilish pack o' thieves and murderers there's never bin, that I kin recollect. Thay fears neither God nor man, and their hearts are as black as tha ace o' spades.

"Lad, keep that money hidden in your sack. Let us go upstairs and git a bite o' dinner and hash thangs out. I'm powerfully curious to know whut your story is, and how a youngin' like yourself gits such a tidy sum o' cash." He smiled reassuringly. "Jeb, on my Ma's grave, ya kin trust me. Ol' Sam will help ya, any way I kin."

Jeb shook his head in acknowledgement, his mind now filled with visions of bloodthirsty bandits in pursuit of his pouch and his life. They climbed the stairs to the second floor.

As they reached the top step, Jeb briefly glimpsed down. He saw the squinty-eyed fella talking in a low, scratchy voice with the barkeep. Jeb had an uneasy premonition about the man.

Sam found a vacant table in the serving area, and they sat down. Sam ordered a meal for the two of them: hot freshly-caught catfish, corn mush, boiled potatoes, dried peas, and a platter of cold pork sausages.

The food, or vittles as Sam termed it, was unlike

anything Jeb had ever eaten. However, he was ravenously hungry. The lateness of the hour, the exertion of the trip, and the exhausting range of emotions experienced since arriving at the tavern all combined to create a monster appetite in him.

Jeb ate with such gusto that Sam thought the lad had not eaten for many days.

The appearance before him of a starving boy, and Sam's false assumption of the same, aided Jeb's cause immensely. Sam took in Jeb's every word as if it were the gospel truth.

Jeb spun his contrived story with convincing sincerity, acting more skillfully than he ever had in a school play. Pulling from his meager mental store of history facts, he was able to concoct a suitable, woeful tale. To cover for the money pouch, Jeb added the plot twist that his pa had been a successful liquor merchant "Back east in the state of Pennsylvania" until new federal taxes "Forced Pa to move our family to Kentucky, then to Tennessee. According to Pa, we settled down many miles somewhere southwest of new Greene County." He added that part in to give Sam a recognizable geographic point-of-reference and make his tale seem even more truthful.

"Sam, all I can recall is we were gathered at the supper table when, suddenly, the Indians attacked us! I remember grabbing my little sister Natalie with one hand, and the money pouch Pa had laid on the supper table with my other. And then...and then...I remember dropping to the floor and covering up the pouch and my little sister with my own body as the Indians around me killed my Ma, my Pa, my older brother and my older sister. I don't know what happened to Natalie. The Indians must have kidnapped her.

"That's the last I recall. I swear, Sam, my memory is gone. My mind has blocked out all knowledge. It was all so horrible. After I fell to the floor with Natalie, from that point on--" he broke off his dialogue and shook his head sorrowfully.

"Well, the next thing I remember I'm wandering on an unknown trail. I honestly don't know how I got there. I don't know why the Indians left me alive. I don't know what happened to my little sis." He hung his head low as if in anguish, but snuck a hopeful glance up at Sam to gauge his response.

Sam sat in stunned silence. He had never heard such a pitiful tale. He doubted not a word of it. After Jeb completed his chronicle of overwhelming calamity, Sam looked at the boy without talking. His rugged, honest face was filled with compassion and pity.

He finally spoke. "Lad, ya have no kinfolk, no friends, and no place to lay your head, in tha whole wide world. Ol' Sam wud be a poor Christian man, if I didn't help ya."

He thought a moment. "Tell ya whut. I want ya to

come live with my family, least for a while. We got room to spare. My two boys wud be happy to have another brother. Thay have three sisters, and thay have always wanted an extra brother so that we wud have three sons in tha family. Ya kin help out with tha farming, hunting, and chores alongside my boys."

Sam halted, as if embarrassed to make his next statement. "My wife, Rebecca, she's tha oldest daughter o' a Methodist preacher from North Carolina. She grew up around finer thangs than a small farmer, such as myself, kin afford."

Sam blushed and hesitated again. "If ya cud see ya way to it, I reckon fifteen dollars to buy a purty dress and fancy tableware to take home wud go a far piece in helping Rebecca see thangs my way, for ya to become part o' tha family, that is." He eyed Jeb ruefully, unsure how the boy would take his request.

Jeb responded impulsively. "Sam," he said, "I don't have anyone else to turn to. I need a safe place to stay. I need a friend I can trust. I know I can trust you. Heck, you can have all the money if you want it."

Relieved, Sam breathed easier. "No, lad, it's your money fair and square. Ya keep tha rest o' it. Fifteen dollars will do jest fine. And I wudn't be asking, except I know how Rebecca is, and whut possibly might smooth thangs over with her for ya to be able to stay. Thankee, son. Thankee."

With that, they finished their dinner, and headed up to the third floor to bunk for the night.

The next morning, Jeb rose refreshed, with the sound of roosters crowing. He'd never willingly gotten up at sunrise ever before. His adventure into the past was beginning to change him for the better. He washed his face from the nightstand basin filled with fresh, cold well water, dressed hurriedly, and went to join Sam for a hearty country breakfast.

After the meal, they walked down to the ground floor and went outside. It was a crisp, sunny winter morning. Sam excused himself, saying he needed to consummate the sale of his hogs and whiskies, and then make all of his planned purchases.

"Jeb, ya kin come along with me, if ya want, or ya kin be on your own. Tha shooting contest won't start for another hour or so."

Jeb choose to check out the premises and people. He stopped first at a blacksmith's shop, watching in fascination as the stocky craftsman hammered out new horseshoes, glowing reddish-orange hot over the anvil. Stacked in the corners, the man had damaged wagon wheels, broken farming tools, and other pieces of equipment to repair for his customers. Jeb noticed the huge knotted muscles on the man's massive forearms.

He next went over to the livery stable and watched the many horses being groomed and fed their early morning mash. Jeb could tell a few of the horses were in high spirits.

After that, he found a large dry goods store. He wandered up and down the aisles happily examining all the many things for sale. *Wow. Things are so different back in frontier days from my own time: the people, their way of life, the lack of technology and modern-day conveniences,* he thought to himself, as he looked at one item after another.

He stopped by the front counter and looked at the various-sized glass jars containing what was obviously candy. "Hey mister, how much, for a couple pieces?" The owner, a sprightly little man with drooping mustache and long sideburns to match his collar length hair, stepped forward.

"Two pennies each for the rock candy, and a penny each for the molasses chips," he said.

"How about three of the rock candies and four of the chips, then," replied Jeb, handing the man a quarter dollar coin. Jeb took his change in one hand and the seven candies in the other, thanked the owner, and moseyed out the door. He quickly learned most of the rock candies were sour, so he began adding molasses chips to balance the taste.

As he wandered around, sucking on the candy bits and inspecting the various sights, Jeb noticed the same person, the squinty-eyed, scraggly-faced traveler he had seen in the barroom last night. The man appeared to be tailing him, keeping a close watch on his every movement.

He stopped and faced the man, who made a pretense of going into the closest building. He studied the back of the man and swallowed hard.

Abruptly, Jeb reversed his steps. Brushing past the staring stranger, he went back inside the sanctuary of the Sloppy Bucket. He sat down at the nearest table, watched, and waited. Sure enough, he saw the person stick his ugly head through the doorway as if ensuring his prey was still there. Then the man withdrew.

A half hour later, Sam returned and collected Jeb. He described his sturdy new plow and Rebecca's gifts with a fair measure of pride. "Rebecca's goin' to be real surprised when she sees this here new dress and all tha fancy tableware. I cain't wait to see tha look on her face," Sam beamed with happy anticipation. "Come on, Jeb. We'll take time to watch a little bit o' tha match before we start home." They went outside together. Sam led way to the area marked off for the shooting contest.

Jeb debated whether to tell Sam of his stalker. Perhaps it was a common occurrence in frontier days for people to snoop on other people, he thought. *Am I being paranoid? Is it my imagination?* He decided, in the end, not to say anything unless the individual did something truly threatening.

The organizer of the contest began announcing the rules and names of the participants, and Jeb turned his attention to the shoot. He forgot all about the scarred-faced stranger. Each of the fourteen contestants had paid twenty-five cents per shot for each of the four rounds. Each man would take his very best aim at the tiny, concentric-circled, bull-eyed targets forty-odd yards away. The closest hit in each of the four rounds earned a quarter of prime beef. There was a bonus prize of five silver dollars for the marksman who won at least three of the rounds.

"All right now. Ya'll got tha rules. Tha best shot in each round gits a quarter o' beeve. And if any of ya scalawags wins three or more rounds, he gits the five dollar silver. All right then. Let her rip!" The portly line judge barked out to the assembled contestants.

Each of the men lined up for the first round and took their shot in turn. As the initial round progressed, it became apparent to Jeb that there were three leading contenders: the clipped-ear, but now sober, victor of last night's brawl; a tall, gangly, gray-bearded mountain man, and the young David Crockett, who turned and winked jauntily at Jeb and Sam as soon as he saw them standing in the crowd.

Having no gun of his own other than an old flintlock pistol, David needed a quality firearm for the shoot. With his outgoing personality and confident demeanor, the teenager was able to convince the owner of the Sloppy Bucket, old Mr. Gibson himself, to loan him the use of Gibson's prized rifle for the contest.

David was sixth in the sequence of shooters. He strode up to the line, shouldered, smoothly sighted his gun, and confidently squeezed the trigger.

In between each effort, the sight judge would amble over to the target to verify the exact location of the shot. He shouted out each result, so that all contestants would know where they stood in the round's competition. A fresh target was set up before each of the four rounds.

Out of all the contestants, the tall mountain man and David both struck nearest the very heart of the tiny center bull's-eye. But the mountain man was a tad closer. He barely won the first round and the first beef.

There was general grumblings and boastings of better shooting to come from many of the losers. Naturally, the ill-tempered chop-eared man, who was one of six inside the inner circle, complained most of all. "If that dern scarecrow thinks he's beating me twice, he's gotta another thang coming!"

The next round began. This time, young Davy Crockett shot dead center. The only one to hit perfectly true. He won the second beef. The mountain man nodded politely in defeat. Clip-ear glared at David.

The third round started. Clip-ear, who was fifth in order ahead of young David, hit "Right in tha middle o' tha middle," declared the sight judge. The contestant stepped away from the line with a smug expression on his sallow face. David grinned at him and said, "That there's right smart shooting. Let's see if my shot kin mount yours directly on top."

He confidently strode up, sighted, and squeezed the trigger.

The sight judge walked to the target. He carefully examined the center, stared at the outer circles, then scanned a second and third time over the entire target, before announcing loudly, "It's a clean miss, boy."

David stood in a puzzled pose while Clip-ear gloated. He politely asked the sight judge, "Sir, if ya wud, please take another peep at tha entry hole in tha middle o' tha bull's eye, for me."

The sight judge did as he was asked. He peered with intense concentration at the little black dot in the innermost circle, his red-veined bulbous nose less than an inch from the surface.

The judge stuck his finger in the top of the bullet hole. He stared, jerked his head back with a startled expression, and then stuck his face close to look in again.

Unbelieving, he called out in a surprised voice, "I'll be a one-eyed possum! There's two bullets in tha hole, one near on top o' tha other."

He nodded his head in puzzlement at the line judge and said, "I reckon this here's a tie. Whutta we goin' to do?"

The line judge chewed his tobacco thoughtfully and

spit out a brownish stream of juice to the ground before replying, "Unless another shooter in this here round also hits tha bull's eye straight on, we'll give tha beef to tha first winner, and tha five dollars to tha second."

David looked at his opponent. "Sounds square to me," he said affably. The two shook hands in agreement, although Clip-ear was agitated, and the round continued with no other exact center hits.

Contestants reloaded for the last round. The tall mountain man won the final match; his was the lone shot right in the dead center. David was barely inside the tiny bull's eye circle, and clip ear was on the line.

As the contest broke up, Jeb's face registered a genuine trace of hero worship and awe. Young Davy Crockett had won a quarter beef and five silver dollars against much older, more experienced marksmen. And Jeb had witnessed everything.

Maybe history isn't so dull, after all. If I ever get back to the future, I will never, ever, take history for granted again or think it's a boring subject.

Sam poked Jeb lightly in the side to break his reverie. "We've got well over half day's travel in front o' us," he reminded Jeb, "and a few mo' thangs to do before we leave."

Jeb turned and followed Sam as he retrieved their various purchases. He watched Sam load up his horse with the new plow, along with Rebecca's store-bought dress and fancy new tableware. It was now half past ten.

A chilly, yet refreshing breeze was gently blowing. It felt really good to be outside. Unlike his fear-filled path coming to Holston, Jeb was looking forward to this trip.

Within the dense forests on the long island and across the shore, he could hear the sounds of a multitude of woodland creatures. The profusion of noise showed that the birds and critters were enjoying the fine winter's morning, too.

Sam and Jeb boarded the flatboat for the other side. Their journey home had begun.

Chapter Seven
THE HANSEN GANG

The beginning part of the trip home was extremely enjoyable to Jeb. The weather was superb, and the walk was very pleasant. The winding forest path was narrow in places but easy to follow, so Sam let him lead. Sam followed contentedly, holding the reins of the packhorse trailing behind them with a slow, steady gait.

As the miles passed, Sam talked about his family, his farm, his past, and his plans for the future. Jeb thought Sam was an excellent storyteller, plus he was easy on the ears. He had a rich baritone voice and he spoke with an unhurried cadence.

"There's eight more acres on tha southwest side o' my homestead that I aim to offer to buy on pay-out. Ol' man Halbert, he lives alone there. He's near seventy-one now. He wants to sell off in another two-three years, and go live in town with his daughter and her husband in Jonesborough. I aim to speak to him once he's ready to move out."

He nodded and aimed a tobacco stream at a bush by the side of the path. "Yessir, Jeb, I want a place for my boys to raise their families close by Rebecca and me. A place for them to call their own after thay are grown up."

Jeb listened carefully to everything, paying close attention to the particulars of people, places, and events. He knew his contrived personal history was razor thin on real details. Whatever the strange source was that kept putting unwanted trivial data into his head he had no control over it. So the more useful facts he learned about the *present*, the better he could supplement his story and keep it believable.

Yesterday afternoon had been so scary and stressful. Yesterday, he didn't know anything about where, when, how, or why he was *here*. Today, his situation and state of mind were much better. At least he now knew the answers to where he was, and when, and had a good guess as to how it happened. *Plus, I have a friend in big Sam. And I have a home*, he thought. A known destination. That meant he had safety and shelter until such time as he could figure out how to return to his dad in present-day Tennessee.

Sam continued to talk. Jeb continued to listen. He learned big Sam had been born and raised in North Carolina, in a small village near the coastline. "I lost one uncle and my oldest brother in tha War for Independence. My Pa got bad-wounded in his left shoulder and arm at that Battle o' Guilford Courthouse."

His mother had died giving birth to his youngest sister. His father had eventually remarried and moved further west within the state.

After limited schooling and years of working on his pa's farm as a young man, Sam had met, courted, and married the oldest daughter of a steel-rod Methodist minister. "Yessir, Jeb, I wound up having to woo tha pair o' them at tha same time!" He chuckled. "I had to work something fierce to win Rebecca's affection. She is mighty particular 'bout who she cottons to. Worst still, I had to win her father over. And let me tell ya, twas the hardest o' tha two." In the end, Sam managed to convince the resistant reverend only by his consistent display of true heart and reliable character.

"Young Samuel, after considerable inner debate and much watchfulness, I have come to the conclusion that you are a good man and worthy of my daughter's hand in marriage," the right reverend had finally conceded.

Rebecca had inherited her father's strong moral backbone and force of will. "Make no mistake 'bout it, Jeb. She's my right hand in everythang I do." Sam knew it, and knew he was a lucky man to have married such a woman; he, just a poor hardworking farmer, and she, a proper school-educated lady. "Tell ya a secret. I don't make any big moves unless I git Rebecca's blessing first. She jest," Sam paused, "has a way 'bout her. She's a strong, smart woman. Got loads o' common sense. And, o' course, she's purty as tha sprang time." Big Sam smiled broadly. "I love her so much."

He described Rebecca to Jeb in detail. She had beautiful, long, reddish-auburn hair that fell down in tresses past her shoulders. When she spoke, he said, it was in a quiet, reasoned voice. She did not have to raise her volume; her speech carried the weight of the divine. Sam was the law in his family. But everyone knew Rebecca was the power behind the law, although Sam was a strapping specimen of adult manhood.

"Pa's second wife, Effie, died jest before he did. After Pa passed away, my two brothers, one's older, tha other's younger, my two sisters, and I sold off tha land. We split up a little inheritance out o' tha ol' farm."

With Rebecca's approval, Sam had moved his family to the frontier state of Tennessee, drawn there by the cheaper land, open opportunity, and excitement of a fresh start. The young state was fertile and growing by leaps and bounds. The threat of hostile Indians was decreasing every year. Churches, small settlements, stores of all sorts, even schoolhouses were being built as more eager settlers poured over the Cumberland and other routes into the region.

"Well, Jeb, I took that inheritance money, and we bought seven be-u-tiful acres, and settled down in tha new county o' Greene. Handsome land, tis. Flat brangs a tear to my eye and an ache to my heart sometimes when

I looks out over tha plowed fields in tha early morning mist." Over the years, he had single-handedly cleared his land, built his home, and put in crops, most for humans, the rest for livestock. All done without hired hands or help of neighboring farmers who continued to come into the area.

"I got me five living children now. A sixth died, stillborn, five years ago. Poor thang." He shook his head at the memory.

Emily, at seventeen, was his oldest. "She looks tha most like me. She's old enough now to be thinking o' marrying, except Rebecca n' me don't rightly see any good bucks nearby. And there's nobody around she fancies," he winked at Jeb.

"Robert, he's my first born boy. He's got lot o' his mother's looks in his face, but he acts like me. He jest turned sixteen. Robert's gittin' to be a grown man now, a real help to me n' his mother around tha place."

Sarah was his next oldest at fourteen and a half years of age. "She's tha purtiest n' has a sweet disposition. She acts like Rebecca. Got her mother's brains, looks, and hair."

Thomas, the younger son at twelve about to be thirteen, was the family clown. "Thomas, he jest wants to have fun and laughs all tha time, that boy. If there's any way he can git into mischief, he'll find it. Ain't got a mean bone in his body, tho'. He jest likes to cut-up."

Ruth, the baby daughter at barely nine years old, was the apple of Sam's eye. "And then there's my darling Ruthie. Lordie, but that little girl has got a way o' laughing that'd make the dead stand up and cackle, too." Any joke or prank Thomas did amused her to no end. "He's always pulling something to git her giggling." Sam winked at Jeb, as the boy half-turned to look at him talking. "He jest wants to hear her laugh. We all do."

Light breezes swirled gently around their faces as they walked. The sun, when it could, filtered through the openings in the thick canopy above to favor them with its late winter warmth. On both sides of the twisting trail, the nearby singing of the birds in the treetops and the constant chorus of other forest creatures provided a relaxing melody. The overall effect was very pleasant. The country path ahead of them seemed to melt away with ease. It was approaching noon.

Next, Sam started telling tales of the War for Independence as fought in the Carolinas, various events leading up to present-day settlement within Tennessee, and accounts of famous people he'd met, heard, or read about. Sam had learned his basic letters and could read a little.

His great adventure was having yet another good effect on Jeb. Dead, dry regional and state history was becoming alive and interesting to Jeb's listening ears. He absorbed every facet, even the smallest minutiae of Sam's narratives. He'd not said anything in response, yet he hung on Sam's every story as they ate up the miles. His head was turned toward Sam as the big man spoke.

Suddenly and without warning, a raucous, whiskey-cracked voice shouted out from the left woods of the oncoming path. "Drop ya rifle right now and run like the wind t'other direction, ya two skunks. Ya might jest live a little longer if we miss our aim."

Sam froze, his rugged face etched in surprise.

Jeb stumbled to a halt, too, his eyes desperately searching the trail ahead for the sound of the villainous, mocking speech. He spied three evil-looking men hiding behind the shelter of some trees lining the trail ahead. All were armed and aiming their weapons at Jeb, the lead walker. He recognized among them the scraggly-faced traveler from the tavern.

"I said drop it, ya yellow-liver'd varmints."

Two shots rang out. Jeb felt a strange tickle in his chest an inch above his heart and another in his lower stomach.

In lightening sequence, Sam reached out, grabbed Jeb, and threw the boy backwards to the ground then pulled the knot on the rope holding the plow onto the horse's saddle. The heavy implement fell to the ground, providing Sam and Jeb a small bulwark as they scrambled behind its shield.

"Are ya hit bad, Jeb?" Sam queried anxiously once

they took cover. He studied Jeb's face and examined his clothes for signs of bleeding.

"No, I'm not hit at all. I'm okay," Jeb replied. "Really," he said as Sam continued to look him over carefully. Sam shook his head in disbelief.

"But...ya got shot dead-center. Thay had tha two rifles pointed right at ya. There's no way thay missed ya that close. I don't see how." He gave Jeb another look-over. Finding the boy amazingly unhurt, he turned his attention to the three deadly killers in front of them.

"Ya stinkin' dirt-farmers. Ya cain't hide behind that ol' plow for long," yelled one of the robbers to Sam and Jeb.

"How tha hades did ya two miss tha boy? Horseshit!"

"Don't worry 'bout it. We'll soon run 'em out and skin 'em. Thay got no place to go."

The two that had fired their weapons began reloading. The third boldly stepped out from the full shelter of his tree and took aim at the stooped figures of Sam and Jeb. Sam leveled his rifle, drew a bead on the partially exposed enemy, and squeezed the trigger. The man's temple exploded in blood and brains.

"No-o-o-o-o! I'll git ya for that, ya sonnabitch!" screamed one of the robbers in a blind fury, while the other stood up, careful to stay behind the cover of the big tree, and shook his fist at Sam. The two men sped up their reloading efforts, anxious to exact vengeance for their fallen comrade.

"Jeb, boy, we're in a little bit o' tight spot here, but we'll be all right," Sam spoke in a low reassuring voice, as he calmly worked his rifle. It was obvious to Jeb that Sam was one cool customer.

Beads of sweat began to trickle down the faces of the two bandits as they worked feverishly to reload their weapons. Sam remained unruffled while he poured in powder. He kept the huge tree where the two men were hiding in his line of sight, suspecting they might try something different.

"Eddie, listen up. He ain't got his rifle ready yet. I'm gonna charge 'im. Ya try to sneak around through the woods to his back side soon as I step out. Ya hear?"

"I hear ya, Charley," replied the other.

The first man got his rifle reloaded. He saw Sam had no gun ready, nodded to his companion, and leaped from his hiding place, his rifle bearing down on his intended targets. "Ya gonna pay for killing Bob. Both o' ya!" The man ran forward, ready to fire.

Unexpectedly, a booming shout rang out in the distance behind the pitched battle. Jeb could hear a horse galloping and a loud, strong voice getting rapidly closer. "Hold on! I'm a coming! Big Ed's on tha way!"

Both robbers froze at the sound of the oncoming rider. The man in the road jerked his head up, his rifle barrel momentarily pointing now in the direction of the new person and not at Sam. The other robber raced back to the safety of the big oak, totally forgetting about the plan to circle behind the crouching victims.

Unperturbed at the approaching rider, Sam finished loading his rifle.

"Oh, damn!" The man realized too late that Sam had his gun aimed. He hastily brought his weapon back downward to sight at Sam and squeezed the trigger. A lead ball plowed into the robber's chest right through the upper part of the heart even as his own shot smashed harmlessly into the middle of the sturdy plow front.

Just then, the horse and the rider rounded the bend galloping toward them. Sam had already starting reloading, his vision still fixed on the last robber cowering in the woods beyond. Jeb, however, making sure his kept his head down, swiveled around to watch the newcomer approach. "Why, it's the big guy from the Sloppy Bucket who was talking to the barkeeper when we were there!" he recalled.

He heard a yell of fright and another rifle shot. Jeb turned toward the sounds. He saw the last robber running pell-mell into the forest thickness. The man had cried out at the prospect of facing another enemy. Leveling his weapon, he had fired in haste. Without waiting to see the outcome of his aim, he had fled in even greater haste.

Oblivious to the rifle ball that had whizzed by just

inches from his broad shoulder, the newcomer leapt from the saddle. His horse was glistening wet, still heaving from the exertion of the forced sprint. He bounded toward Sam and Jeb, his face flushed with excitement, his right hand clenched into a fist, and his left hand holding a long rifle cocked and primed for shooting. He was eager and ready for action.

"I cud hear tha shooting and tha shouting plumb near a mile away, and figured some poor souls were in mortal danger. I put tha whip to my horse and came a riding quick as I cud. Are ya two fellas all right?" he asked.

He examined Sam and Jeb for signs of injury as they stood. Then he strode with large steps to the first fallen foe. The body lay awkwardly twisted, with its face sideways on the path. He nudged his foot underneath and rolled the man over to get a frontal view. He bent down to peer closely at the death-clinched face. His eyes widened in shocked recognition.

"Why, I'll be a hang-tailed 'coon! That there's ol' Charley Hansen, he is. Him, his brother, his cousin, and two or three others, thay are tha Hansen gang, a bunch o' murdering skunks and thieves. I seen 'im jest once after a posse captured 'im three years ago tha other side o' tha Holston in lower Kentuck. I heard he escaped some time later and rejoined his gang. Thay arc 'bout tha worst, blood-thirsty, devilish pack o' killers in southern Kentuck and most o' Tennessee."

He stroked the four-day old stubble on his chin thoughtfully as he stared at the contorted figure. "Aye, thay have murdered women, children, and youngin's. Even preachers. Shot men in cold blood for tha clothes on their back. Kilt people, jest to be killing."

Looking up the trail, he saw the other body, also face down, strewn half inside the tree line, half on the path. The big man walked over, flipped the dead man over, and gravely inspected the partially blown face.

He shook his head at the sight. "I cain't rightly identify tha poor cuss from whut's left o' 'em. Except that--" He leaned in very close. "Lordie, he musta bin truly ugly when he was alive even with all his features intact.

"So how many others were here?" he queried when he returned to Sam and Jeb.

Getting no immediate response, he repeated the question. "How many were in tha gang today that attacked ya?" Sam and Jeb glanced at each other. They shrugged their shoulders and replied only one more that they could see off in the woods.

The huge man stood in front of them, his hands on his hips, and his head turned in a slightly quizzical fashion. The faintest of smiles spread on his broad face. "If tha whole gang had bin here, for sure tha two o' ya wud have bin dead before I arrived. Tha Good Lord above has bin looking over both o' ya today."

He continued, "It's a good thang for ya Big Ed Gibson's here. I reckon we kin travel together for a spell. I don't expect any other members o' tha gang will be coming back here. Jest in case, tho', I'll be a riding along with ya, as far as tha outskirts o' Greene."

He motioned at the two bodies and said meaningfully to Sam, "Not to disrespect tha dead, but thay cain't use anythang any mo'. Come on, boys, let's see whut thay have on em that we might kin take. There's two rifles here, one for ya, and one for me. And let's check their pockets for money. I don't want any o' their clothes."

Big Ed and Sam did the grisly work as Jeb watched the horses. They retrieved and split between themselves the two rifles, two powder horns, a few musket balls, plus a handful of silver half dollars, quarter dollars, dimes, and half dimes.

Because the dead men had attacked Sam and Jeb with clear intent to murder as well as rob, Big Ed deemed it fitting the two bodies should be left, without any formal service or burial, for the wild animals to devour. However, he and Sam did drag the two corpses off the path deep into the side woods, so passer-byes wouldn't have to witness the gory scenes.

Sam repacked his plow. "Mighty glad ya showed up when ya did. Kinda evened out the odds." He shook Big Ed's hand. "Well boys, we best be gittin' along now." Jeb nodded and started walking again, grateful they were still alive. With that, the party of two men, one boy, and two horses returned to their journey.

Big Ed began to whistle with merry disregard as the little band continued. "It's a fine day, boys. Ya got nothing to worry 'bout now, with Big Ed around. Yessiree!"

The trip was not entirely uneventful, as Big Ed turned out to be an even better storyteller than Sam. "One time, I was attacked by two bears all at once. Tha first I kilt with my trusty Ol' Mary, that's my favorite Kentuck long rifle. Tha second one I kilt with jest my hunting knife and my bare hands. Another time, I was ambushed by three Indians whist I was hunting alone. I killed tha one with a shot. Kilt one with my knife. And kilt the last 'un by sidestepping his blow, wrestling his own tomahawk away, and using it on 'im. It'd take a lot to do in Big Ed. By gum!"

The noonday faded into early afternoon and beyond. Big Ed continued to regale them with tale after tale of unbelievable bravery, cunning deeds, and incredible feats wielding gun, knife, ax, fist, and horse, in myriad combinations. He had absolutely no fear of wild beasts or bandits. His booming voice carried far into the forest on either side of the winding trail.

Even Jeb thought Big Ed was a fine figure for a frontiersman. The man's size and shape reminded Jeb of a professional football linebacker. He stood nearly six feet and five inches in his stockings and weighed upwards of two hundred and fifty-five pounds. Though Jeb didn't know it, Ed *was* a giant, considering the average man of the day was easily less than five-eight and one hundred and fifty pounds.

Jeb could sense that Big Ed, for all his colorful boasting and swaggering stories, was an easygoing person who had to be seriously agitated or threatened before his mighty temper flared.

Ed's current goal was to become happily married, he informed Sam and Jeb. "Yessir, I want to find a good quality woman, marry her, and settle down. Fact, I jest got back a couple o' weeks ago. Made a little trip to Kentuck, I did. Went to something thay called a camp-meeting." He turned to them and asked, "Either one o' ya ever heard o' such a thang?"

Sam nodded yes. Jeb drew a blank. *Camp-meeting?*

"Yaw, I'd bin told by several o' my friends it'd be a mighty fine place to meet some purty females, unattached, high morals," Ed explained. He described the campsite to them as a large brush arbor clearing in the woods filled with people who came from miles around. Everyone brought their own food and drink, he said, as well as tents and sleeping pallets. Many brought along their children, neighbors, relatives, dogs, slaves. Some even brought items to sell or trade like it was a marketplace. "Boys, I never seen anythang like it. Hundreds o' bodies all around. When tha meetings weren't goin' on, people were jest a sleeping, eating, talking, funning, and visiting back and forth. Lordie, it was something to behold. I never heard such gossiping, laughing, and loud speaking all my born days. I don't reckon I got more than two or three hours sleep a night tha whole time I was there with all tha commotion."

Having never heard of camp-meetings before, Jeb listened to Ed's tale with great curiosity.

Big Ed had never witnessed such meetings as these either. He mutely observed everything with wide eyes, open ears, and a closed mouth. The fiery sermons and plain speaking of the backwoods Baptist and Methodist ministers touched him deeply. The unrestrained emotions and undeniable zeal of the congregation fascinated him to no end. "Boys, I'm a tellin' ya--believe it or not--I seen grown men and women jest a crying, weeping, moaning, jerking like a turkey with its head cut off, falling down and rolling on tha ground. It was something to behold.

"It was a sight to see," he repeated with conviction. "But so were tha ladies!" He grinned big. "There were some real lookers in that there crowd. One sweet little thang, a red-headed gal, she kept giving me tha once over. Now, if that scrawny preacher hadn't beat me to tha punch," his bass voice grumbled into a string of harsh words about the minister who had cut in front of him just as he had finally gotten up the courage to approach the young woman.

The camp-meeting failure only made him more determined than ever to meet the ladies. He rounded back to his main subject. "Yessir, I want a proper lady to wife. Right now!" He pounded one huge fist into the other big palm. "I'm ready to settle down and raise me a parcel o' Gibsons." He chuckled to himself at the happy image.

Big Ed spent the next few hours peppering Sam with questions about Sam's family, his wife, and the glories of wedded bliss, all interlaced with expressions of Big Ed's vision. "I cain't wait to get my own wife, raise my own sons and daughters on my own farmstead. My boys will all be strong as oxen and good-looking, and tha girls will be tha purtiest around in five countries."

He asked Sam, "So tell me exactly how tha two o' ya met. Give me all tha details."

Sam's eyes twinkled at the big man's enthusiasm. "Well, sir, I had started goin' to tha Methodist church in tha little village close to where we lived. I was nineteen a goin' on twenty at tha time, I reckon. Rebecca was upfront a playing the pianie for tha hymn singing. She was sixteen a goin' on seventeen. Tha first time ever I seen her, I thought she was an angel direct from heaven. Her long hair, her eyes, her face, tha way she talked, tha way she smiled, her perfect figure, everythang 'bout her was, *is*, beautiful to me. Aye, Ed, it took me dang near three years to win her over, and two mo' years to git her father's permission. She didn't think much o' me tha first time she laid eyes on this here rough farmer boy. And tha reverend, well, let's jest say, he was a hard nut to crack. I had to work overtime on him."

Sam clapped Ed on his massive shoulder. "But twas all worth tha wait. I'm a blessed man today. I have tha best wife in tha whole state o' Tennessee and a fine family to boot."

Big Ed listened to every word. He was anxious to find and possess his own heaven on earth after hearing Sam's tale of wedded bliss. While the two men continued to discuss the virtues of a happy home life, the forested path they trod down gradually widened the further south they went. By the time the three travelers reached upper Greene territory, the path had expanded into a broad lane able to accommodate two wagons side-by-side. Jeb looked up and saw the omnipresent, overhanging roof of intertwining tree tops had thinned out. Now the party could see most of the cloudy blue sky above.

The time had come to part their company. Big Ed had distant cousins of Melungeon blood, "Melungin," he called them. "I aims to do some bear hunting with 'em. Yaw, thay all live a far stretch up in tha lower Blue Ridgies," he explained. Hence, he needed to turn sharp southeast. Sam and Jeb, on the other hand, would be going southwest to intersect the rambling Nolichucky River, toward Sam's farm.

Big Ed vigorously shook hands all around; Jeb figured his fingers were permanently damaged by Big Ed's behemoth grip. "Thankee for showing up in tha nick o' time," said Sam. Ed's presence had shaken the robbers and given Sam and Jeb the edge they needed to survive the confrontation.

They watched him mount and ride away, then resumed the last leg of their journey home.

Chapter Eight
THE FAMILY ROBERTSON

Sam had described his brood with such loving detail that Jeb was eager to meet all of them. He didn't know when or how he would get back to Dad and his own time. He would worry about that later. For now, Sam's family was his adopted family, and Sam's farmstead was his home.

They left the remains of the forest trail and headed out into the wooded thicket. Despite the denseness of the surrounding wilderness, sparsely populated in many places and still untamed in some parts, Sam clearly knew the way back.

Here and there, far off on either side, Jeb saw small homesteads; the log cabins perched in the middle of cleared farmland. They looked like toy buildings in the distance. Jeb noticed that the number of people and buildings increased the closer they got to the winding river.

Jeb could hear the Nolichucky before he could

see it. Sam simply called it, "The Nolichuck." The trees thinned close into the river's reedy banks. Sam guided the caravan to a shallow crossing where humans and horse could cross without much difficulty. Afterwards, they followed the mighty stream for about a mile in the same path as the fading afternoon sun. "Purty, ain't she, in tha evening?" said Sam.

He then led Jeb into the thickening forest on the other side of the river. They reached the farm's outer clearing before nightfall. "Here's my homestead," Sam said proudly as they stepped foot on his property.

Six of Sam's acres were neatly plowed with straight rows. The seventh acre lay fallow. A quarter acre of the six was devoted to the family's vegetable garden, which Rebecca and the children tended. The unfarmed ground just behind the home was used for various storage sheds and miscellaneous equipment. The area in front, where Sam and Jeb were approaching, had sixty yards of clearing before the tree line began. The tilled land surrounded his dogtrot style cabins from behind and on both sides.

Jeb saw two rough-hewn, notched-log buildings. Spacing between each log was chinked, or filled in, with a mixture of moss and mud. On the left stood a traditional one-story, one-room log structure measuring twelve by sixteen feet in size. On the right was an unusual two-story structure of the same base dimensions, with a second floor overhang.

The two log homes were separated by an open air space of six feet, with a roofed over passage between the one-story of the two structures. It was obvious to Jeb that Sam had added the second story to the right-hand cabin, sometime after the original construction.

Set twenty-five yards or so beyond the connected cabins was a chicken house and pen, filled with half a dozen restless hens and one very cantankerous red-iron rooster. A water-well lay ten yards to the left of the hen house. To the right of the pen was a long, crudely constructed animal shed with three enclosed walls, simple pitch roof and open front. Less shelter than a barn, more substantial than a lean-to, it nevertheless provided suitable protection and feed area for Sam's horse, his old plow mule, the one milk cow, and Sam's two hunting dogs during the worst of both winter and summer storms. Crops of oats and hay were grown and stored as year-round provender for the livestock.

At one time, they had a small herd of sheep, Sam told Jeb. Two summers ago, he had a fine bull. However, "I had to slaughter it for beef last winter," he explained. Sam had taken five of his hogs to market up Holston way. Still, there were seven hogs with marked ears left, fattening on the forage in the adjacent woods. Sam would buy, or barter, replacement hogs in the spring.

Further back of the well, chicken coop and animal shelter, there were two broad, side-by-side wooden cribs used for storing corn, which was their major food crop. Another final shed held the oats and hay for the livestock. A few yards behind the feed shed, there was a sturdy smokehouse for curing and storing bacon and hog sides.

After the various storage bins, the tilled soil began. The long, immaculately plowed rows stretched to the very shadow of the woods in the distance and continued around the sides of the two cabins.

Fifteen yards on the right side close behind the living quarters was a fully walled and roofed outhouse. It had been built at Rebecca's gentle insistence for the convenience of the family's four females. "Sam," she had instructed him, "I want it set close enough to the cabins to be nearby, yet not too close." The men folk might occasionally choose to go in the bushes and woods with macho abandon like savages, but the delicate and well-bred ladies of the Robertson household required their utmost privacy, year-round.

All in all, even with the bleakness of the late winter season, the modest frontier home gave the impression of warmth, industriousness, and order in the midst of the surrounding wilderness. It conveyed to Jeb a most comforting sense of safety and stability.

He surveyed what he could see from the front property and said, "Sam, your place is really cool. I mean, everything looks," he struggled for the correct words, "very neat, very tidy." Jeb nodded his head in apt approval. "It looks like a real farm to me."

Watching the boy's happy expression, Sam chuckled in amusement. He replied, "Yup. She's a real farm, Jeb. That she is. That she shore nuff is."

Jeb gave a sigh of contentment. Despite the tremendous shock of being trapped in the past, despite the harrowing dangers of the trail, he knew, for the first time in this unbelievable adventure, he had a home.

The youngest, Ruth, spotted them right away. She let out a squeal of pure delight, "Father's here!"

She dashed from the middle of the frost-wilted vegetable patch next to the left hand building where she had been playing games with Thomas and Sarah. Ruth raced around the cabin to reach Sam as he was coming in from the front. She wrapped her slender arms around him in the tightest hug she could. She buried her face against Sam's thick upper stomach and chest; then tilted her head up.

"Father, Father, Thomas found a dead bird and put it down the back of my dress. It stinks to high heaven. And its little beak scratched my back." Her pretty eyebrows knitted together and she pouted ever so slightly.

Jeb picked up on the fact that at nine years of age, Ruth's speech was more polished than Sam's. He supposed her mother's higher education and culture had everything to do with that.

At once, Ruth noticed the unknown boy standing

quietly by Sam. She lifted her face from her father and peered around him at Jeb. As boisterous and high-spirited as she was, she was well trained to be quiet and respectful in front of strangers.

Sam jerked his head at the boy and explained to Ruth, "Honey pot, this here's Jeb."

Jeb nodded at the girl as she watched him with growing curiosity.

"He's a goin' to be staying with us for a while. He lost his family to Injun attack, and he's got nowhere else to go. I met 'im on tha road to tha trading place."

Sam paused and gently raised Ruth's chin up to make sure she listened. "Now, don't ya be a telling your mother anythang. Ya let your father handle that. I need to talk with your mother, all alone, first, 'bout Jeb and explain his situation."

Ruth bobbed her head in understanding, but continued to stare with fascination at Jeb.

Thomas, Sarah, and Robert, who had been doing chores behind the cabins, came up next. They stood side by side, silently eyeing the new boy.

Sam made introductions. "This here's Robert. And that's Sarah. And tha one with tha polecat grin is Thomas." He paused. "Jeb will be staying with us for a bit."

He repeated a bit of Jeb's story to his older children with as soft a voice as his loud baritone could manage. He didn't want his wife to overhear. He needed to get with her, one-on-one, and set the proper stage. Sam explained to Jeb that Emily and Rebecca were inside, busy cooking dinner for the rest of the family.

He knew his wife had a heart of gold. He also knew she could be firm as flint if she perceived any potential slight, loss, or discomfort to her own offspring. The family was not starving by any means. But cash and crops were lean. All too often, wild game was the difference between a full table and slim pickings. Clothing was a continual problem with five growing boys and girls. A permanent extra mouth and body required more food, garments, and other scarce staples.

Sam left the over-packed horse for his two boys to unburden, unbridle, and unsaddle. He noticed the faces of his wife and daughter gazing with curiosity from the front window. They had heard the slight commotion outside, stopped their activity, and lifted aside the animal skin cover to spy out of the one foot square opening.

"I'm a goin' to talk to your mother. Ya youngins keep it down now." Sam squared his shoulders and strode manfully forward.

Meanwhile, Sarah and Ruth had quickly progressed from polite stares to critically examining Jeb with great interest. Jeb noticed that Sarah's expression had the faintest hint of a flirtatious smile.

Ever alert to everything their older siblings did, the two younger children noticed Sarah's flirting look, too. They looked at Jeb, then at each other with barely constrained sniggering. Soon, Thomas was laughing out loud at Ruthie's stifled giggles.

Sarah shot a warning glance to her younger brother and sister. "Hello, Jeb. Welcome to our home. I am so sorry about your family. We are very glad you're safely here," Sarah said in a sweet and gentle voice. Her exceptionally pretty face radiated compassion and more toward the new boy.

Jeb's brown eyes widened and his face began to redden in mild embarrassment at Sarah's attention. He pulled on his shirt collar, thinking it must be getting hotter even though the winter day was becoming colder as it deepened into dusk.

Robert frowned at Sarah's overly attentive display. To compensate, he spoke in a firmer than normal tone, "How old are ya? My name's Robert. I am tha eldest. Eldest boy, that is. I jest turned sixteen." His speech wasn't quite as primitive as his father's or as proper as his little sister's.

Jeb answered distractedly, "I'm, ah, I'm fourteen."

"How many brothers and sisters did ya have in your family?" Robert lowered his volume. He didn't want his father to overhear. "How come ya survived? Why didn't tha Indians kill you, too?" He seemed eager to hear more details of the actual attack.

Instead of answering Robert, Jeb craned his neck

to see in between Thomas and Sarah, who were blocking his view of Sam's discussion with his wife. Jeb watched as she paused in the breezeway with her hands on her hips.

"So, how did ya wind up on tha Trail, the Holston?" Robert asked in a loud whisper. "Did ya see any more Indians between your place and tha Trail?"

"Wait a minute." Jeb waved his hand and shushed him so he could concentrate on what was happening between Sam and his wife. Jeb saw Sam gesturing with great earnestness as Rebecca stood, looking steadfastly at her husband as he spoke. When Sam finished his pitch, she said not a word but pursed her lips. She stared out at the distant horizon and then studied her children in the yard with the new boy. Slowly and deliberately, Rebecca surveyed their property stretching out in front of her. After careful consideration, she replied to Sam. Jeb could tell from the relieved, sheepish grin spreading on Sam's rugged countenance that Rebecca's charitable side had won out.

Jeb smiled. He had a home.

"Sorry, I wanted to see what was going on between your mom and dad. Listen, Robert, I'll tell all of you my story later tonight." He wagged both forefingers at Robert and the rest of the children as confirmation. "All the details, I promise."

Sam motioned the waiting group to come in for

supper. Letting his children pass by, he strolled forward a few steps to speak with Jeb in private, out of earshot of the rest.

"Jeb, my Rebecca's agreeable for ya to stay, maybe through next winter, maybe a lot longer. Winter's a hard time for a youngin' to be all alone without family, no roof over your head, and no steady meals. She's bin raised to show Christian charity. She's a real fine mother, a tender heart, and she'll treat ya jest like one o' our own."

"That's tremendous. I really appreciate it, Sam."

"I reckon ya kin bunk next to Thomas. He's always wanted one mo' brother. If ya don't mind, ya kin help out with chores and such, and hunting for tha table."

Jeb shook Sam's meaty hand in gratitude. Sam beamed and heartily clapped him on the back. "Come on, Jeb. Supper's a waiting." Together, they walked under the dogtrot covering into the left cabin.

The first thing Jeb saw, upon entering the room, was a makeshift bed in the immediate right-hand corner.

Upon Rebecca's request, Sam had created a bedstead in the left dogtrot building for use by passing travelers. The visiting person could sleep comfortably there, allowing the family to maintain their privacy in the right-hand cabin. A large pole had been stuck into the wall, and formed a rail for the outside of the bedstead. The free end was held up by a notched log. A large bearskin covered the top of the mattress, which was stuffed with leaves. Underneath the mattress were six smaller cross-poles laid from the pole into the side wall.

A huge fireplace stood at the other end of the room, filling the twelve-foot by sixteen-foot space with welcome warmth and crackling light. Its long chimneystack was chinked and lined with clay; its massive hearth was made of stones. There was a large, ancient iron pot hanging over the dancing flames. A mouth-watering aroma wafted from the bubbling surface, invading every corner of the small house.

"Wow, whatever it is, it smells wonderful." Jeb sniffed the air.

Rebecca turned and smiled at the newcomer as she and her oldest daughter finalized preparations. "Welcome, young sir. I hope you are hungry," she said.

Although the dwelling was slightly crowded with all seven of the Robertsons and Jeb gathered inside, he considered it very cozy, even comfortable, after the ordeals and outside weather of the two days' travel.

In the middle of the room sat a lengthy wooden table, surfaced with split log slabs and supported by four stout legs. It allowed exactly eight persons to sit down: three on either side and one at each end. Long benches, constructed of smaller log slabs, ran on the sides of the table. Large, hand-carved wooden stools, gently concaved in the seat and surprisingly comfortable, served for the end-chairs.

As their mother watched with approval, Sarah set the table with the new, store-bought tableware and plates, and Emily placed the steaming hot food in the center.

"That looks very nice. Thank you, Father Robertson, for the new china," said Rebecca, smiling at big Sam.

Sam turned and winked at Jeb, glad his purchase had made a good impression.

As was the family custom, the men folk stood in a row behind the ladies' side, in silent patience, watching the meal being served. Once everything was ready, Sam escorted Rebecca to her end-chair and seated her, then walked around and waited behind his chair. Robert and Thomas then escorted and helped their three sisters to their seats on their bench, starting with the oldest through the youngest, than the boys went around to their bench side and waited.

Jeb stood off to the side observing this with great curiosity. Thomas hurriedly motioned for him to take the available end spot on the boy's bench. Jeb trooped over. Not knowing what else to do, he held his hands together across his stomach.

With the women folk seated, and the men still standing, the Robertson clan all bowed their heads while Rebecca said an extended grace over the dinner. Lowering his head yet keeping his eyes open, as he always did, Thomas noticed Jeb awkwardly staring straight ahead. Thomas elbowed him to bow his head, too.

"Heavenly Father, we thank you for your bountiful hand, and for the meal we are about to eat. We know that every good thing comes from above. We thank you for bringing Father Robertson home safely from his trip. We thank you for our young guest, Jeb. We thank you for our blessings, our health, our home, and most of all, for the gift of your Son, our Savior. May every day bring us closer to your divine and perfect will."

"Amen," the whole family said together. The men sat down.

Jeb soon found out the Robertson clan followed this routine for every meal. Although the grace, he learned, was much shorter for the breakfast and mid-day meal. Few frontier families regularly practiced prayer or formality over supper tables. But as Sam later explained to him, Rebecca, being the daughter of a minister, believed virtuous behavior and religious observances were needed in the savage country they lived in.

The family and Jeb sat down to a simple, hearty country dinner. There was a savory stew of freshly-killed wild turkey, along with potatoes, carrots, turnip roots, onions, dried corn, dried peas, and beans remaining from the late fall garden, all seasoned with homegrown dill and sage herbs. Corn was a staple at most frontier meals, and there was a generous platter of hot, mouth-watering hoecakes for everyone. Emily set the table with molasses, made from their own summer cane patch. In late fall and early winter, they still had pumpkin and cushaw squash available, but sadly that supply was recently gone.

Sam had his usual corn whiskey diluted with a generous amount of well water. Although he was partial to strong drink, he had become very moderate in his habits since courting and marrying Rebecca. The two boys were allowed a small taste of the whiskey. Robert and Thomas drank milk from the family cow, but it was mixed with a teaspoon of the corn whiskey and generous honey sweetening for the younger boy, and an eighth shot of whiskey and honey for the older one.

"Water is okay for me," Jeb said. He got a giant wooden mug filled with plain, refreshing water, pulled from the unfrozen depths of the well.

Mother and daughters drank straight chilled milk, poured out of the covered wooden jug which Emily had purposely set outside in the cold to form tasty ice crystals before it was served.

The family and Jeb attended to the business of eating for the next fifteen minutes or so, without any attempt at conversation. Accustomed, as he was, to processed grocery and fast food, the meal tasted a bit wild, yet very good. Jeb found he had a tremendous appetite.

"Mrs. Robertson, this is really delicious. May I have seconds?" Jeb asked. Not to be outdone by the new kid, Thomas gobbled down his last two bites and demanded more. Both his mother and father turned and looked at him.

"Yes, Thomas?" Mrs. Robertson arched her eyebrows.

"Please, may I, too," Thomas mumbled, contritely.

As Jeb dug into another bowlful of the steaming stew and second slice of hot cornpone, he had to admit most modern food didn't taste half as delectable as this first dinner with his new adopted family. Spooning in another big mouthful, Jeb pondered sadly on his own broken home as compared to the togetherness displayed by the Robertsons.

He chewed soft. And contemplated hard.

Chapter Nine
AFTER DINNER TALES

Wow. The Robertsons are so different from my family in so many ways, Jeb observed.

And he knew it was more than the difference between living in 1802 and being back in the year 2014. For one thing, they seem to be a real family. Loving, supportive, and really together. Despite the obvious advantages that time and technology afforded people of today, the Robertsons not only survived, but thrived, even in tough wilderness conditions.

Jeb's frontier experience was helping him see it wasn't the quantity of your life that matters the most, but the quality of it. He reflected that most students at Highland Hill would consider the Robertson to be much poorer, by far, than the worst welfare families in modern day Knoxville.

Jeb was sad about his real family's condition, yet happy to be safe for the moment with his frontier family.

Prayer at mealtime was a new experience for Jeb.

In his own family, religion was not important to either his dad or mom. His father was a nominal Presbyterian. His mother was a non-practicing Catholic.

When Jeb was very young, more so after Nat was born, his parents tried to go to church or mass at Christmas, Easter, and maybe three or four other services a year. But their half-hearted attempts at religious upbringing dwindled and stopped completely after his dad become famous in his academic field.

That was also when, Jeb recalled woefully, *Mom and Dad began fighting more and drifting apart.* Despite his parents' attempts to hide the widening cracks in their relationship, he and his sister understood what was happening.

After dinner, the two younger daughters removed the remaining food, cleared off the dirty tableware and wooden plates, then sat back down. Each person, beginning with the father, spoke to the rest of the family about the events of his or her day.

Normally, Sam, as the patriarch or male head, would start and was allotted the greatest amount of time to talk. However, whenever there was a guest present, as there was tonight, he or she was given the opportunity to speak first.

In the years before Jeb's parents had gotten divorced, it was unusual for all four Cockrells to sit down to dinner together unless they had gone out to eat as a family. And even then, there was mostly stone silence at the table. This was another interesting experience for him.

All eyes turned to Jeb as Sam, in his Carolina backwoods English, explained this other strange custom. "Jeb, if ya want, ya kin go first and tell us little bit 'bout yourself and your situation."

As Sam encouraged him, Jeb reddened in the face and murmured to the group, "Sam has already told all of you my story, I think." He looked over at Robert and Thomas, and mouthed the words, "I'll tell the rest of you more later on."

Sam saw it and smiled. "Jeb, we won't bite, I promise ya. Ya're safe here." He waited a bit longer. "If ya don't want to talk 'bout it now, I understand. Ya bin through some rough times, lad."

When Jeb had nothing more to say, Sam began to recount his eventful journey to and from the Sloppy Bucket.

"I met up with young Jeb here 'bout thirteen miles south o' Holston. Once we got there, a silly fight broke out between two men over a piddling matter. We stayed for tha shooting match tha next morning, then set out. Had jest a little bit o' trouble, though, on tha way home."

Sam was so nonchalant about their life and death encounter with the robbers that he could have been talking about the weather. However, no fact of consequence was left out: meeting Jeb, the fight at the tavern, the shooting contest, the attack by several members of the Hansen Gang, and the timely arrival of Big Ed.

Not a peep was heard from the family. Jeb could tell the two boys were squirming with excitement at their father's story, especially the part about the bushwhacking robbers. He could also see that Rebecca flushed a bit red when Sam came to the part about the deadly ambush on the trail.

Since moving to Tennessee, Sam had experienced similar life-threatening situations, where his quick actions and coolness had saved his family or his own skin. Rebecca knew she must not overreact to the Hansen attack. Living on the frontier meant living on the edge. It was always harsh. And frequently dangerous.

She had learned long ago to trust Sam's abilities in the face of challenges. It had taken her minister father time to see beyond Sam's rough exterior and obvious lack of religious upbringing, to Sam's physical qualities of bravery, strength, and lightning-fast instincts. It was one of the things that made her fall in love with him. Yes, he was a good man. And he was definitely a man's man.

Once he was done talking, the rest shared their day, each in turn. Rebecca, as the female head of the house, went next, followed by the two boys by age, and the three girls in sequence. No event, task or issue was insignificant. If it was deemed important enough to mention, it was worthy of everyone's attention. Even the youngest, Ruthie, was shown full respect as if she was an adult.

Robert spoke about his turkey hunting earlier that day with Thomas. "Tha first turkey we see, Thomas starts laughing 'bout some stupid thang Ruthie did this morning--"

"Robert." A soft word of rebuke came from his mother.

Robert glared at his brother, took a deep breath, then continued, "Thomas starts giggling over something funny that Ruthie said earlier, and he spooked the turkey jest as I shot. So I missed tha first one. And that's why we took longer gittin' back."

Little Ruthie was the last to go. "Sarah and I had to refill hay for old Bessie," she looked at Jeb, "that's our cow," she explained. "And, and," she giggled then clapped a hand to her mouth, glancing at her sister, "and I came around her end, and Bessie farted right in my face." At this, Thomas and Ruth both erupted uncontrollably. Sam cut his eyes up, looked over, and grinned at Jeb.

"Children, that's enough. Ruth, dear, is that proper language for a young lady?" her mother corrected.

"No, ma'am. I'm sorry." Ruthie stifled her laughter, but mirth still sparkled in her eyes.

Jeb was amazed at the natural, friendly interplay between the members. In his family, only he and Nat had a similar bond of togetherness. The deep respect and love exhibited by Sam and Rebecca was something he had never seen with his parents, not even when he was little and his parents' marriage was young.

Once all had spoken, dinner was officially over. It was time for bed. Sam stood up and strolled to the other side to help his wife up.

Mrs. Robertson asked, "Ruthie, do you need to go?" Those who had calls of nature took turns and made their way to and from the one-hole outhouse. Sam stoked the fire down low for the night. Rebecca and the girls tidied up the cabin from the day's activities. Then everyone trooped out, and Jeb watched Sam latch and bar the wood door shut from the outside.

Both cabin doors were constructed of thick pieces of wood fastened to crosspieces. The heavy doors swung open and shut on rugged hinges made of leather. On each door, a deerskin string was tied to its latch and hung outside for use during the day. When the latchstring was pulled, it drew the latch up to open the door. At night, the right door latchstring was hung inside. And on each door, thick wooden bars were put in place to keep the doors shut tight against intruders. But while the right door bar was fixed from the inside, the left door bar was secured on the outside.

At bedtime, the left door latchstring wasn't hung inside; it ran underneath the placed bar, which had numerous porcupine needles embedded up and down its inner side. Sam saw Jeb looking at the secured door and explained. "See, if anyone or anythang tries to pry that bar off, them prickly needles will make a scratching noise loud enough to wake tha dead and let us know somebody, or some big animal like a bear, is trying to break in next door."

"I see. Have you ever had anything try to break in?" Jeb asked with a slightly worried expression.

"Well, we had two Indian braves several years ago who made a ruckus late one night. I came a busting out o' tha sleeping cabin with my rifle cocked and scared both o' them so bad they went a running and a stumbling. Thay were both so skunk-drunk thay cudn't hit the ground itself with their arrows if thay bin aiming right at it. Another time, we had a moose in rutting season that took a fancy to tha door and kept a rubbing his antlers against it until I popped out and shooed 'im away."

Jeb realized that during the day the family spent more of their time in the dining area. The two-storied, right-hand building was where they all slept at night.

For now, the existing housing was workable. But as his children got older, Sam explained, he wanted to add "Another cabin so my boys and girls kin each have their own private room." He also planned to build a second story above the left hand dining cabin, so they would then have twin two-story cabins connected by the dogleg in the middle.

The father and mother occupied the ground level of the right cabin, along with the family valuables-- money, heirlooms, jewelry, finer clothes, tools, and guns they kept in their room for security. Rebecca had her French spinning wheel, "My pride and joy," she called it, next to the fireplace. Sam also stored his better tools inside the space when not being used: the huge felling ax, broadax, adz, froe, wedge, and big mallet. Sam fastened the left door behind him, and the family walked into the right-hand cabin.

As Jeb passed by her, Rebecca reached out and tapped him on the shoulder. When he turned around, she unexpectedly put her arms around the boy and gave him a comforting embrace.

Jeb was moved by the gesture. His mom had never held him and Nat quite like that. She wasn't much of a hugger.

Rebecca said, "Jeb, Father Robertson and I are very glad to have you stay here. I can tell you are a well-bred, young gentleman. And I can assure you our sons are quite delighted to have another boy in our home. They have wanted another brother, a third boy to match the girls, for so long."

Jeb blushed and said, "I'm glad to be here, too. Thank you for putting up with me."

"You are welcome," she smiled and patted his cheek. Sam came beside his wife and slipped his thick arm around her slim waist, a grin plastered on his happy face. He winked big at Jeb.

For now, the children all shared the upper level sleeping area. They crossed the room and climbed up using the steep ladder against the far wall. "Watch your step, Jeb," exclaimed Sarah brightly as she followed him up the ladder.

The ladder led through a three-foot square opening cut into the ceiling.

Separating the girls from the boys was an elongated canvas set in the middle of the room. It was mounted with wooden pins into the opposing walls and had been stitched together from the side sections of two old military tents Sam had gotten from his pa. Although the canvas stretched from wall to wall and provided visual privacy up to six feet high, it didn't prevent the constant flow of bantering, joking, laughing, and innocent carousing that happened almost every night among the room's combatants.

"I'm going to get you back for putting that dead bird down my dress," Ruthie whispered loudly from above to Thomas as he began climbing up the ladder.

"Yeah, well, I have more where that came from," he retorted.

Instead of beds, the children had pallets on the floor. Each had two stuffed mattress piled one on top the other, for optimal comfort against the hardness of the log slabs.

Each also had a heavy bearskin plus a thick handmade quilt for the worst nights of winter. For fall and spring, each typically used just the quilt. In the hottest summer months, they did without any covering at all.

"Say, Jeb, ya kin have my top mattress and my quilt," Thomas generously offered to share. He would make do with just his bearskin.

Sarah overheard and called out from the other side, "Jeb? Oh, Jeb?"

"Yeah, Sarah?" he answered.

"You can have my top quilt, too. I don't need it." She pushed the end of it under the canvas for Jeb to grab hold of.

"Thanks. Both of you." Jeb gratefully accepted everything. It was freezing outside.

"Scoot over," Thomas nudged his brother, who had already lain down. "Robert! Robert! We gotta make room for Jeb."

Robert grudgingly got up and moved his bedding to the right. "I'm still mad at ya for making me miss that turkey," he grumbled.

Thomas ignored his comment and moved over as well. He pulled off his extra mattress, patting the empty floor space. "Put 'er here, Jeb," he said. Jeb made his pallet next to Thomas as the longed-for extra brother. Now, the number of boys equaled that of the girls.

Before Jeb got settled down, Robert called out

from the other side of Thomas, "Now, tell us 'bout tha Indian attack."

Jeb sat up so he could talk better. He angled his body so he would face the stretched canvas in front of him and the two boys on his right, pulling the two heavy quilts around him for warmth as he spoke.

"Well, a lot of my memory has been blocked out. What I do remember is this. We had just sat down to dinner. My father was sitting my right side, and my baby sister was sitting on my left next to me. When all of a sudden--"

"What was your little sister's name?" asked Sarah, interrupting him.

"Umm, her name was Natalie."

"That's a pretty name."

"Let him finish, Sarah," scolded her big brother.

"She is, was, very pretty. And smart, too. We were best friends." He exhaled with a sudden stab of homesickness. Catching himself, he continued ad libbing his story, "Well, anyway, the Indians attacked us just as we were sitting down. They went for Father first. He took three arrows in his chest as he stood up. His rifle was still on the mantle. My sisters and mother all screamed at once. Mother was struck by tomahawk and fell across the table. I don't know why, but I grabbed a money pouch that father had placed on the table from his trading he'd down earlier that day. Then I grabbed Natalie and covered her and the pouch with my body on the floor."

"Oh no," whispered Sarah at the bloody image conveyed by the woeful tale. "Jeb, that's so sad." Her voice was as gentle and soft as a light spring rain.

"I'm fine, now." Slightly ashamed, he roughly wiped a single tear streak off his cheek and stared with a determined look at the two boys. His emotion was for living family members who, for the time being, were as lost to him as if they had all been killed. "Ah-h-h, the next thing I recall is standing in the middle of the old trail. I've forgotten the name."

"It's called tha Holston Trail."

"Yeah, that's right. I don't have any memory in between the attack and the Holston. I don't remember how I got there. I don't know why I was left unharmed. Besides my father and mother, I don't really know for sure what happened to the rest of my family, except to assume they all were killed or carried off by the Indians."

He could see Robert sitting up on his pallet and frowning in deep concentration. "How cud ya not know what happened? I don't understand. Ya were right there. It don't make any sense."

Sarah said, "Robert. Jeb just explained that he lost his memory. Mother has told us stories where people got carried off by the Indians, and later, they couldn't remember certain things when they got rescued and returned to their white families. It's okay, Jeb. I understand."

Her tender nature warmed Jeb. He could feel her compassion flowing through the canvas.

Robert muttered to himself, "Well, it still don't make no sense to me. I wud remember everything if tha Indians got after me." He stretched back down and pulled his quilt and bearskin up under his chin.

Minutes passed. As Jeb lay there, regaining his composure, a soothing state of sleepiness began to settle over his body. He was more tired than he realized. The attack on the trail and aftermath had stressed him out. He listened drowsily as a good-natured war of words started up on both sides. It seemed Emily was too grown up to join the fray.

"Thomas, ya dern fool, ya almost made me miss that second turkey, as well."

His little brother ignored him again. "Hey, Ruthie, did ya like that dead bird today. It was calling for ya. It wanted ya." Suppressed giggling came from the other side of the canvas. "It loved ya."

"Yes, and old Bessie stinks just as bad as you do when you fart, Thomas."

More laughter.

"Mine may smell, but ya cain't hear 'em. Thay's as silent as a graveyard. Ya don't know it's there 'til it's too late."

Ruthie laughed and said, "Robert, you didn't do all your chores today."

"Hush it, or I'll tell mother ya didn't finish feeding tha chickens."

There was a brief silence.

"Somebody likes Jeb, somebody likes Jeb."

"Thomas, you shush now! Go to sleep." Sarah retorted as quietly as she could, but Jeb could hear the embarrassment in her sweet voice.

The friendly rivalry between the Robertson brothers and sisters reminded him of his own sister. He missed Nat so much. He missed Mom, too, but not nearly as bad as Natalie. Now he wished he hadn't started thinking about his own sister! The familiar ache of loss and loneliness began to flare full force in the pit of his stomach. All of a sudden, he wasn't so sleepy anymore. He stared out in the darkness of the logged ceiling, the sibling attacks and counter-attacks lessening as the adversaries dropped off to sleep, one by one.

Next to him, he soon heard the dueling sounds of Thomas and Robert's broken snoring. From the nearby forest, he heard the incessant hooting of an owl and a symphony of noises from the other woodland creatures. Jeb whimpered alone with his overwhelming sadness.

As the night temperature dropped outside, Jeb lay awake a long time, shivering slightly in the cold. Random memories swirled in his head about his sister, his dad, his friends Robert and David, Mr. Mackey, Dora, his grandparents, and his mom.

"Will I ever see any of them again?" he whispered into the night air.

Chapter Ten
SAVAGE ATTACK

When Jeb awoke, it was well past daylight. He stretched and yawned mightily. In fact, he couldn't stop yawning. He had slept hard after finally falling asleep in the wee hours of the morning. Jeb stared at the log ceiling as he mulled over the adventures and close calls he'd had since coming out of the fog and finding himself in the year 1802 on the Holston Trail. *I still don't know how those two robbers missed me. They were only, like, fifteen or twenty yards away. But I didn't get hit or even nicked. That's just weird. And what was that funny feeling I felt when they shot at me?*

And why didn't that big panther attack me when I was all by myself on the trail? I wasn't armed, I couldn't defend myself. Yet it just turned and stalked away. It's all very strange. He pondered whether it was pure luck or some other unseen force at work. An image of the green book floated across his thoughts. *Oh, well, at least I'm safe now.* He glanced over the boys' half of the room.

Nobody was there. He sat upright and called out to the other side.

"Anyone there? Emily? Sarah? Ruthie?"

He was all alone in the top room. The other children had arisen earlier without loud talking or infighting, so as to not wake their tired guest.

"Gosh, I wonder what time it is." He yawned one more time, arched his back and slowly stood up, twisting this way and that to get the kinks out. The single mattress had not totally cushioned the hardness of the slab wooden floor. Jeb had never liked roughing it on the ground and had never slept well with just a sleeping bag on his Boy Scout camping trips.

Rubbing the last of the sleep out of his eyes, he staggered forward and slipped into his frontier shoepacks he'd left at the foot of his mattress last night. Jeb tried smoothing out his wrinkled clothes but to no avail. He then took a look around the sparse room.

The first thing he noticed was a long, low-built cedar chest against one wall. "Hmmm, that must be where Robert and Thomas keep their extra clothes, personal things, and whatnots." It was certainly large enough, he thought.

"I suppose the girls have the same type of furniture on their half of the room."

There was also an enormous, multi-pointed rack of antlers mounted midway on one side wall. Hanging there were two rifles, accompanying pouches, and two heavy coats. He recognized one of the rifles by the fancy silver design on its stock. "Yeah, that belonged to the dead robber who got shot down charging at us," he remembered. He walked over and touched the metal plating on the butt of the rifle.

Turning full circle, he saw the upper level had two windows. On the girl's side, the trace of sunlight shown faintly through the heavy canvass. On the northeast, the boy's side, the strong, early morning sun hit the window's leather flap. It cast an elongated U-shaped shadow that was bordered by a thin stream of brilliant light stretching out on the floor beneath the foot square covering.

Jeb stepped over to the window, lifted the animal skin, and peered out. The day had dawned brightest blue. He saw not a cloud in the sky. The temperature felt at least four or five degrees above freezing. "It feels much better than the last several days," he exclaimed, looking out at the sea of forest surrounding the cabin.

Although he had been depressed when he went to sleep, it was hard to remain sad in the face of such a beautiful morning. He could hear the woodland critters calling out to one another-- birds, mostly, but other creatures and insects, too. "Hey, it's going to be a fine sunny day," he encouraged himself.

Jeb saw a wooden washbasin sitting on top of a thick log pedestal in the corner. He went to it, lowered his head in, and splashed his face and neck. He instantly jerked up. "God, it's freezing!"

Now he was fully awake.

There was no mirror by the basin. A thick homemade towel was folded to the side. Jeb blotted his face with the rough towel and shook his head like a dog to fling off excess water. He blinked his eyes wide open.

He had not taken any of his clothes off last night when he went to bed, but had simply crawled on top of his mattress and covered up with the quilts. He tried again to smooth the sleep crinkles from his outer clothes. "I suppose it doesn't matter back then. Or rather, back now," he said.

How nice would it be if I could go to sleep every night in my clothes in my own bed at home. He grinned to himself. *I could get used to that habit. No muss, no fuss.*

His thoughts were interrupted as he heard voices coming from below. He went to the ladder and carefully climbed down. Sam and Rebecca were gone. Jeb walked over and opened and shut the heavy door. He took two steps across the dogtrot and pulled the latch to enter the dining room.

Everybody was there except for Robert and Thomas, who were outside doing early morning chores and tending the animals: the silkie breed chickens that lay eggs even in Tennessee winters, Bessie the milk cow, Sam's horse, and his old plow mule. Sarah and Ruthie sat at the table while Sam stood. Rebecca and Emily were working together, cooking hominy grits and frying up eggs with bacon. The inviting aroma pervaded the cabin space. Jeb found his stomach growling with morning hunger.

Mrs. Robinson glanced over her shoulder and smiled sweetly as Jeb came in. "Good morning, young sir. I trust our rowdy boys and girls did not keep you up too late. Did you sleep well?"

"Yes, ma'am," he nodded politely. He went to his place at the table and sat down, but jumped up immediately. He had forgotten that in the Robertson household the men don't sit down until the ladies are seated.

She continued, "I hope you like grits and eggs for your first breakfast here." Mrs. Robertson spoke in precise, measured English. "My boys are very excited to have you staying with us for now. They have always wanted another brother."

"I know. Sam told me." Jeb was bashful and hesitant around Rebecca. She reminded him of his own mom in several ways. The careful way she spoke, her professional demeanor, even the coloring of her hair was somewhat similar.

Sam stood next to his chair at the table and spoke. "Jeb, Mrs. Robertson and Emily are goin' to tha Bledsoe's for most tha day. Thay are our closest neighbors, less than a mile away. Their place is due south from our place."

Just then, Thomas walked in and went over to Jeb's side of the table. Full of energy and a bit hyperactive, Thomas paced back and forth as he listened to the morning conversation.

Sam continued, "Husband William came over before daylight saying Mrs. Bledsoe was jest beginning labor for their second child. Mrs. Robertson and Emily are goin' to help out. Robert and I are traveling along to escort tha ladies there. While thay are helping out with tha new baby and all, Robert, Mr. Bledsoe, and I will do some hunting while we wait, putting food on their table so Mr. Bledsoe kin stay close to home over tha next week or so.

"O' course," Sam glanced at Jeb with a jovial expression and the corners of his mouth twitched, "now that we have another boy to help keep watch over Sarah and Ruthie, Mrs. Robertson feels a might easier, leaving tha younger girls home while tha rest o' us go to tha Bledsoes. We should all be home long before dark," he added.

Sam surveyed the children. "I want all four o' ya to stay close to tha house. Ruth kin be mischievous, so boys, ya watch her like a hawk." He gazed over the table and smiled indulgently at his youngest son. "Thomas, stay outta trouble. Don't ya be egging Ruth on, hear me? I want ya'll to git all your chores done. And don't any o' ya go wandering off in tha woods."

He looked gravely at Thomas and Jeb. "Thomas, I'll leave ya in charge for tha day, and Jeb, you help 'im." His commanding eyes conveyed burden and trust on the two boys.

Jeb swallowed. "Yes, sir," he answered timidly.

Thomas, on the other hand, grinned and nodded in shocked approval. This was his first occasion to be given the responsibility as the oldest boy in charge and he was excited.

Robert came in from his chores just as his sisters were putting food on the table. The men waited dutifully behind the girls' bench as breakfast was being served. Jeb got in line next to Thomas. They then seated the women, went to the bench or chair, and stood, as Mrs. Robertson said a quick prayer over the meal.

Once again, Jeb was surprised at how much he liked the simple frontier food and how tremendous his appetite was. "This is so good, Mrs. Robertson," he exclaimed with his mouth half full. Perhaps it was being in another place and time. Perhaps it was being in a primitive wilderness setting. Perhaps it was the stress of traveling back in history. Whatever the reason, Jeb knew he had never been as hungry, nor had food ever tasted as good as right now.

After the morning meal, Sam, Rebecca, Emily and Robert prepared to go to the Bledsoes. Sam and Robert got their rifles, pouches, and powder horns ready for the day's hunting. The women would ride Sam's horse for the short journey of slightly less than a mile. The men would walk alongside. "We'll be back long before sundown," Sam told the others.

The happy party headed out. The womenfolk were excited about the baby, the menfolk, about the hunting. "Ya behave yourselves, now," admonished Sam one last time.

Sarah, Ruth, and Jeb gathered in the front of the dogtrot breezeway and waved goodbye. Thomas stood further out. As he watched the group leaving, he began bouncing up and down on the balls of his feet in sheer elation of being the boss for the day.

"Come on, Jeb, let's git started," he crowed in what he thought was a voice of genuine command.

With her parents departing, Sarah felt freer to express herself. "Well, Jeb," She immediately turned and beamed at him. He reddened in the face a bit, but managed to smile back, saying, "Yeah, it looks like it's just the four of us for almost the whole day."

"Jeb, come *on!*" barked Thomas, stamping his foot.

"Just a minute," answered Jeb. He wanted to spend a little more time with Sarah before starting the work.

Sarah and Ruth had begun weaving projects many weeks ago that they now resumed as one of their morning tasks. Sam had shaved off a generous supply of very slender, long oaken strips for them to use in building their baskets.

Curious, Jeb asked the two girls what chore they would be doing first. Sarah gave Jeb a knowing look and replied, "Basket weaving. Come, let me show you."

Waving to Thomas to be patient, Jeb followed Sarah to the back of the cabin. Ruthie skipped along beside them, leaving Thomas stewing by himself in the front, for the moment.

Sarah pointed, "See here. Every time we do our basket making, we have to soak the strips first in the water trough behind the house." He noticed a large pile of them had been stacked next to the trough.

Sarah and Ruthie each stooped and picked up a handful of the lengthy wooden pieces from the stack and placed them in the water, pushing the strips down to the bottom.

"We have to leave them in long enough to make the wood easier to bend and twist as we weave the baskets." She explained and smiled prettily at him.

Fortunately, the morning temperature was climbing into the upper thirties and beyond, so the trough wasn't frozen. Often, on days like today when the winter weather warmed up, they would restart their project.

Suddenly, he heard a loud grunt. From the front of the cabin, Thomas was calling out in an irritable voice through the dogtrot opening, "Hey, we need to git started with our own chores. Come back over here with me, Jeb!"

"Well, I guess I better go. Your brother's getting

annoyed." He gave Sarah a bashful half-smile, waved bye, and walked back through the 'trot.

Impatiently waiting, Thomas held two heavy axes. He handed one to Jeb and walked across the cleared grounds to the far left side, close to the overhanging forest thickness. Jeb noticed a massive stump that had been sawed flat to form a large cutting surface. Smaller tree trunks and mid to large-sized limbs were heaped around it.

Thomas and Jeb spent most of their morning splitting wood; big pieces for the two fireplaces, and smaller pieces for the family's store of ready kindling.

It was hard work, and Jeb wasn't used to manual labor of any sort. As the morning progressed, he found his hands getting rubbed raw and his arms and shoulders getting very tired and sore.

Although the boys took frequent breaks, Jeb got so weary, he had to be careful he didn't strike carelessly and hit himself, or Thomas, with a wayward swing.

"Ow! Now three of my dang blisters have popped open! Ouch, they freaking hurt!"

Jeb dropped his ax and wrung his hands in pain. His soft hands had formed sores of which several had burst open. The cold, constant wind only made the burning and throbbing worse.

Discovering Jeb didn't know anything about the correct way to chop or split wood infused Thomas with extra energy and newfound zeal to lead by example. "Here, Jeb. Lemme show ya how it's done. Tha proper way. Jest watch me now," Thomas bubbled. The fact that Jeb was slightly older only increased Thomas' swelling sense of pride in being the one in control.

Forty-five yards or so directly in front of the cabins, the family maintained a permanent bonfire clearing where a layered stack of wood was kept ready in the winter months. When the fire was built, it was used for a variety of purposes. It provided a heat source for soap making and similar tasks. Its location kept the resultant toxic fumes, such as lye, away from the buildings. And during the severest winter days, it was a welcome source of comfort to outside workers.

Though it was no longer freezing outside, Thomas decided to start a bonfire just for fun.

A short time after mid-morning, his little sister Ruth came skipping and laughing on her way from the back through the dog-trot to talk to Thomas. She grinned mischievously at Jeb then began speaking to her brother, "Sarah and I have decided we want squirrel for noon dinner. We say you're a cowardly Indian. We say you're too scared to leave us alone, and get me...I mean...get *us* some good food to eat."

She glanced at Jeb, batted her eyes at him, then she continued baiting Thomas. "It's your responsibility as the oldest to take care of the youngest, and that's me."

She smiled at Jeb again and whispered close to him, "My sister likes you."

She turned and skipped, giggling uncontrollably, all the way back to Sarah.

Thomas stood watching her skip away, threw down his tool, and said in what he thought was a voice of authority, "Jeb, you and me are goin' hunting. It's not fair Robert gits to spend tha day hunting and we don't. Now that Ruthie's gone and yakked 'bout it, I'm hungry for squirrel, too. As tha oldest in charge, I say it's our duty to git food for our sisters. You kin use tha rifle father took off that dead bandit. Father has another spare rifle he keeps in his bedroom that I'll git." He had his hands on his hips, scowl on his face, as if he would tolerate no argument from his next in command.

"Your dad, that is, your father said for us to stay close to home and not go in the woods," countered Jeb.

As Thomas folded his arms in protest, Jeb carefully responded, "I don't know if that's a smart idea for us to go hunting." He thought of the Hansen gang, and how Sam and he came close to dying on that lonely country trail.

He shook his head and said, "That doesn't sound like the type of thing Sarah would want us to do, disobey your father and all. I believe Ruthie made it all up by herself. Don't you think so?" Jeb asked Thomas. He remembered Sam's words about Ruth having a tendency to egg her brother on.

"I'm in charge!" Thomas blustered back. "And I say we go hunting. Right now!" With that, he stormed off.

Jeb heard a heavy door open and slam shut. Thomas soon reappeared with the captured rifle, his father's spare weapon, powder horns, and musket ball pouches, plus an extra shirt. He stoically held out to Jeb the deceased bandit's gun and ammunition stock, and the clothing. "You might wanna put on my other shirt, in case you git cold."

Jeb hesitated, wondering if he should remain at the cabins to keep watch over the girls and let Thomas go by himself.

Thomas glared at Jeb. "Let's git!" he said. He shook the extra rifle, slung powder horn, pouch, and shirt in his extended arms, indicating Jeb had better take them off his hand. And pronto.

Jeb accepted defeat, feeling he had no choice. Reluctantly he put on the extra shirt. He slung the horn and pouch over his shoulder, took the rifle, careful to point the barrel downward, and followed the rapidly disappearing Thomas into the foreboding forest.

"Wait up! Hey, wait for me!" Jeb raced to catch up.

As they went deeper into the woods, Jeb deferred to Thomas. He had gone hunting a grand total of three times in his entire life; using a modern gun with a high powered scope and high tech ammunition, and tagging along with a knowledgeable adult, his Dad or uncle, as a mentor.

Thomas, on the other hand, had grown up with a rifle in his hand. From the age of five on, he had learned how to track, shoot to kill, clean, and field dress wild game ranging from squirrel to possum to rabbit to turkey to deer. As of yet, he hadn't shot a bear, moose, panther or wild hog. But he had no dread of any wild animal as long as he had his rifle and enough for another reload.

Thomas was totally in his element. Now that Jeb had acquiesced to him, and once he discovered Jeb was as untrained with the gun as he was with the ax, he became the consummate and considerate guide.

"Now, Jeb," Thomas instructed him in a stage whisper, "when ya see a tail a hanging over a branch, wait until he moves, lead 'im jest a might, then squeeze tha trigger--don't jerk or pull it--squeeze all tha way through. And *Boom*, ya got 'im." They strode silently through the woods, eyes glued to the treetops above.

"Shssssh, now," Thomas' voice decreased to a true whisper. "See up there in tha ol' oak to tha right? 'Bout twenty steps out. Look up left."

"I don't see anything," whispered Jeb, looking up vaguely in that direction.

"No, look all tha way to tha top o' tha tree, then look little bit left. He's coming down tha big branch there. Can ya see 'im? An ol' fat grey." Thomas turned quietly to Jeb. "Ya wanna take tha first crack?"

"Nah, you go ahead. I'll watch," Jeb replied in an equally hushed voice.

Thomas nodded.

He leveled his rifle and dropped the varmint with an easy shot. The boys walked over to the dead squirrel. Thomas reloaded his rifle and then picked up the game. They continued the hunt.

Jeb listened intently and respectfully to Thomas' expansive attempts at field tutoring. They took their leisure in their hunting, stopping often to view the birds, other animals, and the beautiful scenery. They saw a graceful white-tailed doe prancing away in the distance, two sluggish possums, three masked raccoons ambling along, plenty of rabbit, and a family of skunks nosing across the leafy ground.

The weather was perfect. The woods were panoramic. Thomas was in no hurry, and he was enjoying himself immensely being the teacher.

Jeb didn't use his own gun. Obligingly, he let Thomas shoot and reload in succession, bringing down four large squirrels. By the time their hunt was over, Jeb had become very impressed with Thomas' skills. *Gosh, he's way better than Dad even.*

Thomas reloaded a fifth time before turning to Jeb. "Ya 'bout ready to call it a morning?"

With the sun hitting high noon, they began to

saunter back in the general location of home. Suddenly, from a distance, they heard panicked screams--one muffled and one high-pitched. Jeb and Thomas stared at each other in shock.

"Sarah and Ruthie are in trouble. Let's git!" Thomas broke into a dead run, weaving his way zigzag fashion through the looming brush, thicket, and trunks. The four dead squirrels strung over his shoulder swayed violently to and fro as he dodged through the trees.

Jeb followed behind as best he could. By the continuing screams, he knew the girls must be in serious danger.

Jeb's heart was in his throat. His face flushed with fear, and his side began to stitch from the exertion of the race. Soon he was out of breath. "I'm coming. I'm coming," he called out as Thomas sprinted ahead.

Thomas burst into the clearing ahead of Jeb. He could see three persons, one nearby, two off in the distance entering the forest. All three were dressed up like Indians, whether Cherokee or Chickasaw or other, he didn't know. The closest one was kneeling by the side of the right cabin, attempting to set it ablaze using a burning limb taken from the bonfire. The other two held his sisters captive and were dragging them off, screaming and kicking, into the woods.

The girls were alive.

"Leave my sisters alone!" Thomas shouted out in

anger. He braked to a stop and threw the squirrels to the ground, freeing up both hands. He quickly leveled his rifle. In one fluid motion, he sighted, cocked, and shot at the kneeling Indian who had begun to stand up at the sound of Thomas's yell.

His round hit the man in the left side of his gut. The Indian dropped his rifle in pained surprise and cursed at the top of his lungs. Thomas believed he sounded a lot like a white man. Jeb thought he looked vaguely familiar, too. *Where have I seen that face before?*

Forgetting about his fallen rifle, the Indian twisted and ran, crouched over in intense pain, stumbling to catch up to his comrades.

Jeb ran to where the cabin was beginning to blaze. He pulled off his outer shirt, and frantically beat at the flames. "I gotta put this out before it burns your home down."

"Don't worry 'bout that now! We gotta save my sisters!" Thomas rushed up beside him and grabbed the Indian's unused gun off the ground. "Here, take mine!" he yelled. He tossed his now unloaded rifle to Jeb to carry, and motioned him to follow. Intent on what he was doing, Jeb let the rifle bounce off his shoulder and side as he hunched over, feverously working to extinguish the last of the fire. With the flame extinct, he picked up the empty rifle in his left hand, held his own unused rifle in the other hand, and raced after Thomas.

Once the real action started, Jeb's anxiety left him. *Here I am, chasing after real live Indians, and I'm not the least bit afraid.* His own life was at risk, yet he had no sense of peril. It was as if he had somehow gained an unknown measure of courage and fortitude, going back into frontier time.

In the shadows of the woods, they caught up with the wounded Indian. As the man turned and glanced over his shoulder at his pursuers, Thomas swung the butt of the rifle with all his young strength at the man's head. There was a loud crack and a yelp of pain. The Indian collapsed to the ground, not moving.

They ran further into the thickening forest chasing the other two Indians. Thomas and Jeb broke into a clearing and abruptly halted, momentarily paralyzed at the scene before them. To the left, lay the crumbled figure of Ruth. An Indian moved away from her still body. His breeches were already pulled down his waist in his lust for play.

"Hot damn, we gonna take real good care o' you, missy," he cackled as he literally tripped over himself to join the other Indian. To the right, Thomas and Jeb saw the second savage kneeling with a drawn knife over the sobbing and prone form of Sarah. Her clothes were torn and her body was partially exposed.

"Go help Sarah!" Thomas shouted at Jeb, who was standing by his side, rooted, still holding a rifle in each hand.

So focused were the two men on their evil plans, the arrival of the boys caught them off guard. At the sight of Thomas and Jeb, the first Indian stumbled backwards in desperation to retrieve his rifle lying on the ground next to little Ruthie's quiet form. Encumbered by the crumbled breeches now fallen around his legs, he awkwardly crawled then lunged for his gun, grabbing it, aiming in haste, and firing off balance. Thomas had hesitated, waiting for the man to stop moving and present him a better target for a clean shot.

Thomas' body jerked backwards with the sudden hit. A small blood patch appeared on his left shoulder. He staggered, but regained his footing and determinedly raised his rifle, gritting his teeth with the pain of motion. His shaky return shot only grazed the Indian. Howling, the savage pulled his breeches all the way up, yanked out his knife, and dashed at Thomas in a blind rage.

Sarah's name propelled Jeb to action. He had never shot at anyone in his life, or ever had reason to. Certainly, he had never killed another human being. All he knew of killing what was he saw in movies and TV. This was real. But in his heroic desire to save Sarah from this savage, he forgot all fright, all apprehension.

While Thomas and his foe exchanged shots, Jeb sprinted up to within five yards of the other Indian, who abruptly stood up over the weeping girl. The man picked his rifle off the ground and leveled it at the oncoming boy.

Jeb flinched and closed his eyes for the expected impact. The blast at close range was deafening. He felt the same funny tickling sensation in his chest he had experienced facing the Hansen killers.

Jeb threw Thomas' unloaded rifle aside and leveled the other unused weapon, steadying his aim straight at the man's heart. *At this close range, even I can't miss.*

He gritted his teeth, held his breath, and pulled the trigger before the savage could jump out of the way. As soon as he had shot it, he threw the empty weapon down like it burned his hands, horrified at what he thought he'd done.

Nothing happened except the sound of his shot, followed almost simultaneously by an unknown second gunfire. The man fell sideways on top of Sarah, dead, even as his body hit the ground. There had been another shot right after his.

"What?" Jeb yelled in confusion and turned. Out of the corner of his eye, he saw a fourth man standing with a gun and a trailing horse off in the thick of the woods perhaps sixty or seventy yards behind them.

Jeb didn't know who this new person was or why he was there. Distracted, he spun back around searching for Thomas.

The first Indian had his prey on the ground. Thomas' countenance was chalk-white as he struggled for his life.

"I'm a' goin' to scalp ya, boy. Hear me! Slit your throat. Skin ya like a possum, ya little bastard!" the man said in ragged gulps. The breath of the Indian stank horribly of bad tobacco and cheap alcohol. His wicked hunting knife hung suspended, inches and moments from slicing into Thomas' wide-eyed face, as Thomas frantically fought with his one good arm to push the blade away.

"No!" Jeb darted and leaped onto the back of the kneeling man. "Get off Thomas! Let him alone!" shouted Jeb. The man's body odor was rancid with accumulated sweat and grime. Jeb grabbed ahold and yanked the Indian's greasy brown hair with all his might, forcing the man to let go of Thomas and stand up to dislodge his new enemy.

The Indian thrust his knife violently again and again behind his head and around his side to try to cut Jeb. "Argggggh! I'm gonna git ya! Cain't keep...a dodging me...ya little piss ant," he said determinedly.

Jeb hung on for dear life, twisting this way and that to avoid the stabbing stokes. He had to do something more than hold on; he had to fight back.

The Sloppy Bucket. Gouge his eye out. Before Jeb's thumb could find its prey, though, Thomas had grabbed a spent rifle off the ground and rammed the Indian hard, right in his groin.

"Ohhhhhh!" the man groaned loudly.

Teeth clenched, eyes blinking in excruciating pain,

he convulsed forward with Jeb still on his back, dropping his knife. Thomas picked it up. He stared mercilessly into the face of the Indian now stooped in agony. Thomas rammed the blade into the middle of the man's hunched chest.

"You hurt my sisters. Ya red devil. Ya hurt Sarah and Ruthie." Tears streamed down the sides of his face, while his eyes burned with vengeance.

Blood splattered his knife hand and unto the ground as he stabbed again and again with his good arm, until he could thrust no more, and his body shook with exhaustion, and he fought for breathe. "I hate you, I hate you, I hate you!" he yelled in fury.

The Indian toppled over as in slow motion. Jeb slipped off his back as the man fell, face-first to the ground, mortally wounded.

Meanwhile, the unknown man, observing everything, had stalked silently up behind them.

Chapter Eleven
CHEROKEE JIM

"Aye, ye want to be a taking it easy with tha sharp knife, ye do. Jest turn around, laddies. Nice and slow."

Behind them came a tranquil, even voice. "Ye needna worry. I be a friend. I won't be a hurting ye. I promise," the stranger said.

In a daze, Jeb turned to meet this new individual. He saw a light olive-skinned man of medium stature and build with a closely shaved head and face. Unlike most of the locals, he wore store bought trousers, jacket, and quality hunting boots. Cradled in the crook of his left arm was an expensive, handcrafted Pennsylvania long rifle that drew Thomas' admiration. Jeb could tell he had a touch of Scottish brogue in his speech. The man seemed like a well-to-do person, engaged in hunting, perhaps, or casually passing through the area.

The stranger surveyed the entire battle scene. He saw the still body of Ruth on his left, the crumpled man lying at Thomas' feet, the relatively unharmed condition of the two boys, and the twisted form of the Indian he had shot splayed over the still whimpering Sarah to the right. He checked to make sure the Indian before him was truly dead.

"'Tis staying here ye are," the stranger commanded.

He strode decisively over to the fallen body on top of Sarah. Without glancing once at the partially uncovered girl, the stranger bent down to make sure the second Indian was lifeless, too. He stepped over the prone figure, grabbed the man's arms, and pulled his dead weight off the sobbing girl. Then he dragged the heavy body deep into the thicket of the woods behind.

The boys watched his every move, hypnotized. The adrenalin effect of their fight to survive and protect the girls was wearing off. Thomas swayed on his feet; Jeb reached out to steady him. *Gosh, I feel really wiped out myself.* His movements were groggy and his brain felt stupid.

The stranger returned from carting off the dead Indian. He stepped into the clearing and motioned Thomas and Jeb over to Sarah's side. "'Tis dead as a graveyard ghost these evil men be. Ye're safe now, and ye ought come, lads, and help tha two lassies," he said.

At that, the boys snapped out of their lethargy and rushed to Sarah's side. Unsure of what he should do or say, Jeb stood mutely by, as Thomas knelt down by his sister. Jeb kept his vision locked on Sarah's beautiful, but bruised face, forcing himself not to look below at her torn dress.

Thomas gingerly took her hand. His eyes clouded with fresh agony and he whispered as softly as he could, "Sarah, please. Look at me. It's Thomas. Your brother, Thomas. Tha bad Indians are dead. Thay are all dead, Sarah. You're safe now."

"Sarah..." Thomas moaned as his bitter tears trickled onto her upturned face. Her petticoat skirt had been pulled violently up to her waist, and the front part of her smock-dress had been torn apart, by hand or knife, he couldn't tell. He reached to gently pulled her skirt down, and took off his outer shirt and covered up the torn dress top.

The sides of her face were bruised and purpling from the slaps and punches she'd received to stop her initial struggling. The linsey-woolsey shawl that had been roughly ripped from her head lay two feet away.

"Sarah, please be okay. Please, please be okay," Thomas rocked back and forth with his head bowed over his fallen sister, weeping in anguish.

Sarah fluttered her eyes open. She stared, unfocused at first, at her kneeling brother. Thomas sobbed uncontrollably now, his hands shielding his brow.

At the sound of Thomas' weeping, try as Jeb might, tears of compassion began welling within his eyes.

"Thomas?" Sarah was coming back to reality. She reached up and touched her brother's arm.

"What? Sarah? *Sarah!*" Thomas removed his hands from his swollen, reddening eyes to grasp his sister's outstretched limb.

"He tried to...he was going to..." she shuddered, and her wide eyes sought out Jeb.

"Jeb saved me. Jeb killed him before he could... before they both could..." her voice trailed off. "Where's Ruthie? What did they do to my sister?"

Her urgent concern for her little sister shook Jeb into action. He wiped the tears from his cheeks and hurried to Ruth's still form, grateful for something to do. Jeb dropped down on one knee and put his hand to her forehead. It was warm, almost hot. "Thank God!" he exclaimed with relief to the others. "She's alive."

He noticed a swelling, ugly bump on her forehead where she had been struck, probably with a rifle butt. Gently picking up her wrist, he searched for a pulse. It was strong.

Ruth had fought like a wildcat: biting, scratching, punching, and kicking. The two men had fully intended to kill and scalp both girls anyway, but wanted to slake their sexual desire first. Fortunately for her, Ruth was deemed too young to rape. The girl's ferocity kept the first Indian from joining the fun with Sarah, so he had brutally knocked Ruth unconscious.

Jeb looked up to see Sarah standing on her feet, though somewhat unsteadily. Her skirt was pulled all the way down as it should be, and she was wearing her brother's shirt tightly wrapped around her top. After the ordeal she had been through, it alarmed him to see her standing so soon. "Sarah, you shouldn't be doing that. You're hurt," he cautioned her. "Thomas, don't let her get up yet."

Without replying a word, she turned around and faced him. Painfully and slowly, Sarah walked with halting, but resolute steps over to Jeb. Once there, she waited for him to get to his feet. Then she unexpectedly threw her arms around him. She hugged him so tight Jeb could hardly breath. He could feel her silky skin and luxurious hair pressed hard against the side of his face. One searching hand squeezed the nape of his neck.

Her voice fervently whispered in his ear, so low only he could hear her, "You saved me. You rescued me, Jeb boy. I thank you so much. Mother talks constantly about, about the virtue and duty of a Christian woman. I owe you. Both my virtue and my life." She kissed him so gently on the cheek, then she pulled inches away, still holding him, staring mistily into his shocked brown eyes.

"Oh, Jeb. Jeb, Jeb, *Jeb*."

Nearby, her brother Thomas was watching it all with even greater shock showing on his freckled, baffled face.

Sarah's eyes penetrated Jeb's. Of all the things

he had encountered in his short existence, Jeb had never experienced such an intimate display of feminine emotion. Even Nat, when forced to move with Mom to Atlanta, had controlled herself in front of her brother. She had not cried until mother and daughter were thirty thousand feet in the air. And even then, she had wept silent tears. Girls were a foreign universe to Jeb. He had no knowledge, no skills, and no innate wisdom to rely upon. He was as helpless as a newborn baby. He looked back into her eyes, getting more and more lost in them, as she continued to hold him, so close, face to face.

After what seemed like forever, he replied in barely audible words, "You're welcome."

His face flushed and he felt really stupid as the words left his mouth, but he didn't know what else to say. However, his inadequate reply didn't seem to bother Sarah one bit. She just kept looking sweetly into his wide-open eyes.

It was at that moment, Jeb remembered. It was not *his* gun, but the nearly simultaneous shot of the stranger that had killed the Indian and saved Sarah. He thought to himself, *I totally missed him. Even at point-blank range, somehow, I couldn't hit him.* He knew it. He also recalled he felt a weird tingling sensation at the instant of the Indian's preemptive rifle fire. The same strange feeling had happened during the Hansen attack. Once again, the image of the green book darted ever so briefly into his mind.

At their feet, Ruth was coming to and stirring fitfully. At that, Jeb broke away from his thoughts and from Sarah. "Let me check on Ruth," he said, as she reluctantly let go.

Sensing it was no longer an intrusion, Thomas joined him. He kneeled alongside Jeb, and together they tenderly helped Ruthie first sit, then stand. "My head hurts bad," she whimpered.

She had a powerful headache where she was struck, some scratches on her face, and her right arm and hand were quite sore from hitting the Indian so hard so many times. Otherwise, Ruthie seemed relatively unharmed.

The stranger, meanwhile, had moved the body of the stabbed Indian into the forest thicket, placing it next to the one he had shot, so both were now out of the view of the boys and girls. Searching, he found the gut-shot and rifle-butted third Indian in the far woods' edge, the man nearly dead. Mercifully, the stranger finished him off with his knife. He carried that body to add to the pile of corpses. He then stripped the three bodies of guns and other valuables.

Jeb and the others watched him as he toted the last Indian across the clearing and disappeared into the dense forest edge.

The stranger was undecided whether he was going to return later and dig a mass grave for the dead attackers. In his opinion, they certainly didn't deserve a decent burial. He returned to join the others. "Och, tis getting ye back to ye hoose I want," he calmly said.

He brought his great stallion over and very carefully assisted the two wounded girls in mounting his horse. "Step up, little lassies. Climb up on ol' Lightning. He winna buck with me aside ye. Easy now. Easy. There ye go. Come on, Lightning," he took the reins and coaxed the big horse into a slow walk.

Turning to the boys, he asked, "Now then. Where we be a goin', laddies? Where's yer hoose?"

Thomas pointed behind them. "Back that way." Guided by Thomas, the stranger led the bedraggled group out of the woods back toward the cabins.

Once inside, the stranger dressed Thomas' shoulder injury as best he could. The family had a small supply of basic medicines and natural herbal remedies stored in the kitchen cabin.

"Och aye, lad. That should stop infection and ease tha pain a bit," he said. Luckily, the shot was a clean flesh wound, passing through without hitting bone or sinew.

He also examined Ruth's bludgeoned forehead and Sarah's battered face. Without proper poultices or salves, however, there was not much the stranger could do for them but let their bruises naturally heal. The blow to Ruth's head, while sufficient to knock her out and cause a headache, wasn't serious.

The stranger pointed to the long table. "Let's all be a sitting down and collecting up our wits 'bout us. Ye laddies and lasses have been through a rough patch, ye have, but ye be safe now," he spoke with kind authority.

Obediently, the two girls went to their side of the table and numbly sat down on the bench. The two boys followed suit on the other side. The stranger pulled out the stool and sat at the head. Once they were all seated, the stranger broke the lingering silence, "If it's all right with ye, I'll be a staying until yer folk return, jest to be a making sure ye stay safe."

They stared at him, not replying, their bodies fatigued to the point of exhaustion. The stranger continued. "Tha three men that attacked ye warna Indian. Thay were but white men poorly dressed up as Cherokee braves, thay were" he explained.

"I knew that Indian sounded white!" exclaimed Thomas, finding his voice.

The stranger acknowledged Thomas with a gesture. "Aye, they were all white."

He looked around the table. "I know. Because I've lived most o' me life with tha Cherokee peoples. Me name is Cherokee Jim."

Both boys raised their heads from their stupor and peered at him funny. The man didn't look or sound Indian. He seemed white and sounded Scottish.

He saw their questioning glances and smiled. "Och aye, looks can be deceiving, lads. Canna be judging a book by its cover alone."

Cherokee Jim told them his story. "Me grandfather, Benjamin Colbert, still living, is a Scotsman who went to live with tha Cherokees. He married a Cherokee woman by tha name o' Ahinawake. That means *Laughing Eyes* in English. Their son, Robert, was my father. He married a white woman. He was killed by tha Chickasaws shortly after I was born."

He continued, "Me mother was in fear for our lives afterwards, but she coudna go to tha white settlers for protection. Tha few whites close by had nothing to do with her because she had married a half-breed. We went to live with me grandfather and Ahinawake instead. And so, I was raised as a real Cherokee on Cherokee lands west o' here, I was. And though I can be speaking Cherokee as good as a full-blood, I never lost me Scottish accent when I use the English.

"Me grandfather's brother married a white woman. His son married a white woman and their family settled close by to yer hoose here. I wear me white man's clothes and visit me white cousins every year or so. I was a goin' there when I chanced upon yer troubles."

He looked at the children. "I knew immediately thay warna Indians. Jest white men a doin' bad, and a hoping to pass off tha blame for their evil ways."

"I knew they weren't Indians!" Thomas slapped his leg using the hand of his good arm. "And I know tha Colberts, too. They live jest three or four miles from us. They have a boy 'bout my age."

Cherokee Jim nodded solemnly at Thomas and said, "Jack be his name." He resumed, "I be assuming none o' ye knew these men who attacked ye?"

Jeb frowned in concentration and spoke, "I've seen one of the men before. The one that Thomas shot in the gut. I know I have."

It suddenly dawned on him. *It was the man who escaped.* Out loud to the group he said, "Sam and I were attacked by some outlaws called the Hansen Gang, as we were coming home on the trail from the Sloppy Bucket. Sam shot two of them. But a third person got away. He was one of the made-up Indians today."

He thought some more and said, "One of the men Sam killed was at the Sloppy Bucket the night we came in. At the time, I kinda felt like he was eavesdropping on our conversation or something. I saw him talking later to the bartender, who would have known our names and where we were from, because Sam told him everything. The hotel, I mean the inn, was crowded that night, and Sam was trying to boost our case for the one remaining bedroom."

"Ye think tha one man learned yer name and where ye were from?" asked Cherokee Jim.

"Yes, sir, I believe so," Jeb answered.

Cherokee Jim reasoned, "Then tha one that got away told tha others. I have heard o' this here Hansen Gang. Thay be very wicked people, even for whites."

Now Cherokee Jim was putting the pieces together. "It must be tha rest of tha gang came for vengeance, thay did. It would be easy, even for white men, to track ye down here to yer hoose."

A light of comprehension grew on his face as he said, "Twas not yer time and place to die, children. He that lives in tha clear sky with tha sun and tha clouds, tha Great Spirit, creator o' all things, made Cherokee Jim ride by, jest when ye needed him, jest at tha right moment."

He raised his right hand for emphasis, "Och, we Cherokee believe death canna be hurried or cheated. Only when tis appointed, will death come to us all."

His face began to glower with anger.

"Aye, thay were dressed up as Cherokee, so tha local law and tha government army would blame innocent braves." His fists and face tightened up. "Twas killing thay wanted, and killing thay got! Tis glad I am. Thay were tha worst kind o' whites who deserved to die."

The great fireplace, left unattended since mid-morning, was burning low. Cherokee Jim got up and added more logs, stoking the blaze back to strength. He returned to his seat as the fire regained its intensity.

Jeb stared at the luminous interplay of changing

colors and ascending sparks. He looked across the table. The two girls, particularly Sarah, still seemed to be in a state of shock from their ordeal. He glanced over. Next to him, Thomas sat in a stupor, slumped, and exhausted. He was hurting from his wound, Jeb could tell.

For several minutes, everyone sat quietly, watching the dancing yellowy-orange flames with their soaring blue tips breaking off into the air. Except for the constant crackling, popping, sizzling, and snapping of the blazing fire, there was silence in the room. Finally, Cherokee Jim spoke. To pass the time waiting for the rest of the Robertson family to come home, he told them many things.

He spoke more of the Great Spirit creator, "Called by tha Chickasaw *Tha Beloved One Who Dwells In Tha Blue Sky*, and by tha Cherokee *Tha Great Man Above*." He told them, "Each warrior has his own guardian spirit. Tha sun, tha thunder, and tha four winds are powerful gods o' tha upper air."

He instructed them that certain animals were said to possess magical powers. Cherokee medicine men combined spirit worship with native healing practices. Tobacco was frequently used in certain religious rites. And the corn spirit was esteemed within special ceremonies.

As the afternoon lengthened, he told them the old Cherokee folk story about the lazy hunter. "Many years ago, a young brave once courted a pretty maiden.

But she would have nothing to do with him, telling him her husband must be a good hunter or she would remain single. One morning this young brave went into tha woods and by pure accident happened to kill a deer. He lifted it onto his shoulders and carried it into tha village, a making sure to pass right by tha door of tha pretty maiden's home.

"As soon as he was out of sight, he circled back into tha forest, and a waited until evening. He lifted tha dead dear up and carried it past tha maiden's door, as he had done in tha morning. He did this tha next day, and tha next, until tha girl thought, surely, he must be a killing all tha deer in tha woods.

"She thought he *must* a great hunter and told her mother. So her mother, who was tha matchmaker, went to tha young man's mother to be a talking things over, and making arrangement for a possible marriage.

"When she arrived at tha home and greetings were done, she said, 'Yer son must be a good hunter.' 'No,' replied the other mother, 'he rarely kills anything.' Surprised, the young maiden's mother explained, 'But he has bin killing a lot of deer lately.' 'I hinna seen any,' replied tha brave's mother."

"'Why, he has bin a carrying deer past our home twice a day for three days now,' exclaimed tha girl's mother."

"'Why, I dinna know what he did with them. He

never brought them home to me,' answered tha brave's mother, a shaking her head."

"Then tha maiden's mother knew something was wrong. She told her husband, who followed up tha young man's trail into tha woods until he came to where tha body o' tha same deer was hidden. O' course, tha body was a stinking by then, and had to be thrown away. And so, the lazy hunter was found out!"

As exhausted as he was, Jeb still laughed out loud at the end of the tale. "And so, he never married the pretty maiden, right?"

"No, and he didna marry any o' tha other girls in his village, either," smiled Cherokee Jim.

He brooded for a minute and then became serious. He said, "Contrary to what white settlers be a thinking, most Cherokees are as civilized as tha better classes o' whites." He said that within the state called Tennessee by the whites and within other neighboring states, as well, the Cherokee tribes still had their own lands that were apart from white society.

"Many o' me people have very large farms and orchards, they do" he said. He noted that a few of the wealthiest kept Negro slaves, even as white plantation owners did.

"We raise tha finest cattle, sheep, and horses," he said, proudly. He explained that the Cherokee nation used the best farming methods and tools in growing cotton, tobacco, corn, wheat, oats, potatoes, and indigo in abundance.

Although much of their cotton crop was made into cloth for home use, a fair number of enterprising Cherokees shipped their surplus to New Orleans. U.S. Army garrisons stationed in Cherokee territories often bought milk, butter, eggs, apples, and other staple items from neighboring tribes.

He boasted, "Unlike tha lands settled by tha poorer whites, Cherokee lands all be a having good horse paths, good wagon roads, and tha best trails for traveling."

Cherokee Jim himself belonged to a modestly wealthy family. Although he was just quarter Indian by ancestry, he considered himself a true Native. "Aye, lads and lassies, everything good in me life I got from tha Cherokee side: the way I think about things, physical habits, religion, wife, neighbors. All Indian.

"I educated me two sons and daughter in all tha Indian ways. At home and around other members o' tha tribe, we speak only Cherokee. Tha children speak it as well as their mother," he added proudly.

"I always wear some pieces o' traditional costume except when I be a traveling outside Cherokee lands. Then I wear all white clothing, especially when visiting tha white folk."

As Cherokee Jim continued to talk, Jeb's thoughts wandered to his recollections of the Indian past. All at once, he began to feel a sinking sensation of shame in his heart. Poor student that he was, even Jeb remembered enough history to know the Cherokee Trail of Tears would be happening a few short decades after 1802. During the interim years, the Cherokees would make major strides in their written alphabet, political unification, and material attainment as a nation of peoples.

Tragically, all of their farms, the tidy plantations, the civilization, the abundance, the culture, the unique way of life, everything would be uprooted, turned out, and destroyed in their forced inhumane relocation. Worst still, many women, children, and old people would die in the terrible travail of the difficult journey to Oklahoma. All because the white settlers and white governments couldn't stand to have civilized, wealthy, forward-thinking, autonomous, protected Indian lands within their midst. The Cherokee nation's crime was being red skinned instead of white.

And for the second time that afternoon, Jeb got hot tears in his eyes.

Chapter Twelve
RECOVERY

As the sun dipped toward late afternoon, the sounds of several voices and a single approaching horse filtered into the room. Outside, they heard Cherokee Jim's steed whinny at the presence of another horse.

Cherokee Jim strode swiftly to the square window. He lifted the covering and peered out. Turning to the children, he said, "Tis a man, woman, boy, and girl a coming."

Thomas found his voice, "That's our father, mother, big brother, and sister."

Cherokee Jim nodded. He went back to his seat and waited.

Sam entered first, cat-like for a well-muscled man, rifle at the ready. He surveyed everything in seconds. His eyes narrowed at the nasty contusions on his daughters' faces, the bloodied bandage on his son's shoulder, the ashen color of Jeb's countenance, and the solemn visage of the unknown stranger.

His natural instinct told him this man was friend,

not foe. He stepped aside from the doorway to let his wife, eldest daughter and son enter the room. The two older children gasped at the scene of their hurt brother and sisters. The mother said not a word, maintaining her outward composure. But Rebecca's eyes mirrored her inner maternal pain.

Before the mute stranger could say anything, Sarah blurted out, her voice quaking with emotion, "Father," she faltered and collected her wits before continuing, "Three men dressed up like Indians attacked and kidnapped me and Ruthie. They were going to kill us. They were going to..." her voice trailed off.

"Thomas and Jeb had gone hunting," she added.

Sam scowled fiercely at Thomas, who turned his head away to avoid his father's glare.

"But, Father, it was all my doing," Sarah hurried on. "It was my fault. I asked them to get us a few squirrels for noon dinner," she said.

At this, Ruth stared at Sarah and vigorously shook her head *No*. Sarah ignored her, determined to take the blame for her little sister's instigation.

"Thomas and Jeb rushed home. In the very nick of time. And Jeb risked his life to save me." She looked over and blushed at Jeb, then turned back to face her father. "He kept them from, from," she took a deep breath and hardened her resolve to tell everything. "He kept them from doing something *very bad* to me."

Her lips trembled ever so slightly and she began crying. "And they were going to scalp us and kill us. Jeb and Thomas and Cherokee Jim fought them. They're all dead now, Father." Sarah dropped her head, folding her hands in her lap. She had exhausted her last reserve of inner strength.

Sam stood thunderstruck, unable to completely comprehend the unexpected evil that had come so close to taking his younger son and daughters. Finally he blurted out, "Who *were* these men? Who were these men who hurt my family? Ya say thay were whites dressed up as Indians? Why wud white men attack my place and harm my precious daughters?" He shook his head at the stranger for answers.

"Mr. Robertson?" Jeb spoke hesitantly.

Sam turned his focus on Jeb as the boy explained. "They are, I should say they were part of the Hansen Gang. Or what's left of the Hansen Gang."

Seeing the grim expression on Sam's face, Jeb hurried along. "Do you remember the robber who got away? In the woods on the trail? Well, he was one of them. And the ugly-faced man you killed when we were attacked. He was in the Sloppy Bucket the night we were there. He was one of them, too. I saw him talking to the bartender. He must have found out who we were and where we were from, and he told the others who attacked us on the trail. The last man that got away in the woods must have informed the remaining members of the gang where we lived and your name. They must have tracked us down for revenge.

"At least," Jeb looked up at the big man, "that's what I believe happened."

Usually, Sam was firm but never harsh with any of his children, even when Thomas or Ruth did something troublesome or exasperating. But upon hearing the tale of the Indians, his square-jawed face now locked in mounting fury as he confronted his youngest son. His deep baritone voice cracked like a loud whip through the small room. "I told ya to stay home with your sisters! I told ya not to go into tha woods, Thomas. I told both o' ya. Your job was to be there to protect your sisters. Sarah and Ruthie were nigh kilt and...and....and almost *raped*. There, I said it! All because ya didn't obey me!" he raged.

Thomas bowed his head, staring at the packed dirt floor, salty tears of shame starting to drip down between his feet.

Sam gathered his breath to continue his tirade. Abruptly, Rebecca laid her hand on his brawny forearm and he halted at once. She quietly looked at him, then at Thomas, then at each of her children and Jeb. Understanding her cue, Sam quit his anger and waited for her to say her mind.

"Father Robertson, I believe Almighty God in His infinite mercy saved the lives of our children and the virtue of our daughters by turning Thomas' willful disobedience into a real blessing. I'm of the mind that these evil men, had they encountered any resistance or met any males of the family, would have slaughtered all without hesitation. When they found two young, unarmed girls, their evil plans turned from quick murder to base lust," she said.

"They meant to carry our daughters away from the cabins out of sight, and to dishonor them first, then slay them later. Unknown to these foul creatures, two very courageous, young men were racing to their sisters' rescue at the very instant our Good Samaritan, Mr. Jim, was passing close by the place of attack."

Rebecca looked tenderly at her three youngest children, and especially at the two boys. She said with a forgiving tone, "God in His all-knowing goodness preserved the lives of all, as well as the chastity of our daughters. All because the boys disobeyed and were in the woods, wrongly hunting, when the bad men came."

Her husband stared at her in wonderment. Clearly, he had not reasoned everything out or considered all the possibilities before losing his temper. Rebecca's logic and wisdom were infallible. His quick wrath evaporated as his wife spoke.

He cleared his throat heavily, and somewhat sheepishly said, "Your mother's right, as always. God does work in mysterious ways."

He gave a rueful smile and said, "I reckon He did

save your lives by your disobedience, after all. I am proud o' ya, Thomas, and ya, Jeb, for fighting to save your sisters. Not many grown men cud have done whut ya two boys did today, against three savage killers such as tha Hansen gang. Jeb, with nary a scratch. And Thomas, with jest a little flesh wound. Yes, boys, I'm proud o' ya for standing up to these evil men.

"But," he continued in his normal loud voice, "that there don't mean ya kin generally disobey your father and think thangs will always work out. Or think I won't git ya. Ya are to obey your father and mother."

Thomas raised his head, his confidence slightly regained for the time being.

At that, Mrs. Robertson took tender charge. She carefully examined Ruth, Sarah, Thomas and Jeb, each in turn. "Nothing is wrong with me. Seriously, I'm not hurt," Jeb protested. He remembered he had said that very same thing to Sam when they were attacked on the Holston Trail.

Rebecca lovingly dabbed generous amounts of old-fashioned spirit of turpentine on her girls' bruises. She kissed them on the top of their heads and hugged each very gently. Sarah in particular she held close for several minutes. She again murmured a heart-felt prayer of gratitude that their lives and more had been spared, "Lord above, thank you."

Next, she doctored and redressed Thomas' shoulder

wound using fresh clean cloth and their available home medicines. "Don't be fidgeting with this bandage now. You leave it on, until I tell you it can come off," she smiled at her youngest son, knowing full well how antsy he could be. Thomas nodded his head and meekly submitted to a long motherly embrace.

At the same time, Sam and Cherokee Jim took digging tools and their horses and went to bury the three bodies. They would travel some distance and dig a deep mass grave much further out, where, hopefully, the boys couldn't find it. The wooded area where the corpses were currently stacked was too close to the homestead, Sam decided. He didn't want any stench or tangible reminder of the dead men to bother his family, in any way.

"Tell me again where ya dropped tha game?" Advised of the location from his brother, Robert went to retrieve the four squirrels Thomas had killed and left at the wood's edge. He would skin and clean them, along with two rabbits he had shot as the party was returning home from the Bledsoe's, for family supper that night.

Earlier, he, his father, and Mr. Bledsoe had field dressed all the game from their late morning hunt. Meanwhile, Mrs. Robertson and Emily had assisted as midwives during the noontime arrival of the new baby, Samuel Edward Bledsoe. Afterwards, mother and daughter had taken the kills and prepared many days' worth of food for the Bledsoe family. The meals would last without spoilage in the near-freezing temperatures.

Rebecca had sat beside Mrs. Bledsoe's bed at the time, holding the newborn in her arms for the mother to see. She said, "Susan, dear, Emily and I have fixed enough food to carry you into next week, while you are recovering and unable to cook. I just want you to rest and regain your strength. So you'll be able to take care of that handsome, new baby boy."

When Robert returned with the squirrels, Mrs. Robertson and Emily took the skinned game from him and began working on their supper meal. "Thank you, dear," his mother said. She hugged her oldest son tightly, thinking how he and Emily could have been home at the time of attack and in jeopardy, too.

An hour later, Sam and Cherokee Jim came back. Rebecca looked up kindly at Cherokee Jim as the two men entered the cabin. "Dear sir, we request that you stay for supper. It is the very least we can do, to show our gratitude," she insisted.

Cherokee Jim respectfully accepted her offer, but made it clear he should have been at the Colberts by mid-afternoon. It was now mid-evening. He stressed he must leave immediately after eating.

That night, the Robertson's mealtime ritual of saying grace and recalling the day's events was much more poignant than usual. All heads bowed as Rebecca began her heartfelt prayer, "Heavenly Father, we are so grateful for your wondrous hand of protection, your almighty hand of mercy this day, on our precious children. You, in your infinite grace, gathered the boys and Mr. Jim together at the right time, and gave them strength to fight to save our daughters. You spared them all from death and more. You brought everyone home to us."

She continued, "Now, Lord God in Heaven, we thank you for your bounty and the meal we are about to eat. We know every good thing comes from you. We thank you for your blessings revealed again today, for our health, our happy home, and most of all, for your Son, our Savior. Bring us, dear Lord, ever closer to your perfect will." Fresh tears sparkled in her eyes as she raised her lovely head.

"Amen," the family said, in unison.

Even Cherokee Jim was touched by the sincerity of this white woman's prayer.

An extra wooden stool kept for the purpose was brought out for their guest, who squeezed in between big Sam and Robert at the table corner.

Sam clapped the guest on the back and said, "Dig in, Cherokee. It's all good. And I wanna say, thankee so much, for helping save my girls and my boy. And saving Jeb, too, o' course," he added playfully. Now that the initial shock had subsided and all his family was safe, Sam was in a right jolly mood.

The supper proved to be especially delicious and

comforting that night. Familial warmth filled each heart. The cruel events of the day brought a fresh appreciation to all of the gifts of life and close companionship. Cherokee Jim sensed that this family was different from almost all of the whites he had previously known.

Jeb, too, breathed in the abundant atmosphere of home and hearth. Though it was only a few brief days of 1802 time since he had been flung into the past by the green book, he thought, *Gosh, it feels like I've been with the Robertsons for a much longer period. Almost forever, actually.* He had experienced and done things he could never know or do in his modern day world.

It seemed to him he had grown-up considerably. *It's like I'm a different person altogether.* He felt like an intrepid adventurer, an older and wiser teenager, very nearly an adult. He had a whole new level of inner confidence.

As he ate, Jeb reviewed his experiences to himself. In his mind's eye, he told himself, *Hey, I came up with a fantastic storyline, acted the part, and totally convinced Sam. I faced death at the hands of killer robbers. I fought that Indian, uh, robber, and helped rescue Sarah, too.*

He smiled as he basked in his happy thoughts.

I've got a wonderful new friend in Sarah. She has knockout looks. She's nice to me. She's got a sweet personality. Not at all like the mean girls at school. More than that, she seems to really like me.

He smiled so big that he caught himself and

nervously looked around to make sure no one else had noticed the sloppy grin plastered on his face. Thomas, as usual, had his head down, shoveling food as fast as he could into his gaping mouth. Emily and Mrs. Robertson were taking petite lady-like bites, although he saw the Mother occasionally stealing a loving glance at her three wounded children. Robert was listening to Cherokee Jim and Sam discussing various hunting tips and tricks. Only Sarah had eyes for him, and she returned his lingering smile from across table.

Yes, he had gained the budding friendship of a beautiful young lady. Something he had yet to accomplish with any of the girls at Highland Hill High School.

As soon as supper was over, the visitor left.

He thanked Sam for his hospitality and the ladies for their exceptional cooking. He praised the boys and girls for their bravery in the face of such danger. He shook Sam's hand with true respect. Jeb felt Cherokee Jim's demeanor was more genuine and gracious than a lot of adults he had come in contact with, except perhaps for his dad, who was the most courteous person he knew.

Sam and Rebecca again expressed their gratitude for helping rescue their girls and boys. Big Sam, in particular, pressed his parting thanks on the visitor. "I know I'm a white man and not Indian or part Indian," he fumbled for the words. "But if ya ever need anythang at all, ya jest call on me. Anythang at all, ya jest let me know. I owe ya a debt o' gratitude for whut ya did for my children today."

After Cherokee left, the family prepared for the night. Tomorrow, surely, would be a better day.

Chapter Thirteen
CIRCUIT RIDER

After breakfast the next day, Rebecca kept the five Robertson children and Jeb at the table. During the late fall, mid-summer and long winter months, unless the urgent demands of crop planting and harvesting prevented it, they had lessons, taught by their mother, one morning each week. This included reading, writing, spelling, arithmetic, and proper etiquette, with some ancient history of the Greeks and Romans, plus a little Latin, thrown in. Rebecca remembered her childhood Latin lessons with fondness.

Which day it was varied from week to week, according to the amount of early morning chores each child had to do. In addition to this ad hoc class, every Sunday evening the children's regular education class was held year-round.

Of course, Sunday morning was devoted to Godly learning. The entire family participated in Bible reading, Bible stories, and prayer. In this respect, their home was quite different from the typical Tennessee pioneer family of the time for which formal religious attendance and observance played a limited role.

The Robertsons had not yet joined, nor did they travel to, any church. There were only a few tiny log cabin worship facilities within ten miles of their homestead. There were a handful of small, but zealous, congregations in Greeneville, the closest town. Elsewhere in the eastern and mountain regions, within the more populated villages and cities, places of worship were springing up along with other evidences of civilization. Religion was neither well organized, nor highly regarded by the common man, in the rough and rowdy environment of early frontier Tennessee.

As the lessons proceeded, Jeb found that, except for the Latin, he had to feign ignorance at the easiest questions to safeguard his cover.

"Emily, that is correct. You did very well." Mrs. Robertson praised.

"Jeb, it's your turn, now. How do you spell the word, *impractical*? Here's an example of it. Trying to chop firewood with a knife is impractical," Mrs. Roberson quizzed him.

She waited patiently for him, and then repeated the word, "Impractical."

Jeb didn't dare let them know how advanced he was in comparison to the elementary level of the Robertson children. He had to protect his contrived story, which certainly didn't allow for someone of his age and situation to have the equivalent math and reading knowledge of a beginning college student in the year 1802. He glanced around and grinned at Thomas before beginning.

"Uhmmm. Let me see." He tapped his forehead. "Let me see."

"Impractical." He spelled it very slowly, "I...m...p...r...a...k...t...i...c...l...e. Impractical." He put a smug look on his face and winked at Thomas and Robert, as if he knew he had gotten it right.

"That is a fine attempt, Jeb. However, the correct spelling is as follows: I-m-p-r-a-c-t-i-c-a-l. Now, all of you repeat after me...." Mrs. Robertson had them say the spelling and use it in a sentence, even little Ruth, over and over, until she was satisfied each had mastered the word.

As the lesson progressed, Jeb dutifully repeated the rote phrases as Mrs. Robertson taught them. He allowed himself to answer just enough questions, when asked, so that his level of learning was perceived to be closer to that of Robert and Emily, than to Thomas, Sarah and Ruth.

For him, the three hours dragged on. He ruefully recalled how much he disliked school before this adventure. *Hey, compared to this boring stuff, my modern day classes aren't so bad, after all.* All at once, they heard the sound of a horse and rider outside.

Sam was out in the back with the animals, and

Rebecca was still skittish. The events of yesterday afternoon were fresh on her mind. She shushed her children silent and went over to the moose antlers on the side wall, pulling down Sam's spare rifle. Expertly, she checked to see the gun was ready, primed, and loaded. On the wild Tennessee frontier, even the womenfolk had to learn how to use firearms.

She motioned the children to sit down. Over the protests of Robert and Thomas, she ordered them in a hushed voice, "Stay where you are. I will go and see." Holding the rifle with the barrel up, she stepped out of the door into the breezeway to face the visitor. "Yes?" She said.

"Hello, ma'am." The traveler smiled big. "It's another fine day tha Good Lord's given us, don't ya agree?"

The stranger was a fairly young man, astride a wiry, glistening, coal-black stallion. He had a black hat on his head and was dressed in a plain white buttoned-up shirt, dusty black frock coat, black trousers, and heavily worn boots.

His rifle was sheathed in a saddle holster. In his right hand, he held a big black Bible resting open on top of his thighs, as if he had just been reading it. He held the horse's reins loosely in his left. He beamed at Mrs. Robertson, undisturbed by the presence of a weapon in her hands.

"A blessed morning to you and your family. My name is Mordecai Smith," he jovially said.

"I am newly appointed by tha Bishop Francis Asbury o' tha Methodist Episcopal Church to travel in these here parts. I go from tha mountains west through Greene and Hawkins area to help preach and teach tha gospel o' our Lord Christ Jesus. I jest arrived from Virginia four weeks ago." He smiled again and nodded his head.

Mrs. Robertson intently studied the man's face as he spoke and determined he was who he said he was. She lowered the rifle and called out to the children peeking around the open wooden door that they could come out and see the visitor for themselves.

The youthful preacher smiled even more broadly, if possible, at the sight of the children. He said, "I will be helping tha regular preachers in Greeneville, Jonesborough, Rogers, Elizabethton, and other chapels round 'bout. And I will be helping other settlements start their own churches."

"In between, I go home to home, place to place, throughout tha countryside. And I jest share with people. I especially love to preach tha message to persons and families who are too far out to attend services o' any kind."

Mrs. Robertson considered his words. She replied courteously, "Preacher Smith, the Robertson family is a Christian family. We would be honored for you to come inside, rest a bit, and give us a fine sermon, if you wish."

In response, the young preacher gaily nodded his

head and dismounted. He led the horse to the dogtrot opening beside Rebecca.

She turned and instructed Ruth to go tell her father to finish his chores as fast as possible and come to the cabin. Then she asked Emily to prepare refreshments with the food remaining from the recently completed breakfast meal.

Jeb stared curiously at the black-suited man standing in front of him. The preacher looked to be in his middle twenties. He was thickset, almost stout. He had medium length, sandy blond hair, an infectious smile, unending cheer, and the kindliest demeanor Jeb had ever seen. His eyes radiated benevolence and compassion. His voice had a pleasing, melodious quality; he was very easy to listen to. Upon dismounting, he appeared almost six-one in height.

Jeb could tell, straight away, he probably was an excellent, as well as entertaining, speaker.

The rest of the family and the preacher gathered inside the dining cabin, waiting on Mr. Robertson. Emily reset the table with biscuits, honey, ham slices, and drinks according to age. The preacher accepted plain well water, plus two flaky biscuits filled with honey.

Sam came in, moments later. "How do, sir. We'll be glad to hear ya message." He shook hands with the circuit preacher and motioned everyone else to the table.

The family sat down in their regular places, except

for Sam, who moved his log chair over next to Rebecca's, so everyone could face young Mordecai standing at Sam's end of the table. The family nibbled on their second breakfast, sipped their respective drinks, as the preacher finished his tasty snack. There was silence except for the slight sounds of munching, drinking and coughing.

So he would know the Robertson family trusted in the providence of God, Rebecca shared with the preacher the dangerous yet fortuitous events of the previous day. As she spoke, the young man took in every word of her story as if he had no doubt the outcome would be blessed in the end.

When everyone was ready, Preacher Smith stood up, large black Bible in hand, and faced his small audience. He smiled warmly before beginning.

As Jeb expected, the preacher was a gifted storyteller.

The preacher began by sharing his own story. "I growed up in ol' Virginia right before, and during, tha late War for Independence. My pa, he's now dead, bless his poor soul," the preacher paused, "he was a mean, mean drunk when I was a boy. He was a slave to tha bottle, and he had a mighty bad temper. He used to beat Ma and my brothers and me something fierce. So, I ran away from home at tha tender age o' eleven to become a sailor."

He recounted difficult years spent as a young, teenaged seaman sailing on various vessels from the Virginia coast. Life was harsh, treatment was brutal, and pay was poor. As he grew into manhood, he became enslaved, he said, by many of the same vices he had despised in his father.

On his twenty-first birthday, he took shore leave, wildly intent on abusing strong spirits and weak women with a few of his shipmates. Then, "A bold man o' God, one Jonathan Manville o' tha Methodist persuasion, came near and began to preach and quote scripture from tha Holy Book."

Mordecai's companions had mocked and cursed the preacher. One even physically threatened him. But there was something about this man's conviction, his peace, and his words that cut deep into Mordecai's spirit. His shipmates and their female consorts had stumbled drunkenly away from the man. Yet young Mr. Smith had stayed.

He soon sobered up. He experienced a genuine conversion and followed the preacher to the local town chapel. "It was there I started a whole new chapter. Found new and better friends. Learned another trade besides tha sea. Over tha next two and a half years, I was able to complete my education with tha help o' a dear, sweet ol' lady who went to tha church. She taught school when she was younger.

"And then, one o' tha happiest days o' my Christian life--tha Good Lord called me to be a preacher o' tha gospel." The young reverend's eyes lit up with joy at the sweet memory. "And tha best part is I was able to lead my pa to tha Lord before he passed away."

Having told his own conversion account, Mordecai next livened up his audience with tales of humorous things that had happened to him or befallen other ministers. His funniest personal episode occurred when he was preaching at a big camp-meeting over a year and half ago. In the throes of evangelistic ecstasy, he recalled, "I leaped on top that ol' wooden pulpit to deliver my message from on high, only to have it collapse under me before I got my next word out!" He was left, he said, to continue his sermon in the middle of the wreckage and the hoots and the hollers.

Without skipping a beat, Mordecai cleverly worked into his broken discourse a new theme, ad libbing to the laughing camp congregation, "Tha only sure foundation is God our Father. Stand on His eternal Word! It will not crumble beneath ya, like this pulpit did, or like tha works o' man will! In God, and God alone, do we all trust, brethren!"

Preacher Smith was now ready for his current sermon. Opening his Bible, he read Romans 8:28 from the Holy Writ: *"God causes all thangs to work together for good to those who love God."*

He looked up from his reading and beamed at the seated family. "Tha events o' yesterday showed tha Robertson family loves tha Lord. And it showed tha

Heavenly Father most assuredly loves tha Robertson family. His sweet hand o' protection was on your daughters and sons to save 'em out o' tha hands o' some very wicked men. There are situations when bad people and bad thangs come into all our lives. But tha Good Lord can turn whut was meant for evil into blessing, jest as long as we do our best each day to obey His Word!"

Preacher Smith explained, "The steps of a righteous man are established by tha Lord. God's mercy, kindness, and attention are shed abroad toward us, every day, in every way. He is concerned 'bout tha littlest thangs in our lives. He cares so much for all o' us. He loved us before we even knew Him. He loved us before we accepted His gospel."

He paused for effect before his next statement. "Four and a half years 'go, he put Preacher Manville smack dab in my way. Tha Heavenly Father wud not let me go on without hearing His message o' salvation," he said with firm conviction.

The morning progressed pleasantly.

Mordecai Smith preached a complete sermon in his own entertaining, enthusiastic, and engrossing style, as if he had a church full of rapt listeners. His little congregation hung on his every word. His melodic voice impressed upon all, especially upon Jeb, the depth of God's love through Jesus Christ His Son, as demonstrated in His wonderful plan of love and redemption.

When Mordecai finished his talk forty minutes later, all the ladies had moist eyes. The three boys were unusually contemplative and quiet. Even rugged Sam appeared to have something caught in his throat. Jeb had never heard such preaching.

He had never gone to church much, and this was a new experience for him. He remembered what Big Ed had said about the preachers and the people at the camp-meetings.

The whole Robertson family got up from the table. Sam and Rebecca each generously thanked the young circuit rider. "I greatly appreciate you for stopping by and sharing with us on such a beautiful morning," said Rebecca.

"Emily, would you please wrap up the remaining biscuits and put some tasty ham pieces and bacon strips in the middle of each, for our good preacher to take," she asked.

Sam commanded his oldest boy, "Robert, go git his canteen and fill it with fresh well water for him to take."

Before leaving, Preacher Smith prayed for the family's safety and blessings, "Lord, we thank ya again for your loving hand o' protection. Send thy guardian angels to watch over tha Robertson family in tha days to come. Keep them from any more evil doers. Shower them with many blessings. Coming in and goin' out. May their crops this sprang be plentiful. May thay all be in perfect health. Draw 'em ever closer to ya. May thay always live by your Word and your perfect Commandments."

"Amen," said everyone together.

When he finished his final prayer, the entire family and Jeb followed him outside.

"Thankee, Preacher. We are very grateful to ya for stopping by this morning," said Sam, and he meant it. He vigorously shook young Mordecai's hand anew.

Rebecca added, "Good sir, you are most welcome to come any time and preach again at our humble home. We thoroughly enjoyed your fine sermon." They watched and waved enthusiastically as he mounted, turned his horse, and rode off into the thick woods bearing southward.

"Bye!"

"Goodbye!"

"Please come again!"

"Ma'am, your biscuits are 'bout tha best I've ever had," he mumbled with his mouth full of another big bite, just as he disappeared into the forest.

Chapter Fourteen
A HOUSE-RAISING

A newly wedded couple named Nelson had very recently moved into the area.

Almost all the local farming inhabitants were poor in money and valuable possessions. Still, most were willing to share the little they had to aid newcomers, particularly a young couple starting out. Two of the neighboring families had generously offered to let the Nelsons stay at their own homes, until a patch could be cleared on the Nelson's property and a lean-to could be built as a temporary abode.

That being done, those same two neighbors had then helped Jonathan Nelson cut and hew logs from his land. These would be used in the construction of his future dwelling. Two other neighbors had also generously assisted. They hauled some freshly felled and trimmed logs off their own land over to the Nelsons' property, adding to the couple's supply of building logs.

Sam had promised the Nelsons and their four

neighbors he and his family would be available for the house raising, which was scheduled for the next day. A bountiful dinner and late night dance would follow the cabin built-out.

Mordecai Smith's unexpected arrival had delayed the family's chores and preparations to be gone. But Sam didn't begrudge the morning hours devoted to young Mordecai's powerful preaching. After the calamitous events of the last two days, and the obvious occurrences of what he and Rebecca both viewed as divine interventions, Sam was more inclined than ever to the importance of spiritual teaching.

The arrival of Mordecai Smith seemed perfectly timed in Sam's estimation. "Tha Heavenly Father has certainly bin grabbing my attention lately," he told his wife that night as they both got ready for bed. "And I am grateful for His keeping our children safe. Mordecai was right. God has protected and blessed us in tha midst o' real evil intent."

Since Sam believed the entire murderous, vengeance-seeking Hansen clan was now finally eliminated, he deemed it safe to leave the homestead, animals, and possessions unguarded for the festivities. In any case, all his family members, including Jeb, would be with him, protected by himself and the presence of other adult settlers.

He and Rebecca looked forward to the evening's

activities after the house-raising. She delightedly told him, "It's been almost three years. Remember, Sam, the last time we danced? Most of our neighbors will be there. And I will get to wear that lovely new dress you bought me. We'll have such fun. And after all the cruel dangers our family has suffered through. Oh, Sam, I'm so excited." Her eyes sparkled with anticipation. It was not often the drudgery and demands of their daily work were relieved by gaiety.

Although conditions were always demanding in the Tennessee frontier wilderness, settler families and singles still found ways and means to relax. Corn-huskings, log-rollings, house-raisings, quilting-parties, and such, were universally accepted excuses for men, women, and children to join together for a work hard, party hard occasion. People often came from many miles around to join in the affair.

Sometimes during house-raisings, the men would cease the real work long enough to conduct impromptu shooting matches, or hold contests of physical strength or speed. Then everybody, big and small, young and old, after performing their fair share of the day's labor, would gather inside the newly constructed home itself, or meet at a participant's designated cabin, to enjoy the massive feast prepared by the women and girls during the day.

After the grand meal, the adults and older young people would dance until well past midnight, only to go home in the early morning hours for breakfast and perhaps a rare sleeping in.

The Robertson girls got to dress in their finest clothes, as thrilled about the evening activities as their mother. "What do you think, Jeb," cooed Sarah, batting her gorgeous eyes at him as she twirled once in front of the cabins, modeling her lovely pink cotton dress with the bright rose sash.

Even the boys were getting in the spirit of things. Notwithstanding, Sam and the boys wore their usual attire, since they would be doing heavy labor all day and into the evening.

"Everybody *finally* ready? Ya sure?" Sam said, looking at the ladies with a big grin on his rugged face. "We should've bin gone two hours ago. Well, let's git!" he called out merrily.

Rebecca and Ruthie took Sam's horse; Emily and Sarah rode the old, yet still reliable, plowing mule. The men went on foot.

Thankfully, the day had dawned fair and sunny, warming to the mid-forties and beyond. If the weather held, the plan was for the women to do all their cooking outdoors on two big campfires. The meals would be served on three long makeshift tables freshly constructed for the event. The evening's dance would also be held outdoors on the cleared grounds next to the newly built structure. If the weather turned bad, all meal preparation, eating, and dancing would be done at the Sullivan's double-wide facility three quarters a mile away.

"Now, even if it pours rain, we're gonna keep on raising that cabin," Bill Sullivan had admonished and spread the word to all the participants. "'Less it starts lightning something fierce, we gonna keep on keeping on."

The house-raising party could occur the following night after the new home was finished. In this instance, however, everyone involved had agreed beforehand to get the job done during the day and have their meal and dance that very same night.

When the Robertson clan arrived, there were four families, the Sullivans, Hunbricks, Lamberts, and Cartwrights, plus the newly wedded couple, the Nelsons, already busy. The five men plus the three oldest boys, between fourteen and eighteen years of age, were busy at work. Some were cutting down and sawing trees for additional timber. Some were finishing out the necessary trimming and notching of previously hewn lumber, making the logs ready for use. The five wives and four older girls were handling the cooking.

Sam, Rebecca and their brood plus Jeb joined the fray.

"Howdy, Sam. Rebecca. It's nice to see your bunch, again. It's bin a spell," called out Bill Sullivan gaily as he saw them arrive.

With the temperature hovering in the mid-forties, Bill had still managed a deep sweat with the late morning's work. He pulled a faded red handkerchief out of the inner brim of his hat and mopped the sides of his jowly face and his patch of balding forehead. He then gave his instructions to the newcomers, "Sam, if ya wud, go help Joe and Ben's crew with cutting timber. We need 'bout ten more logs felled. Me and Tom's crew are stripping and notching tha cut logs. Robert, I reckon ya kin go with your father."

Sam paired Jeb up with Robert on the adult crew. Watching the two boys leave, Thomas stomped his foot in prideful irritation and protested stoutly, "Father, that's not fair! I'm near as old as he is!"

Thomas reluctantly joined the remaining group of younger children. The twelve boys and girls ranging from six to thirteen years old were given auxiliary tasks appropriate to his or her age. For them, the day would be mostly play or idle time.

Jeb stopped and looked around. The crews were all busy at their tasks. He saw that the designated location for the Nelsons' new home lay on the back edge of a sparsely timbered patch within the otherwise thick forest. The workers were taking advantage of this natural partial clearing by removing all the trees and hewing the larger ones into building logs. Beyond and to the sides, other suitable trees were being targeted by the logging team as well. Overall, this had the added benefit of providing the Nelsons a tillable starter plot of land for their inaugural spring planting. After the house-raising, both the supper and dance would be held on this newly cleared space.

Already by the first tree and eager to get started, Robert motioned and called out to his partner, "Hey, Jeb, over here!"

As the day progressed, Jeb found himself engaged in the most demanding manual labor he had ever done. Nevertheless, he thoroughly enjoyed it. Welding the heavy ax, he found his blisters were now turning into hardened calluses in only two days frontier time and was proud of it. "My hands are really toughening up!" Jeb said to himself. He was learning valuable lessons he would take back with him into the future. Hard work is usually its own reward. Helping others is often a greater gift to the doer than to the receiver.

Jeb had never worked harder physically, or liked it more. "Gosh, if Dad could see me now," the boy mused.

He laid his axe down for a breather. Impulsively, Jeb flexed his right bicep and felt it with his left hand. A loud guffaw immediately issued from the other side of the tree. Jeb saw Robert observing him and shaking his head. "Go on with ya!" The two boys' eyes met. They both laughed out loud. Jeb continued chortling and picked up his axe to resume chopping.

"Come on, Jeb, I'll race ya. I bet I cut my side faster than ya cut yours," challenged Robert. The two boys hewed away, felling the big tree and watching it land between them. Their competition continued.

A little later, though, Jeb started thinking, sadly and seriously, about Nat, Dad, and his mom. He didn't know what prompted the thoughts about home. He tried to block out the inconvenient and painful recollections, but found he couldn't. His mind simply refused to obey.

As he brought the ax up for another blow, Jeb became flooded with his old despair. He wondered, *Will I ever get back to my real family?* He shook his head and wiped tears from his eyes, careful now to hide his face from Robert chopping on the other side of the thick tree. Resolutely, he tried to force all images, all memories, of 2014 out of his consciousness.

I can't dwell on my old life. The boy gritted his teeth with fierce determination. *I can't do that anymore. It gets me depressed. I'll go crazy if I think too much. Besides, I don't know for sure if I'll ever return to my own time. So I might as well forget about Nat and Dad and Mom. Forget I ever lived in the future.* Jeb threw himself into work with blank-minded, renewed intensity. The more he tried to not think about his family, the more he thought about them. It was an impossible situation.

Fortunately for Jeb, right at that moment, the

ladies called out for noon-dinner. "Ya'll come in! It's time to eat a bite."

The meal gave him the opportunity he needed to rein in his raw emotions, unwatched by Robert or Thomas. Although they both called out his name, he made a point of sitting apart from them in between two burly men, so he would be hidden. Once Robert and Thomas began eating, he knew they'd be too busy feeding their faces to notice him.

Though lunch was a brief repast, it allowed Jeb time to gather himself together. The evening supper, after the raising, would be a big celebration. Everyone else would be ready to celebrate, and he wanted to be in a good mood, too. When labor resumed, Jeb had his memories corralled enough to work unimpeded.

Hard labor and hard drink were mutual by-products of the wild Tennessee frontier, so it was no surprise that several of the participants had brought their best whiskey and other fine liquors to treat their fellow workers, as the afternoon progressed. A fancy jug was passed to him, and Sam gladly took a gigantic pull.

"This is," he allowed, "among tha best Kentuck whiskey I've had for quite a spell."

He smiled broadly and took a second, third, and fourth swig. Sated, he passed the jug to Robert, who was allowed a small sip as a member of the men's crew. Robert offered it to Jeb, who merely shook his head.

"No thanks, I don't like the taste of alcohol," he said. Robert shrugged his shoulders and stole two more quick tastes when his father wasn't looking.

Emboldened by the effects of the tasty spirits, a friendly, raucous rivalry broke out among the six men and five teenaged boys as they labored. Now that a sufficient number of logs were cut, stripped, and notched for building the cabin, the three available mules could be harnessed up to start uprooting the leftover tree stumps in and around the site. Thomas was added in, to create three crews of four people per mule. Every stump had to be removed, and there were several dozen littering the area.

The three pulling teams began each contest at the same instant, ensuring hotly competed races with fervent betting on every outcome.

"Hot damn, ol' Methuselah!" shouted Ben Lambert, along with his members, as their mule pulled hard.

"Come on, boy!" yelled the Sullivan crew to spur their animal.

"Ho, Big Johnnie, ho!" Now, Tom Cartwight's team was urging on their big glossy brown. "Git up, git!" they called out.

"Hurrah! Hurrah, there, Methusie!" The four humans on the Lambert team pushed and dug and hacked into the hard roots to attempt to remove their first stump ahead of Tom and Bill's equally straining teams.

The pulling contests continued until all tree stubs lay piled in a tremendous heap by the edge of the forest. Tom's team barely beat out Bill's crew, with Ben's group finishing last. The men searched and found a mini-clearing beyond the stump hill that was devoid of heavy undergrowth and also had patches of soft bald earth. This they dug and carted over to fill and pack the many gaping root holes, providing a uniform and safe surface all around the site.

"See, this way, nobody's gonna break their legs when thay dance tonight," Robert explained to Jeb, as they shoveled dirt into one of the last stump holes. "'Course, ya may be such a clumsy oaf ya still fall down and bust ya ugly face," he hooted and slapped his knee.

"Yeah, well, I don't really dance much anyway," replied Jeb. He felt way too tired now to defend himself.

Jeb had to pace himself. The next round of hard labor was about to begin. It was nearing time for the workers to set the logs in place and erect the walls. Naturally, more contests followed.

Once the prepared timber was carried to its side of the cabin site, they stopped real work for another game. The builders once again strove to outdo one another in feats of strength and speed. This time, the men and older boys competed in teams of two to see who could pick-up and toss their upright log the longest forward distance, one person on either side lifting up and throwing in unison. As before, there was enthusiastic betting on each event.

"Ho, lookie there at my Jacob and Tom. They dern near beat out ol' Sam's team on that one." Bill boasted on his oldest son's performance.

After several competitive rounds of this "upright lifting," as Sam called it, the workers settled down to the final task of completing the walls and roof of the structure. Around the four sides, teams of two or three people, lifting in sequence, meticulously fitted the heavy notched logs, interlocking each new layer snugly into place from the ground level up. It was heavy labor, but they knew what they were doing.

Even at this later stage, any careless actions or mistakes were met with jokes and boasts. "Tom, ya big id-jit. I figured a grown man your age wud know how to properly notch timber," cackled Ben Lambert with gentle humor. "Ya got tha cut facing down on one end and facing up on tha other."

The women, girls, and younger children temporarily stopped their cooking and other assigned chores to witness this beginning phase of putting the logs in place. Many called out encouragement to husband, father, son, or big brother. "Michael, Michael!" yelled little Bonnie to her oldest brother. She eagerly watched his crew settle a big front-wall log into place. It was a fine thing to see the cabin rising.

The surrounding crowd dispersed as the construction continued. Everyone returned to their own projects. The laborers quieted to their tasks, while the early evening breeze mingled with the peaceful sounds of the forest and the tranquility of approaching dusk.

"Steady. Lay it in nicely, lads. Easy...easy," sang out Thomas Cartwright to the work crews.

Of necessity, as the walls and top went up, they discovered some logs were unusable due to crookedness, poor quality, bad trimming, or inaccurate notching. Replacements had to be fashioned on the spot.

Less than three hours later, with the onset of nightfall, the sides and roof were built, leaving only the cracks in the walls to be chinked and the dirt floor to be foot-packed by the new couple after they moved in.

The construction workers stepped away from their labors with immense satisfaction. A few strode completely around the structure to check for defects and admire their handiwork.

"Well, boys, we did it. Looks mighty fine to me. Real fine, in fact," crowed Joe Hunbrick, arms folded, as he and Sam moseyed around the new home. "What say, Sam?"

The men treated themselves to more whiskey and a much deserved rest in the lightly chilled breeze. Several sat down on the ground and propped up against the front walls, so they could comfortably watch the women setting the tables.

One or two brave souls catcalled light-hearted jokes to the ladies about a particular item of cooking. "Bertha, whut's this I heard from Joe 'bout your 'possum stew where ya forgot to put in tha meat? Kinda thin, weren't it?"

Or they repeated juicy gossip overheard. "Sally, did ya hear there's a young new peddler in Greeneville they say is mighty partial to redheads? Hey, Ben. Ben!"

"Huh?"

"Ya best be on tha lookout. Take real good care if ya see that peddler sneaking around your place. He might be selling something ya don't want."

Each time, the quicker-witted females responded with even better retorts. "Thomas Cartwright, did you know your mule has got more God-given sense than you? Every time you open your mouth, your mind shuts down. Why don't you stand up, and take a load off that poor brain you've been sitting on?" the sharp-tongued Mrs. Lambert retorted, as Amy Cartwright poked her best friend in the ribs.

"Thomas, you're about as funny as a horse turd," chimed in Amy, "and almost as smelly. Sakes above, I can't believe I actually live with that man!" They sniggered together at the bested male.

Soon, all the men wisely watched the ladies in polite silence. Great expectations arose. A bountiful feast was about to begin.

The celebration meal was a smorgasbord of delicious meats and winter-available foods. There were two giant cast-iron pots of bubbling stew, filled with a potpourri of venison, pork, rabbit, and squirrel, along with potatoes, carrots, dried peas, onions, dried corn, turnips, and dried herbs. There were also succulent venison steaks, mouth-watering pork loins, and individual roasted potatoes.

Six heaping plates of hot Johnnycakes, with mounds of churned butter, were placed strategically on the three tables so that every person could reach and replenish his or her own serving. Mugs were constantly being refilled with the drink of choice: full whiskey, water, cow milk, buttermilk, or sweetened water-cut whiskey.

Appetites were enormous after the day's work, with food enough for all. Hunger was such that all the jousting between the sexes and friends stopped during the serious repast. Big Sam ate enough for three normal men all by himself.

With dinner done, more logs were added to the two cooking fires, turning them into blazing bonfires, driving away the darkness in front of the newly constructed cabin and its clearing. The stupendous meal was followed by a short period of relaxing to allow full stomachs to partially settle. Then at last, the real evening's excitement could begin.

After a restful stretch of thirty minutes or so, Joseph Humbrick and Benjamin Lambert went to their horses.

Each man retrieved from his saddlebag a worn leather carrying case of similar size. Each removed the contents, tightened up the instrument and rosined up the bow. As they tuned up, the distinctive high-bass cries of the two dueling fiddles echoed throughout the neighboring woods upon the cool night's air.

There had been many hours of grueling labor, followed by a delicious, well-deserved supper. But now the long-awaited party was about to start. There was a carefree dance for the older ones and a frolic for the younger ones, until the wee hours of the morning.

Thomas Cartwright, with his muscular son's help, placed a tremendous kettle on one of the fires. "This here's my special brew," he called over his shoulder to the others.

He had blended a potent concoction of many gallons of one-third water and two-thirds strong whisky, liberally sweetened with maple tree-sugar, plus added spices and fresh butter. Although spices and seasonings in late winter were scarce, two of the families had meager stores they donated for the refreshment. The drink was mild enough that the older children over ten could enjoy in careful amounts if generously diluted with well water.

Unusual for a gathering of six pioneer families, there were no aged people present. Except for old man Halbert, who had declined to come, there were no other elderly persons living in the area. It took youth and fortitude to handle the harsh frontier. Over the last five years, the adults, along with their children, had infrequently joined together for rare festivities such as this.

The two self-taught, yet expert fiddlers struck the beginning chords of a popular Virginia reel. "Gents, face your partners. Now, here we go!"

"Come, Sam," Rebecca took his meaty hand and excitedly led him into the dance area.

In no time, all the adults were enthusiastically stepping their way through the patterns, the women's skirts ruffling with the rapid dance motions, the locks of their hair blowing with the sweet evening breeze.

Emily and Robert joined the older teenaged group, which claimed its own dance area within the clearing. Here, though, just one couple was attempting to dance. The rest were mingled, carrying on and laughing, or else looking wistfully on. Further out, the thirteen younger boys and girls gathered near the outskirts of the clearing, among the three long dining tables.

Ruthie ran up behind Thomas and stuck a pinecone down his shirt as he turned to talk to Jeb. "Hey, what the--" She pushed the cone burrs firmly into his bare back and then ran around to the other side of one of the tables, giggling. Thomas took off after her while Jeb watched in amusement.

Thomas circled the table, only to have Ruth counter by running the opposite direction, darting back and forth, keeping the table between them, then crossing over to the other table and daring Thomas to catch her.

His shout could barely be heard amidst all the other noises, "I'll git ya, Ruthie! Ya cain't keep away from me forever."

"You can't catch me. You can't catch me," Ruthie teased her brother in sing-song, as she ran, first this way, then that way, skillfully avoiding her brother's clutches. "Dead bird! Dead bird! I told you I'd get even." she called out. "Na-na-na-na-naaa-nahhh."

As Jeb viewed the festivities, there was a soft tug on his sleeve.

He turned around. Sarah's tilted face was inches from his, her bruises barely visible in the flickering light from the two fires, her features still extraordinarily pretty, and her eyes as bottomless as ever.

"Do you want to dance?" she said and looked full into his face.

He felt an immediate heat flushing from his head downward, as he stammered, "I...I don't know your type of, I mean, I don't know how to dance. The way you dance," he lamely finished.

"It's easy to do."

Her eyes kept drawing him in closer. "Let me show you," she took his hand and gently pulled him toward the older teen group and away from the tables.

Without warning, Henry Cartwright, who had

recently turned fourteen, bumped deliberately into Jeb from behind, knocking him forward a half step. Next to Henry was his constant sidekick, closest neighbor, and only good friend, Timothy Lambert.

Henry elbowed Timothy, who stood gawking as Henry smirked at Sarah, "My God, gal, whut happened to ya?" Henry leered at the girl and said, "Your face looks like your ol' worthless mule stepped all over your head."

The two ruffians howled and slapped their knees.

Henry had always coveted Sarah's beauty the times their families had met. But she hadn't fancied his appearance, his personality, or his attitude one bit. And she made sure he knew it. Jealous of Jeb, and eager to extract vengeance on Sarah for rejecting him, Henry seized the opportunity to bully the smaller boy and humiliate her at the same time.

Unfortunately for Sarah, Robert and the other older boys were all engrossed in having their own fun. Thomas was still chasing Ruth. And with the cover of darkness, the noise, and the activities of their own dance to distract them, none of the adults could see, hear, or care what their children were doing.

Henry gave Timothy a sloppy grin, then turned back to Jeb and shoved him roughly in the shoulder. "So, boy, whut ya gonna do 'bout it?" he growled.

"I think you're jest plumb chicken, boy." He looked over at his buddy for support. "Hey, Timothy! We gotta scrawny little chicken here and an ugly-faced squaw there."

Henry shoved Jeb with even greater force. He hesitated briefly to see Jeb's reaction then cocked his ham-like fist to strike a blow. Sarah cowered behind Jeb.

Jeb went into a strange fighting stance Sarah had never seen before. She watched him in amazement.

Chapter Fifteen
FIRST KISS

Jeb blocked Henry's relatively slow punch, then side-kicked him in his solar plexus, between the stomach and chest, knocking Henry down yet without seriously hurting him.

Henry's eyes bugged out in shock. He struggled to catch his breath from the unexpected blow. "Ya done it now. I'm a goin' to hurt ya bad, boy!" he shouted hoarsely.

Pulling in ragged gulps of air, Henry sprang from the ground in rage, motioning Timothy to join the fight. "Go git 'em!"

Henry hurtled himself at Jeb, wildly launching punches. Jeb deflected all the strikes and got inside the swinging fists. Snapping his right arm straight, he smashed the palm of his hand into Henry's onrushing exposed nose. Henry fell, clumsily and backwards, onto his rump, landing with a loud thump. "Umphh!" he cried out as he hit the ground.

Staring up at Jeb in utter disbelief, his thick stomach

facing the sky, Henry began scooting away reverse fashion on his feet and hands, with his considerable bottom dragging on the leafy turf. He resembled a defeated crab. When he got out of range, Henry leaped up.

"How'd ya do that?" he mumbled. He threw one last look of mingled surprise and fear at Jeb, then grabbed his nose, turned, and ran into the crowd of kids beyond the last table.

Before Henry even hit the ground, Jeb had swung around to face the second foe now rushing in. "I'll do 'em good for ya, Henry. Don't worry."

Timothy awkwardly attempted to mimic Jeb's technique by kicking out at him. Jeb simply turned his body sideways, causing the strike to miss and leaving Timothy's launched left leg temporarily suspended in the air. His body weight was now supported by his single leg only. Jeb side-kicked Timothy's right leg out from underneath him, dropping him like a sack of potatoes to the earth.

"Oomph," he cried out, twisting his leg beneath him as he fell. Timothy, too, turned and limped from Jeb, as fast as he could on one good leg.

Unbeknownst to Henry and Timothy, Jeb had been taking Tai kwon do lessons from a trained professional since he was seven years old right up until five months ago. Last fall, when he had tried out for the school basketball team with his Highland Hill buddies, Robert and David, he had stopped going to his martial arts class altogether. But before that, he had averaged a little more than a session a week for the previous six and half years.

I know I'm not all that skilled, he mentally conceded, watching his two foes scoot away. He didn't have the exceptional fighting ability of the more advanced students. And he hadn't worked very hard at Tai kwon do. Prior to quitting, he had only earned an upper level green belt.

However, when used against unskilled frontier boys who had never experienced, heard or dreamed of such fighting, Jeb's lightweight training in martial arts had come in quite handy. He had been considered a bit of a slacker and a weaker fighter by his higher achieving Tai kwon do peers. Yet Jeb's skill level was more than enough to defeat cowardly bullies such as Henry Cartwright and Timothy Lambert.

I don't know for sure if I can beat Brent if I ever made it back to the present, but at least all those lessons paid off against these dudes.

Yet somehow, Jeb's wild frontier adventure was infusing him with increased confidence, especially in his fighting ability. *Boy, if I could just face Brent right now.* Jeb replayed his last battle with the bully in his mind and pictured what he would do differently the next time. *Yeah, if there is a next time.*

Nobody else had paid attention, or even noticed

the short shuffle. Grateful for the chance to enjoy some needed recreation, the adults were oblivious to any activities outside their dancing fun. The older teens had their own clique formed next to the grown-ups. And the younger kids were all playing around the dinner tables or in the woods close by.

Neither of the attackers was noticeably injured; mostly they had been frightened, not beaten, off.

I know I hit Henry hard enough to do some damage. That punch should have broken his big nose. Or bloodied it, at the very least. After the hard palm smack, he could see Henry's nose was red, but it was definitely not broken. And there had been no blood dripping down Henry's face that Jeb could see.

That's just strange, pondered Jeb, as he watched the two ruffians scamper away. *Really odd. It's like I can't hurt people here. But then, they don't seem to be able to hurt me, either.* He recalled the several gunshots fired at him by members of the Hansen Gang, and how he remained totally unscathed. The image of the green book reappeared and disappeared in his mind.

Jeb's train of thought was interrupted by the warm touch of two hands: one resting gently on his shoulder, one on the back of his neck. "Jeb?" That soothing, sweet, feminine voice he found so appealing was calling his name.

He turned around with expectation. Even in the

deepening dusk, he could see the shining in her wide, liquid eyes.

"Jeb? You're not hurt at all, are you? And you fought off both of them, all by yourself," said Sarah, gazing up at him. "What were those strange moves you made?" An inquiring expression lingered on her pretty face. "I've never seen anyone fight that way. Did the Indians teach you that?"

"No. No, I didn't learn it from the Indians." He couldn't tell her about martial arts.

Her breathing was as gentle as her voice. "I've never known any boy like you," she whispered.

He was getting lost in her beautiful eyes again.

"First, you save my life. Plus, you saved my virtue. Now, you've saved me from being tormented by that horrible Henry. Mother has a name for a man or boy who is not a gentleman. She calls them a scoundrel. That's what Henry Cartwright is. A scoundrel. He has absolutely no respect for ladies.

"But Jeb, you are the most perfect gentleman. You're like," she searched for the right comparison, "like a Knight of the Round Table. Mother has read stories to us about King Arthur. You are gallant and brave and kind and respectful."

Jeb didn't know how to respond. He'd never gotten a complement before from any girl, except from Nat, of course. As Sarah continued to talk, his inner self shifted into overdrive. *I'm not overly brave or gallant. Or at least I'm not in the year 2014.*

He knew all of the popular girls in his time merely laughed at him. Or they didn't speak to him at all.

Jeb also knew that, at best, he was only average at Tai kwon do. While he'd always liked the feeling of serenity and well-being he sometimes experienced after a good workout session, he didn't particularly enjoy the sparring or fighting itself. Outside the martial arts studio, he avoided confrontations whenever he could.

However, in this exciting world of 1802, he felt like he'd traveled to another dimension and become a superhero.

Jeb marveled at how radically different, how much better, his life was with Sam, Thomas, Sarah, and the rest of the Robertsons, versus his stinky reality.

Apparently, here, nothing could physically hurt him. *I get to fight the bad guys and beat them. I have the best looking girl interested in me.*

In his real existence, at Highland Hill, he wasn't sure where he stood on girls, whether he could like a particular one as a girlfriend, or just have one as a simple friend. At Highland Hill, he hadn't yet entered the mysterious realm of women. But in this pioneer adventure, it was unbelievable what was happening to him.

Inside, he felt four or five years older than his actual age, a teenager who was approaching manhood. He had lived in frontier Tennessee for less than three full days; however, each day seemed an entire year of adventure unto itself.

There was no doubt in Jeb's mind that he cared enormously for Sarah. Already, he had strong emotions--romantic sentiments he had never before experienced. There was something captivating about her. If he had been born in 1788, and had met Sarah under similar circumstances, Jeb was quite sure they would have become the best of friends and likely fallen in love.

Here in this frontier past, he mused, *there is something special happening inside me. I feel like I could take on the whole wide world.* Jeb could sense it! As a person, he was developing, maturing, building confidence, learning valuable lessons about life, about himself, and about love. All in ways he would never have experienced in 21st century Knoxville and Highland Hill School. Best of all, these changes were becoming a permanent part of him.

Jeb was lost in his rumination. Sarah had continued speaking to him, mistaking the intensity of his expression as evidence he was listening attentively to her all along.

"Jeb, do you like me?" she gently asked.

He didn't answer and she repeated the question.

"Jeb, do you like me?"

"Yes, what?"

Her bold heartfelt query snapped him back to reality. He blinked hard. Twice. Jeb studied her upturned face for a full minute without replying. Choosing his words with care, he finally said, "Well, yes, Sarah, I really like you."

Jeb looked down at his feet, drew a deep breath to still the pounding of his heart, and looked back up. "Sarah, I've never met any girl at Highland...I mean, I've never known any girl who's as pretty and as nice as you. Honest. I'm totally blown away that you would even like me."

Jeb didn't mean to be *that* honest, but somehow the words tumbled out of his mouth before he could stop them. He thought about Melissa and her snobbish group of girls at Highland Hill who admittedly were good-looking, but who were also shallow and mean-spirited. Sarah was much prettier than they and so much better as a person.

He gazed into her lovely eyes and said, "Sarah, you're drop-dead beautiful. You're very sweet. You're very considerate. You have a great personality. How could I not like you? How could any boy who's normal and with half a brain not like you? Gosh, I like you. A *lot*." Jeb blushed at his statement.

He took another deep breath and said, "You're awesome." His voice held wonderment that such an attractive female could be so smitten with him.

Sarah positively radiated. Her gorgeous smile filled her face with even more loveliness, evaporating the ugliness of her bruises. She took Jeb's hand once again. "Come on, sweet knight."

She gently pulled him off to the left, under the covering of the darkened and thick woods--away from the dining tables, the dance, noisy teenagers, parents, and away from the continued scrutiny of Henry and Timothy. Obediently, he allowed himself to be led.

They walked hand in hand about seventy-five yards into the deepening forest and stopped behind a massive oak. Its wide trunk would further shield them from prying eyes. Sarah turned to face Jeb, her soft dainty hand nestled inside his. Just the feel of her warm feminine hand excited Jeb to no end.

She gazed solemnly into his unblinking brown eyes for what seemed an eternity. Mingled together, he could hear the sounds of the insects, the night birds, the small varmints passing by, and the branches lightly blowing in the tree tops above.

When she finally spoke, her choice of subject surprised him.

He had vague expectations of romantic, mushy conversation. Instead, Sarah told Jeb of her family's move from their old farmstead in North Carolina to the new Tennessee territory. She said, "I remember it was in the early spring, after the winter thaw. I had just turned nine. Ruthie was not yet four years old. When I think about it, it seems like it only happened yesterday.

"I can recall it being very difficult on everyone. All of us worked our fingers to the bone, doing what we could, except for little Ruthie, of course. Father had to plant our crops and build our cabin--that's the one we use for cooking and meals now--with a little help from mother and Robert. In the beginning, there were very few neighbors.

"That first winter was just terrible. There was barely enough harvest to last our family and our farm animals until the spring. We made it through because father was always able to kill enough game for the table. But there were so many days, too many to count, that I was very hungry.

"There never seemed to be enough food. Father often did without his share to leave more food for the rest of us. And here, he worked harder than all of us put together. There was real danger from the Indians back then. Father had two fierce battles with them in that first year. One happened in the far back end of our cornfield nearest the woods. Four braves jumped Father early in the morning as he was hitching up the mule for plowing. Thank goodness, he carried his rifle and had his big hunting knife.

"Father is very strong and very quick. He shot the closest brave. Then he used the brave's body to shield himself from the gun, arrows and knives of the other three Indians. He knocked down one, stabbed another, and used that Indian's fallen rifle as a club against the last brave.

"Another time, he was coming back from Greeneville and a small band of Cherokees hidden among the thick trees suddenly attacked him. He has an ugly scar from a stab wound he got in that fight.

"I deeply respect my father. He is a very good man. I only hope I can find someone as good as he is when I marry." Sarah looked coyly up at the boy, her pretty mouth opened in a small circle of wondering.

Jeb gave her a half-smile, but felt totally inadequate to the conversation. Compared to big Sam, he had a long ways to go.

Sarah spoke of the time when she turned ten. Her father and other settlers had luckily discovered, battled, and contained a forest fire in its infancy, keeping the flames from reaching their houses. "They put out the last of it just a hundred yards from the back of our place. Robert and Thomas both helped them."

The fire had been caused, she explained, by a thunderstorm's lightning strike into the virgin timber. Unfortunately, the accompanying rainfall had not been heavy enough to extinguish the blaze and it had begun to spread.

She told many stories about her father and his bravery, resourcefulness, quick reaction, and cool thinking under attack. One day when hunting by himself, her father was surprised and attacked by two vicious panthers together. This was virtually unheard of. The beasts usually avoided man. They almost never hunted together, being solitary predators. They were a secretive species.

"Father shot one at close range, just four feet away, with his rifle, as the other landed on his back. He fought and killed the second cat using his big hunting knife. He still has ugly scars on his back, arms, and a few on his chest.

"There was another time last year. He and Robert were out hunting. They got ambushed by two renegade braves. Since we came here, Father has seen and faced all kinds of dangers. But he always seems to get through them in one piece."

Sarah confided all her girlish hopes and future dreams to Jeb. All the while, he listened with rapt attention. He didn't speak a word in return, but managed to sagely nod his head at just the right moments.

She finally halted, looking at him sweetly. She waited for him to speak. Jeb kept silent, so Sarah asked simple questions about his past and his ambitions. "Was it as hard for your family when you first came? How long ago was that?"

"About three years ago," he lied.

Sarah was a romantic young lady, but also very practical. "Father has always wanted to be a farmer," she said. "What do you want to do or be, Jeb, when you grow up? What did you say your father did for a living?"

Jeb sighed and frowned slightly. It was one thing to fib to Sam in order to find a place to stay. He would have been absolutely lost in this frontier if Sam Robertson had not kindly taken him in. However, it was quite another thing to make up stories to Sarah. He liked her a great deal. Plus, it felt much worse to lie to a girl than to a man.

He looked at her and shook his head from side to side, as if to say, "I can't talk about it."

Sarah nodded with a gentle smile of compassion.

"Oh, Jeb, I forgot. You lost your whole family, didn't you, and you don't want to think or talk about it. I'm so sorry about your loss. I understand. I truly do understand."

She edged nearer to him. "There are just no good boys around these parts. And then you come along. And I'm so glad you did. You saved me."

Jeb's heart was beating very fast now.

"You are so brave...to go through...what you went through. So very, very brave you are."

Sarah whispered the last words. She leaned close in, then closer still.

Her eyes were moist with tender affection, her face infused with longing, her breathing deep and slow. Jeb could feel her sweet breath on his face. She continued to lean closer in. He could almost count the number of lush eyelashes. She was now less than an inch away. Their lips met, touched, ever so gently.

Pure electricity shot through Jeb's body. The sensation was entirely new. And mind-blowing.

Now, she kissed him more strongly. He began to kiss back. They wrapped their arms around each other. Every particle in his body and brain exploded--alive with ecstasy. Jeb forgot where he was, who he was, how he came to be there. All he knew was this one fathomless interval of being, this all-consuming span of time, as his kisses and arms merged with those of Sarah.

He had never known such intense feelings. Whether it was minutes or hours they were locked together in such ardent embrace, he did not know. All he knew was he didn't want it end!

Suddenly, Jeb had a weird tingling in his right side, between his stomach and back, just below his ribcage.

Where had he experienced that strange sensation before?

Startled, he pulled away from Sarah's loving arms, his face momentarily white with surprise. Her puzzled eyes searched his as he continued to release her.

He felt the tingling in his lower side again, even stronger. And it happened a third time. Jeb suddenly recalled, *It's the same type of feeling I had when the members of the Hansen gang shot at me.* A dream-like mist began swirling, surrounding, and seizing his mind.

Jeb felt himself falling, motionless, into a trance. Somehow, Sarah's beautiful face was fading. The Tennessee woods were disappearing. The background noise of the happy house-raising dance was becoming dimmer.

"Sarah!" he yelled out once to her dissipating image.

His body was tumbling, tumbling to an unseen ground.

Chapter Sixteen
INTRUDERS

TJ awoke out of the fog.

He found himself lying face down on the hardwood floor next to his dad's desk in the left wing of the master bedroom.

TJ laid perfectly still, his brain racing to catch up with his body, as he strained to hear any familiar frontier sounds, hoping against hope he was still with his Sarah, still with the Robertson family, still at the dance. Still in the year 1802.

He stared at the underbelly of the desk and the wall beyond.

The green book was on the floor to the right of his prone stomach. It was open, and its pages were now blank. TJ didn't dare to make contact with it again. Instead, he reached out and touched the closest leg of the compact desk. He rubbed his fingers up and down it. Unfortunately, it was as solid and as real as his body.

"I'm back," he whispered, with mixed feelings of

disappointment and relief. "I can't believe it. I'm back and I didn't do anything. It just happened." For all his homesickness about his sister and his dad, for all his erstwhile longing to return to the future, a big part of him had become right at home with Sarah and with the rest of the Robertsons.

But, TJ had to face the truth. There was no doubt. He had gone forward to the present. He was back in his dad's bedroom, where the incredible adventure had started. Cautiously, he raised himself up, his ears tuned to catch any strange sounds within the house.

At once, TJ recalled the funny tingling he had in his side. The same odd sensation had occurred twice before in his brief frontier experience. Then, it had happened again while he was kissing Sarah. In a flash, his mind and body had gone back into that same hazy, trance-like state that had begun his adventure.

The first time TJ had felt the weird tingling, someone in the Hansen Gang had shot him pointblank, to no effect. He reached around to probe his right lower side where the latest sensation had occurred. "There's nothing there. No blood, no wound." He couldn't feel any scar tissue, either. However, he noticed his shirt was torn, with multiple slits, around the spot.

TJ glanced over at the chair that was now several feet behind him. The leather barrel-back chair had apparently rolled back with some force over the carefully polished hardwood boards and slammed against the beginning edge of the thick bedroom carpet. It was now oddly positioned eight or nine feet behind the desk and sitting askew, as if he had abruptly fallen out of the chair and it had scooted backwards as his body fell out.

Something awful had been attempted on his helpless, immobilized body in this room. His brain fairly leaped to the conclusion. *Someone in this house just tried to hurt me bad. And whoever it is may still be here.*

How he knew this, he couldn't yet fathom. But somehow, he just knew.

The few days he had spent in the 1802 frontier had sharpened his mental reflexes and survival instincts, even into the present. TJ no longer thought as a careless, relatively spoiled, over-protected, 21st century boy would. His mindset was that of a hardened wilderness traveler. *Hey, I've faced bloodthirsty bushwhackers and survived. Battled would-be savages in hand-to-hand combat. Helped save a beautiful girl. Fought two bullies my age and won.*

TJ had experienced peril and adventure. He had seen things he would never forget. Now, his newly heightened perception alerted him that somebody else was in the house.

Somebody's here who doesn't belong here. He gritted his teeth. *Someone just tried to hurt me. This intruder probably thinks he killed me since I'm just slumped on the floor like a dead person.*

He got up and stalked as quiet as an Indian to the doorway, listening intently.

He could hear muffled footsteps on a carpet further down the hallway. *That's coming from Nat's room.* TJ concentrated on the faint noises, trying to decipher how many other people were in the house.

He breathed easier. *At least there's only one person upstairs.*

Hurriedly, TJ looked around his dad's bedroom for anything, any tool or any object he could turn into a weapon. He kept his ears attuned to the slight sounds outside the door, all the while carefully scanning the room. He stared into the adjoining master bathroom, trying to remember any items Dad kept there that could be used against the intruder.

As TJ urgently searched for a makeshift weapon, the awareness surged through his being. *I'd be helpless if this had taken place even a week ago. For sure, I'd already be dead, if it wasn't for the green book.*

He should be scared. But somehow he wasn't.

TJ reasoned that, however its power worked, he was no longer under the protection of the green book, now that he had returned to his own century. Yet he still wasn't afraid. He was simply determined to fight for his home and the Cockrell property, no matter what.

He wondered if the intruder had a gun or knife,

whether there was another accomplice working the downstairs. It didn't matter.

Then he saw it. One of Dad's larger-sized academic awards sitting on top the big chest of drawers against the far wall. It had a sturdy base to hold on to. It was a foot and half high, thick and heavyset. Best of all, it had a wicked top that could do a world of hurt if applied with enough force to the side of somebody's skull.

This'll do just fine, he grimly thought.

He lightly stepped over to the chest of drawers and quietly removed the heavy award, cradling the base like a short baseball bat in his two hands.

He could hear someone still moving around in his sister's room. As silent as he could, he crept out into the hallway and stalked down the corridor to his sister's old bedroom.

He paused outside the door.

Hearing the shuffling sounds inside, TJ calmly weighed his options. He knew he had one huge advantage--the element of total surprise. Whoever it was likely thought TJ was dead and out of the way. He had to catch the person unaware, reach him, and land a knockout blow before that individual brought his gun or knife into play.

He could have remained motionless on the floor, trusting the burglar wouldn't enter Dad's bedroom again. Or if he did, that he wouldn't examine him closely to see if he was really dead. *I couldn't do that now, just cop out. Not after the adventures I've had.*

The new TJ couldn't possibly remain sprawled beside the desk, playing dead like a cowardly human possum. The post-frontier TJ would take it to the thief. *Just like big Sam would have done. I want to fight and I don't care what the odds are.*

Ever so cautiously, TJ craned his neck to peer around the door. The burglar had just opened his sister's closet, and was inspecting the various contents stored inside. Luckily, the burglar's back was to the door. With stealth born of sheer desperation, TJ dashed through the doorway to take on the unsuspecting intruder.

The man heard the slight noise of TJ's movement behind him. "Bob, that you?"

He pulled out of the closet and turned, the hand holding the wicked blade now arcing around to face the boy. His face registered complete and utter shock as he saw the body running at him. "What the hell? But you're dead."

Even as the man was turning, TJ had begun his swing. "This is for all those innocent people you've murdered," he whispered through clenched teeth, putting all the speed, all the strength he could muster into the blow.

It caught the man full on the side of his head. There was a resounding crack, as the thickly set trophy shattered into half a dozen pieces. TJ could tell the intruder's skull had probably cracked a little, too. He knew he had hit his opponent's head too sharply, too flush, and in too perfect a location for there not to be a serious injury.

The man crumpled to the ground, unconscious, though perhaps not dead. There was the tiniest trickle of blood on the side of his head.

Without checking him further, TJ grabbed the knife from the fallen man. "You won't need this anymore."

Careful to make no additional noise, he ran quietly out of the room to the top of the stairs, straining to detect any evidence of downstairs intruders.

"Mason!"

A harsh voice lashed out in a carrying growl from the first floor. "Mason! Mason! Answer me. What was that noise?"

A brief silence, then the second robber snarled, "You pecker-head. You drop something valuable and break it?" There was no reply.

"Dammit! I can't depend on you for nothing."

There was another pause. "I'm coming back up. You better not have broken anything valuable."

TJ could hear the intruder grumbling loudly to himself as he moved toward to the stairs. "I want to finish this freaking job and get out of here before the cops or somebody else shows up and we have to take care of them, too.

"I told you that hitting a house so early in the evening was chancy...but no, you thought we had to change our pattern of doing it in early morning hours so as to throw off the cops."

The downstairs thief reached the staircase and began to climb up, huffing and puffing a bit. TJ could tell he must be a large man.

Instinctively, TJ raced across the head of the stairs to the other side. The hallway to the left of the stairs had banisters where a person coming up the second flight of stairs from the landing could see anyone standing in that section of corridor. But the hallway to the right had a solid wall. The approaching burglar could not see TJ hiding just around the right hand corner.

He heard heavy, labored steps coming up the staircase.

TJ grabbed the knife handle with both hands, edging as close as he dared to the corner next to the stairwell. His hands were sweaty. He gripped the weapon so hard that both sets of fingers were growing numb.

But he was ready. Every nerve in his body was throbbing with anticipation.

Just a few more steps. Two more. One more. C-o-m-e on.

The man, a wide-bodied, bearded individual, took the final step onto the hall floor. Lucky for TJ, the burglar turned to go to the left, because his upstairs accomplice had started with the master bedroom, down the hall in that direction.

TJ reacted with survival speed. Just like Thomas

had done to the Hansen Gang member, TJ violently thrust the knife multiple times into his foe.

"Umph! Umphhh!" TJ grunted with the sheer force of each exertion. He struck deep into the lower right side of the exposed man. In a fighting frenzy, TJ stabbed, pulled out and stabbed, as fast and as furious as he could.

The stricken man swore horrible oaths as he feebly attempted to face his attacker.

He groaned, "What the hell--" and tried to turn with his gun in his hand. But TJ had struck too often. The weapon went off once, twice, into the facing wall before the huge man crashed like a small elephant to the floor. Bloodstains soaked through his shirt and onto the carpet beneath him, as he lay dying.

In a flash, TJ sped downstairs, the knife still in hand. He was too hyped to even think about grabbing the gun.

If there was a third burglar, *I'll meet him head-on just like I did with these two bozos*, he raged, regardless of the danger and the foolishness of his gesture.

Now, TJ knew, to some extent, what a soldier in combat experienced. He felt alive as never before, exhilarated and nauseated at the same time, all of his senses magnified in the face of imminent death or life.

He raced through every downstairs room, his chest heaving and his heart pounding. "There's nobody else, no other burglars," he wheezed to himself. There were only the two motionless thieves, upstairs.

His breath was coming in long ragged pulls now, as the tremendous adrenalin rush from the back-to-back battles began dissipating inside his body, leaving behind a pervasive numbness. "I've got to sit down...lay down...stop....rest. I can't keep moving..."

All of a sudden, he felt dizzy and disoriented.

Stumbling, TJ entered the formal study room off the long hallway, closest to the garage door. There, he knew vaguely, he would be able to hear his Dad coming in from the garage.

"I guess they really...really were...the Al-Qaida Burglars." His mind flowed slowly and with great difficulty. Every movement, every exertion was costly and labored.

Wearily, he sunk into a sitting position; his legs sprawled awkwardly on the plush carpet, body slumped and motionless as he waited for his dad to get home.

"I'm so tired. Just so tired."

His entire being was saturated with exhaustion beyond measure. He was relieved to be alive, but petrified at what he done to stay alive. He was still sitting, staring off into space, the bloodied knife held loosely in his hand, when his dad pulled into the garage twenty minutes later.

TJ heard the garage overhead closing. He heard the beeping alarm. The sound of a door opening and shutting. A deadbolt locking in place. Then footsteps.

"TJ? TJ, boy! Dad's home."

Chapter Seventeen
BACK AGAIN

Walking down the hall, Vern Cockrell loudly announced himself, "Anybody here?"

Out of habit, he did this every weeknight as he entered the house, even though it was unlikely that TJ could hear him. Vern knew his son could be upstairs in his bedroom with his Walkman turned up. Or he could be asleep. Or he could have the small TV blasting in his room or the big screen TV in the living room. Or he could be on the phone with a friend. TJ knew to call and get permission if he wanted to stay at a friend's home after school. So he assumed TJ was somewhere in the house.

It didn't matter much to Vern whether Tege heard or answered him immediately. It was just psychologically satisfying to call his son's name out when he got home. Especially now that it was just the two of them. It was akin to an individual who was single being glad to see their dog or cat as soon as they got home.

He spoke again as he walked down the back hallway toward the living room.

"TJ? Are you here?"

As usual, his father had passed the door to the formal study without looking in. Vern strode briskly, briefcase handle and keys gripped in one hand, his attention briefly focused on reading the document held in his other hand.

TJ didn't call out as his Dad passed by. He couldn't speak. Not yet, anyway. He just sat there in a daze, vaguely aware of the receding steps. His thoughts remained confused, swirling, and sluggish. He would wait for his father to discover the horrible secrets upstairs. His father would come searching for him, eventually. In the meantime, it felt so good to sit still and rest. Simply rest. He had never been this tired. Even more so than after the Indian attack.

Unconcerned, Vern Cockrell went to the kitchen. He set his briefcase, keys, and papers on the dining table, then grabbed a clean glass from the top cabinet shelf, stepped over to the refrigerator, and pressed the glass against the ice and water dispenser.

"Tege? Hello? Anybody home?" raising his voice even more, he yelled loud enough to be heard in the upstairs rooms. He sipped his ice water slowly. He peered out into the living room and shrugged his shoulders.

"He must have fallen asleep. Or maybe he went

over to David or Robert's house. He should have called me first and gotten permission, though."

"Umm," Vern grunted, "he said he had a history test tomorrow he needed to study for."

He sipped his water some more, set the glass on the table then began to climb up the stairs to check on his son. He reached the landing, put his foot on the second flight...and froze. There was a man lying at the top of the stairs. His face was down on the landing, and his large body was blocking most of the hallway.

"What's going on?" Professor Cockrell sprinted up the remaining stairs. As he reached the prone figure, he gasped in horror. The man's side as well as the carpet underneath was saturated in blood. He held a gun in his rigid right hand. And he appeared to be dead.

"No. Oh, no!" the professor gasped and gingerly touched the man's shoulder. As he looked up into the hallway, he saw the two gaping bullet holes in the wall. His initial reaction was, *This is one of the killers on the news.* His voice quivered, "Where's TJ? What have they done to my son?"

He stepped over the man's big body and raced to TJ's room. He saw the computer, ceiling light and desk light all turned on. But no TJ.

He darted down the hallway, past Natalie's old room, headed for the master bedroom. Abruptly, he skidded to a halt. Out of the corner of his eye, he had seen the torso of another prone body in his daughter's bedroom, half hidden by the chest of drawers, as he flashed by.

He quickly backed up, and cautiously entered the bedroom. "TJ? TJ? Are you in here?"

He gingerly walked over and examined the still unconscious form, seeing the tangled remnants of his award lying on the floor. The man's head was bashed in. The professor put his trembling hand on the man's chest. "He's still breathing, at least. But where's my son?"

Vern swallowed hard. His heart was pounding deep in his chest. Sweat beads shown on his forehead. He had to call the police. But before he did anything else, he had to find his son. What had they done to TJ? Where was his son?

He licked his lips nervously and jerked his hand away from the body. He stepped back into the hallway and stumbled, zombie-fashion, into his bedroom. He saw the chair askew against the carpet edge.

Then, he noticed the green book lying on the floor.

Vern groaned. His heart skipped a beat. "This was entirely my fault, all my fault," he whispered through gritted teeth. "If I had just remembered to lock up that damn desk this morning."

Rubbing his furrowed brow, he stared off into space, in hard concentration. "Think, Vern, *think*! If TJ is out *there*, who fought these men? He'll be safe if he's out there, but someone was *here* who fought with these men."

His mind raced, filled with a torrent of thoughts, each one more foreboding than the last. Finally, he deduced his son must be here, somewhere. *He has to be here. TJ is the only one who could have done battle with these men.* There couldn't possibly be anyone else at home. Before he called the police or did anything else, he had to find his son first.

But they're hardened killers, criminals. TJ couldn't have been the person responsible. Surely not! Not my Tege. His mind couldn't comprehend it.

"Maybe..."

Getting down on his hands and knees, Mr. Cockrell desperately looked under his bed. He hoped, but no, his son wasn't hiding there.

He rushed through the master bathroom and its two large walk-in closets. "TJ? Tege? It's Dad." No one was there, either. He hurried out of the room and literally sprinted down the hall to the bathroom at the far end. Still, he found no TJ.

He ran to the stairway, stepped over the big body, and darted down to the first floor. "Son? Hello?" He searched the first level bathroom off the kitchen and the half bath in the back hall. He looked behind, under, and around the couch, the two loveseats, and the recliner chair in the living room.

Now, Vern was as equally perplexed as he was

worried. Fear mounting in his stomach, he retraced his steps down the long hall toward the garage. *Where could TJ be?*

There was only one room left unchecked in the entire house. His breath caught as he saw his son slumped on the floor in the master study. The door was open wide. He'd not looked in when he came in from the garage.

"TJ! Son!" he exclaimed. Vern Cockrell stared in horror at the bloody knife in his boy's hands and at the red splatters on TJ's clothes.

Tenderly, he knelt down in front of his son. "Son? It's Dad. I'm here."

At the sight of his father close by, TJ awakened out of his lethargy. He let go of the bloody knife. "Dad... Dad!" He began sobbing uncontrollably, his raw emotions finally flooding out. TJ and his father hugged each other with all their might.

"I'm so glad you're home," mumbled TJ, his head buried in his father's shoulder. "Dad, those two men upstairs. They're the Al-Qaida Burglars. I know they are. And I know one of them thought he'd stabbed me to death because he started to say something right before I surprised him and smashed him upside his head."

TJ had to make his father understand. "I didn't want to kill them. But it was them. Or me. Dad, I *had* to fight," he said through his sobs.

Anguished over having taken the life of fellow

human beings, even in self-defense, he pulled away from his father and asked, "Are they both dead?"

"Son, I believe the one at the top of the stairs is dead. I was too nervous to properly check for a pulse, but he appears to be. The other is knocked unconscious, I think. He's still breathing and alive. I don't know how serious his head injury is."

He outwardly examined his son for wounds and asked, "Did you get stabbed, or shot, or hurt in any way?"

TJ nodded, then shook his head. He didn't really know how to answer. "Well, yes. And no. Yes, I did get stabbed when I was still in the past. I also got shot at several times. But no, I didn't get hurt. The green book must have protected me," he explained. "I have no wounds I can see or feel from a bullet or a knife. I don't know how the green book does it, because I really should be dead now."

Vern inhaled big and stared at his puzzled son. Now that he knew TJ was home and uninjured, he began to get his own emotions and thinking under control.

He considered all of the facts of his son's situation, and how they would appear to the authorities if everything was fully divulged. He knew certain things had to be kept secret, no matter what.

He looked down at the exhausted boy again. "Tege, I want you to stay here. I need to go and find some cord to tie the one burglar up, in case he comes around. I won't be gone long."

"Don't move," he repeated. "I'll be back as quick as I can. Okay?"

He held his son tight once more, ignoring the bloodstains he might get on his brand new suit. Then he left to attend to the burglar in Nat's old room.

Without getting up off the floor and without waiting for his father's probing questions, TJ started at the beginning as soon as his dad came back into the room. He had to get it all out, everything. It was too much to keep bottled up inside. He would simply explode if he didn't tell someone. His natural confidante and confessor, Nat, wasn't there, so his father would have to do.

TJ gave his dad the whole story, hesitantly at first, then with increasing urgency. He told about finding the green book, landing on the Holston Trail, and meeting Sam Robertson. "If I hadn't bumped into big Sam, I don't know what I'd done. As it turned out, he was a life-saver in more ways than one."

TJ continued his tale of adventure; no detail was left out. "At the end of the trail, we stopped at a place called the Sloppy Bucket. A couple of drunken men got into a fight. One got part of his ear chewed off. The other got one of his eyes poked out. It was really gross to see it, and I threw up a bunch of times in front of Sam."

He told his father about their adventurous trip home and the murderous Hansen Gang. "They shot at me twice at close range, and somehow I didn't even get hit once." He could tell his dad wanted to say something at that point, but his father held his tongue.

TJ described the Robertson clan, their wonderful togetherness and unique traditions, with fond remembrance. "They were really nice people, really tight with each other, you know, the kind of happy family that I wish we--" TJ saw his father's sudden pained expression and caught himself.

He recounted the brutal Indian attack, from the moment of hearing the girls' screams until the battle was over. "They weren't really Indians, you know, just members of the Hansen Gang dressed up in native clothes and war paint. They also used some type of gunk to darken their face, neck, arms and hands. From a distance they looked like the real thing."

Next, TJ talked about Cherokee Jim, Mordecai Smith, the cabin-raising, even beautiful Sarah Robertson--he blushed a bit here--the brief fight with the two bullies, and the life and death struggle with the two burglars in their house; nothing of consequence was left out.

As TJ spoke, Vern listened intently, without interruptions. He also carefully watched the face of his boy, like a physician studying a patient. When his son finished his account, Vern continuing kneeling in front of TJ, his mind lost in analysis of the circumstances.

It was clear to him the force of the green book had protected his son from the multiple bullets and the

Jack King

stabbings. The same way it had kept him safe during his forays into the past. He had known that it would. Thankfully, it was also evident the experience had given TJ a daring and hardiness beyond his fourteen years. TJ's wild frontier adventure had matured and equipped him to defend himself against two armed intruders, even after the power of the green book ceased to operate.

Having found his son safe and having heard TJ's tale in full, Vern knew it was time to call the authorities. But, first, they had to sync up their stories. Certain facts could not be told. Certain secrets had to be protected at all costs.

"Son, I want you to lie down here, on the floor," he instructed. "You're still very tired, I can tell. Don't pick up the knife again. Leave it alone where it is. Try not to handle or smear the blood on your clothes. Please don't get up and wander around. Just stay here. Rest some more. Sleep, if you can." He paused. "Do you want a drink before you lay down?" he asked.

TJ shook his head.

Vern continued, "TJ, when the police get here I don't want you to tell them anything--*anything at all*-- about the green book. It would be utter nonsense to them. And they wouldn't believe you, anyway, even if you gave them the truth."

His bespectacled light-gray eyes penetrated his son with the seriousness of this instruction. "Also, don't tell them about the burglar stabbing at you. They wouldn't understand how you could possibly be unhurt. Or how you could know you were being stabbed at, if you were unconscious at the time. I'm sure they would draw the conclusion that you were simply making up a story for some ulterior motive. Or that you were hiding additional facts from them. Or that you were protecting someone else. Or whatever."

He looked at TJ and repeated sternly, "Again, this is very important. Whatever you do, don't tell them about the book. Don't tell them about your adventure. And don't divulge the fact you were attacked," he iterated.

He pondered for a second and said, "Tell the police that you heard some noises, downstairs, and that you went and hid under my bed. Tell them the two burglars were in a hurry. They missed you when they searched my bedroom. By the greatest of miracles, you caught each by surprise. You were able to disable one with the trophy, then kill the other with the knife you took from the first burglar. Please, son. Whatever you do, just stick to this story when you speak to the police."

TJ nodded his head, laid down, and wearily closed his eyes.

Vern Cockrell dialed 911.

In a surprisingly short span, the street and the sidewalk in front of the house became a media circus. One detective, three policemen, and one coroner in three separate squad cars soon arrived to investigate the crime scene. The police were followed by two ambulances, one for the deceased and the other for the injured burglar. Next, reporters with their camera crews came bustling over from each of the three major TV stations, the four independent channels, and the two leading radio stations.

Naturally, the media had all received immediate inside tip-offs from their various law enforcement contacts. This was truly big news. A major breaking story. Yet another attack by the dreaded Al-Qaida Burglars, but this time the killers had been foiled. Doggedly, the competing reporters scrambled to be first to uncover the juicy facts.

"Don! Don! What did you find out about the number of suspects captured in the house?" called out one television cameraman to his top field reporter.

"Carl, get a wide angle view of the front of the house, followed by close-up of the door." A senior journalist from another station stood by the side of the heavily equipped news truck and barked out orders to the head of the video crew.

"Say what? Bill, come here! You heard that one of the robbers is dead? No fooling?" A man from a third TV station queried a roving reporter who had some juicy information.

"Were any of the occupants hurt?" The crew chief

of an independent channel was asking his men what they had found out.

They all were shocked and delighted when they learned the killer duo had been thwarted by a mere kid. "You say he's only fourteen years old? You've got to be joking." Standing in a small group of crewman, Bob Matthews couldn't believe the news he was hearing.

Don Overton, his lead reporter, exclaimed, "What a great story!"

Incredibly, the boy happened to be the son of a prominent University of the South professor. "Andy, you know that history professor over at the university who got nominated for the Pulitzer Prize three years ago? He wrote a couple of bestselling books? Well, it's *his son* that did it. The dad wasn't even home at the time."

"Hey Mike, I got the latest scoop from McCluskey, the chief detective. Man, this gets better and better. The kid bashed in the head of one guy with one of his dad's trophies. And he killed the second guy with the knife he took off the first. Frigging unbelievable!" Bill Mason, roving reporter, had gleaned important facts from Chuck McCluskey, an occasional golfing buddy of his.

As they gathered the available tidbits of news, the crews began to broadcast live with their respective field reporters. It was a race to see who would make the biggest splash with their coverage. Of course, none of the press were allowed into the house, so they milled around outside. This was still officially a crime scene investigation.

In talking to the detective and other policemen inside, Vern Cockrell omitted the green book and the part about TJ being stabbed at and not wounded. His account matched his storyline instructions to his son. When chief detective McCluskey later questioned the boy, he had no reason to doubt TJ's account.

"Now, tell me again, son. Exactly where were you, about what time was it, and what were you doing when you first knew for certain burglars were in the house?" The grizzled investigator leaned forward, along with the senior policeman, to listen closely as TJ repeated his tale.

TJ replied, "I had just stepped out of the upstairs bathroom when I heard voices coming from the living room area. I remember looking at the alarm clock on the nightstand next to Dad's bed. It was 7:42pm, 7:43pm, something like that. Anyway, I ran into my dad's bedroom, thinking I was going to lock the door." The senior policeman bent his head, scribbling notes on a pad. McCluskey leaned further in, his hard-bitten face boring holes into the boy as he spoke.

They had gathered in the wing off the kitchen, standing around the little dinette table. The sound of scratching pen on paper seemed amplified in the packed space. The noise was a bit disconcerting, but TJ continued. "Then I realized that would be a dead giveaway to the intruders that somebody else was in the room. So, I hid under my dad's bed instead."

The detective said nothing. He kept studying the boy's eyes as if he could read his mind. TJ hurriedly explained, "Officer, there just wasn't enough time to call 911. Besides, at first I was scared."

The detective motioned impatiently with his hand, "What happened next, son?"

"Well…I heard the one burglar coming up the stairs and into the bedroom. I could see his shoes as he walked around, picking things up. I don't know what all he took." TJ squinted convincingly at the detective. This would be his best acting job ever.

"After the burglar left the room, I decided to defend my home. I don't know why. The idea popped into my head. And I went with it. From that moment on, I wasn't scared anymore. Gosh, I was just mad! I thought of the other people they had already killed. If I was going to die anyway, at least I could try to take one of them with me," said TJ with conviction.

The two policemen were astounded, as TJ finished his tale. How could an unarmed, unequipped, untrained fourteen year old kid possibly defend himself against two murderous adult criminals: one with a knife, the other with a gun? They shook their heads in amazement at his luck and pluck.

The on-site interrogation and search for evidence,

including examination and removal of the two thieves, took several hours. During that time, the reporters, still hovering outside, jockeyed each other for all the exclusive information they could get. Toward the end of the investigation, the detective allowed them to briefly interview Mr. Cockrell.

"Okay, boys, in a few minutes, you can each talk to the professor one-on-one, with your crews, out on the front lawn. But you gotta stay the heck out of our hair and away from all police activity."

McCloskey spat on the ground. He scowled at the assembled group standing in front of him. It was obvious he had a somewhat unenthusiastic opinion of the rank-and-file news professionals. "This is still a crime scene," he growled. "We're obtaining evidence and we don't need any of you tea-sippers to muck it up. You can take pictures of the front of the house only," he commanded. Later, he relented a little and they were allowed to snap shots of both the father and son, separately and together.

Local programs were interrupted with the breaking facts of how a young boy was able to take one of his famous father's trophies and turn the tables on the murderous Al-Qaida Burglars. The complete story made the ten o'clock local headline news on all three major TV networks. It was picked up by many cable channels in Knoxville and across most of the state. It also got national coverage in other major markets. Soon, the TV coverage was recorded on YouTube, and the story became a viral internet sensation overnight, with hundreds of thousands of hits. After all, it was an amazing tale of bravery and determination.

TJ had spent three nights and part of four days in the year 1802. Parallel, in the year 2014, he had been gone over an hour and a half, from shortly after six o'clock in the late afternoon to seven thirty-nine that night. His father hadn't gotten home until close to eight o'clock.

TJ had interacted with, spoken to, been touched by the people in his adventure. At the same interval, his present-day body was in a deep, senseless state, slumped upon the small desk in the master bedroom. When the burglar had stabbed at TJ multiple times in the side, his shirt had been slashed open by the knife, and his unconscious but unhurt body had slipped off the chair to the floor, thrusting the barrel-back chair up to the carpet's edge.

The protective power of the green book had kept him physically safe in both worlds during the course of his journey.

The next morning at his Dad's insistence, TJ got up and got ready for school. His dad said, "Tege, I think it would be better for you if you had the support of your friends. I'd rather you keep busy and have people around, rather than staying home. You went through a terrifying ordeal last night. I don't want you brooding about it at the house all alone today. I know it'll be hard to go to school, but I still think that's best for you."

He reached out and fondly tousled his son's hair. "Tege, even if I didn't go into the office today and tomorrow and stayed home with you, there'd just be the two of us during the day." He gave a wry grin. "You know how easily you get bored being around your dear old Dad. I wouldn't be a lot of help. Basically, you'd still be left with all those thoughts rolling around in your head. I think you want to keep your mind occupied with normal activities and other things, as much as possible."

He became more solemn. "Frankly, son, it's going to take time for you to heal from your experience."

"Sure thing, Dad. Yeah, whatever you say," conceded TJ.

He couldn't tell his father how much he disliked going to school most days, with the bullies and ridicule and dreary classes. TJ had never confided in him about his problems at Highland Hill.

Other than his son's poor grades, which he learned from progress reports, Vern Cockrell knew nothing of Brent, the humiliation from other students, the discouragement felt in not making the basketball team, TJ's lack of friends, and his lingering depression over the divorce.

"Listen, I'll make arrangements to come home much earlier over the next two nights. That way, you'll only be by yourself a short time before I get in. Alright?" His father's concern was etched on his face.

"I'm extremely proud of the courage you exhibited facing those men here at home, proud of how you rose to the occasion each time you faced danger during your adventure." He ruffed TJ's head again and laughed. "You better go fix your hair before you leave. You don't want to disappoint all those pretty ladies at school."

The lines of TJ's mouth tightened at the mention of girls, and he looked up at the ceiling. Resigned to his fate, he went to Highland Hill that morning, as usual.

Chapter Eighteen
HIGHLAND HIGH

Over the course of the first few periods, the tale of TJ's battle with the two thieves spread through the school like wildfire. Most students in his grade didn't listen to the nightly news. And not all of them spent much time on their parents' computers except for doing occasional research for school, or getting onto Facebook, or chatting with friends. However, their parents, older brothers and sisters, school administrators, teachers, and coaches did. By late morning, every student and adult had heard the story repeated and embellished considerably. For the first time in his young life, TJ was a celebrity. As was his father before him, he was self-conscious, even uncomfortable, with the new found fame.

Even stuffy old Ms. Primm attempted a half-twisted smile when he entered first period class. "Good morning, young man," she unexpectedly said. Ms. Primm had never spoken nicely to TJ before, and her elongated horse-face looked like it was pure agony for her to turn the corners of her mouth up instead of down.

"Good morning, Ms. Primm," said TJ, taking his customary seat near the back. *Whoa! I bet it's been ages since she last cracked a smile.*

Thankfully, Robert and David stuck to him like glue. They badgered him endlessly for more details about the fight, "Tell us again how you surprised the big guy, how you hid around the corner, and how you iced him with the knife!" But they also helped as bodyguards to give TJ some peace in the hallways and lunchroom from the crush of unwanted well-wishers and backslappers.

Boys TJ had never spoken to, even the *in* kids and athletes, came up to him and clapped him boisterously or made a show of shaking his hand in front of their entourages. They bothered him constantly in class and especially in the hallways.

"TJ! Wait up! How you doing today, buddy?"

Brad Simmons, the rangy starting quarterback of the football team, was grinning from ear to ear as he approached him with huge Tom Murphy, the starting center, by his side. Brad jovially slapped TJ on the shoulder and looked him up and down, as if he were seeing TJ for the first time. "I didn't know you had it in you. Hey, you might even think about coming out for the team next fall."

He shot both his forefingers at TJ like two guns

and exclaimed, "You the *man!*" Among the athletes, Brad was one of the nicer ones. His dad was the assistant football coach. Brad seemed to have more natural inbred confidence and didn't need to put on airs or be a snob like some.

TJ knew he wasn't nearly talented enough to try out for the team. He was flattered, but all he said was, "Yeah, I'll think about it."

"Hey, you do that!" Brad looked at him with newfound respect and stomped off with Tom to class.

Even girls who previously didn't know or care that TJ existed now approached him, offering insincere or inarticulate praise and batting their eyes. Others stood by, giggling while their friends struck up totally artificial conversation.

Melody Winters, the head majorette, made a point of passing close by him in the hall with all of her band friends and smiling big. "Hi-i-i-i, TJ." It was the only time she had ever acknowledged him that he could remember.

Robert elbowed TJ in his side and grinned, "Hey Tege, you really need to start following up on some of these connections." He glanced back at the departing group of girls. "I bet Melody would go out with you now. She's hot! Pretty nice, too." He looked over at David and asked, "You think she'd go out with our big hero?"

David shrugged his shoulders and replied, "It

wouldn't hurt to try. All she can do is say no."

To the girls, whether attractive or not, all TJ could do was blush and mumble inconsequential comments such as, "Thank you for the compliment," or "I was just lucky, believe me," or "It was nice talking to you."

Finally, the thing he'd been dreading all morning happened.

Melissa Carter, Amy Bradbury, and Jessica Smith cornered him in the hallway after the third period. They called themselves the Highland Hill Angels: the bleached blonde, the natural redhead, and the light brunette cuties of the drill team squad.

Melissa started in with her usual loud voice, thoroughly enjoying being the center of attention as other students stopped to listen. Whenever Melissa was around, the onlookers knew a show was about to begin.

"Gosh, TJ, I had no clue you were such a good fighter! I mean, we all knew you took karate and all..."

"Actually, I've been taking Tai kwon do," TJ softly corrected her.

Melissa didn't even acknowledge TJ had spoken. She talked non-stop over him. "...but we had no idea you were so good! Listen, I'm sorry I said those thangs yesterday."

The crowd around the three girls began to grow rapidly, blocking traffic and causing more students to stop to see what was going on. Melissa loved it. "You know I was only joking, right? Well, I was. I was just kidding. I was just playing with you."

She turned and gestured to her entourage. It was obvious they had planned this setup. "Hey, you want to join the three of us for lunch today?"

TJ looked over at his pals. David rolled his eyes in disgust, but Robert was panting like a dog. Robert had the hots for Amy. But of course, she barely knew he existed. Robert was only a second team basketball player. And Amy chased after the first team football studs.

"Uh, thanks, but no thanks. I'm going to eat with my friends," TJ forced a smile as she stared at him incredulously.

Watching among the outer layer of surrounding students was Brent Hasselbunt, along with his shadows, Stephen and Johnny. Brent pushed roughly though the crowd when he heard TJ's response.

"Hey, hey, hey! What's this? You think you're such hot stuff now, that you can dump on three," Brent looked over and winked at Jessica, whom he had recently dated, "of the loveliest ladies in the entire school?"

He turned back to face TJ, his face a scowl of contempt. "Hero? Ha! I say you got stinking lucky last night, Ninja boy. You snuck up on both of them. That's what I heard. You know what else I think? I think I can whip your punk ass. Right here, right now," Brent challenged him with a sneer. "I've let you get off easy far too long, *Cock*-rell. It's time to settle our business, once and for all!"

As he said this, the three girls, David, Robert, and the mass of spectators began backing up, creating a three quarter circle arcing out on either side from the wall of lockers. Like magic, the news instantly spread from hallway to hallway there was going to be a fight. More and more students flocked to see the action, forming a tightly packed cordon around TJ and Brent.

Up to now, TJ had let Brent and other bullies harass him for much of the school year, avoiding them whenever he could, and refusing to seriously fight. Waiting for his friends yesterday outside the gym, he'd had no choice but to face Brent. He remembered being very nervous and tentative. Somehow though, TJ's incredible frontier adventure had given him an undeniable measure of genuine confidence and courage. This time, he felt different inside. This time, he was relaxed.

TJ was ready.

"Let's see what you got, dick-head. I'm not playing around. Now it's for real!" Brent was deadly serious, determined to whip and embarrass TJ in front the assembled crowd.

He threw his books to Stephen and Johnny as they lounged against the lockers. "Catch." Then he snarled, "Let's go!"

Brent rushed forward with a flurry of punches,

hoping to end the fight before it began. TJ stood his ground, moving inside of the bigger boy's reach, turning to face his bigger opponent as Brent maneuvered for position, ducking when necessary, and skillfully deflecting all but the last swing, which barely grazed his cheekbone. TJ shook it off. Now his eyes burned with even greater resolve.

Brent retreated and tried the same tactic again, throwing as many blows as possible. Bobbing his head and rotating his hips and shoulders, TJ slipped three right crosses and two left hooks. He cleanly blocked all the lower jabs and body blows. Gasping a bit for breath, Brent tried to overwhelm his opponent yet a third time, flailing away with even wilder, harder swings.

After parrying all of Brent's attempts, TJ stepped back, calmly waiting.

Flummoxed, Brent reared back for a massive blow. TJ dodged the big punch, firmly grabbing Brent's arm as it swung inches from his face. Suddenly, he dropped with his back falling to the floor, catching Brent flush in the stomach with both feet, holding tightly on to the arm, and flipping Brent over with head-knocking force to the hard terrazzo tile floor beneath.

Thoroughly embarrassed, Brent leaped up and charged in a blind fury. Again, TJ ducked under a roundhouse blow, stepped to the side, and delivered a strike to Brent's Adam's apple.

Brent staggered. Dazed, he backed away, clutching his throat and coughing for air.

Brent regrouped. Clearly, his kamikaze approach wasn't working. He gathered himself and began circling TJ. He finally landed a hard punch to TJ's ear.

Shaking the pain off, TJ steadied himself. Sensing an opportunity now, Brent pressed the attack and began another wild barrage. TJ parried the right cross and left jabs. He caught Brent's left leg in the thigh just above the knee with a sharp frontal kick that doubled the bigger boy over. TJ twisted around full circle and executed a perfect roundhouse kick.

This time, he didn't miss.

The kick caught Brent flush on his outreaching chin. Arms slung out, eyes rolled up, Brent slammed backwards, knocking Johnny and Stephen along with him into the wall lockers.

"Oh, my gawd!" shrieked Melissa Carter, her hand to mouth in disbelief, as she watched Brent zoom by her. A collective gasp was heard from the surrounding crowd of kids.

Looking straight at Melissa, TJ coolly said, "I'm sorry. We're not going to be joining the three of you for lunch today. Maybe Brent, Johnny, and Stephen can eat with you, when they're done kissing the lockers." A very uncharacteristic smirk appeared on his face. Turning his back on the three shocked girls, he said, "Come on, guys. Let's go."

From that moment, TJ Cockrell had no more trouble from Brent or any other wannabe bullies at school. He and David and Robert nonchalantly strolled away to the lunchroom as the crowd dispersed. Hurrying past the three boys, a hall monitor and teacher sped the opposite way toward the now vacant scene of the fight. Of course, none of the students present ever admitted to seeing a fight. And nobody cared to snitch on their new hero.

TJ hadn't looked for a fight, but he hadn't backed down either. He had merely defended himself, which he reasoned was the constitutional right of every American.

Except during the fight, TJ's mind kept slipping away to memories of Sarah. He remembered her pretty face...her liquid eyes...her sweet, caring voice...the caress of her dainty fingers upon his neck and face...the feeling of her soft hand held in his...and the warmth and wetness of her kisses.

"Sarah," he whispered, lost in his memories.

"What'd you say, Tege?" asked David, as the three of them slowly walked to the cafeteria.

"Oh, it's nothing. Just thinking out loud," he shook his head, sadly knowing he would never see her again.

The more observant of the two friends, David couldn't help but notice TJ's continued woe-struck expression. He didn't speak more than ten words all during lunch even when people kept coming over to their table to talk to him. He maintained a hangdog look that concerned David. On the way back from the lunchroom David tapped Robert on the shoulder. He jerked his chin in the direction of TJ when Robert looked around.

"Hey, what's up? Tege, is anything wrong?" inquired Robert, glancing first at TJ then at David.

David asked TJ, "Seriously, are you all right? You don't look so good. If you need to talk about something, we're here for you."

TJ feebly punched David in the shoulder and said, "I'm okay, I guess. There's nothing either one of you mug heads can do to help. And it has nothing to do with the robbers or Brent," he added. "But thank you guys…for being good friends. I really appreciate it."

TJ hurt tremendously inside, as if he were suffering the pangs of deep unrequited love. This pain was just as overwhelming, but somehow different from the harsh loneliness he felt at the loss of Nat and Mom. The sharp feeling was new to him. His memories of Sarah were both intense and bittersweet. He had to force himself to focus on the present tasks. After all, he still had to take the history test right after lunch.

As he entered the classroom, the history teacher immediately pulled him aside. "TJ, you can wait to take this test one day next week. That's perfectly fine with me." His graying eyebrows knitted together in concern. "You've been through quite an ordeal."

TJ thanked Mr. Smith for his generous offer, but

decided to take the scheduled exam despite not having studied. Afterwards, he felt he did well on the majority of questions that dealt with details of early Tennessee pioneer life, but not so well on actual events and dates.

TJ also had that five-page Tennessee history paper due next week. However, he was confident that he could get a high grade on the paper. That would certainly be a first for him. He knew exactly what he was going to write about. *My topic will be on how early frontier people lived in the eastern part of the state and how their lives differed from people today.*

The rest of the day was a blur. He forced his mind to stay in the present. Yet it seemed forever until the unending school day was over. He needed to go home to the one person in the entire universe who could understand and totally relate to his time-travel experience. *I really need to talk to Dad.*

As last bell rang and the crush of students filed past him, TJ didn't stay until the end of basketball practice for his usual ride with David's Mom. Instead, he took the school bus that afternoon, something he hadn't done since early middle school. He couldn't wait to get home and see his Dad. After being let out at the corner street, he walked the block and a half to his house. He slid the key into the front lock, opened the door, and went inside.

He found his father home early, sitting on the big

couch in the living room, waiting for him. Dora had worked late, too, and was just leaving.

She immediately walked over and gave him a warm lengthy hug. "I saw the news," she said. "I'm very proud of you, TJ. So proud. Your father is, too." She squeezed him extra tight before she released him. "But, oh, dear me!" She put her hand to her throat in fearful imagination. "Oh, dear me!" she exclaimed again. "What if something had happened to you?"

Her kind eyes glistened with tears. "Then I thought about my grandkids and thought what if those men had broken into my son or daughter's house when neither was home and the young ones were by themself."

Dora reached out and tenderly held TJ's face in her sturdy grandmotherly hands. There was the faintest mixture of pleasant food, kitchen, and cleaning aromas on them. She clucked her tongue in wonder. "You can thank the Good Lord above, TJ. That's all I can say."

The old lady patted his cheekbone. "Sugar, I left you a grilled cheese sandwich in the fridge. I know you like to eat it cold." She gathered her things to leave.

"Bye, Professor Cockrell. Bye, TJ."

After Dora left, TJ shut and locked the door. He hung his coat up and turned to face his dad. His father sat observing him for a minute. "Son, how was school today?"

TJ responded with a slightly bewildered smile. "It

was kind of embarrassing, to tell the truth. Kids I'd never spoken to before were coming up and bugging me all day long. Girls who normally wouldn't have anything to do with me. Well, you know..." he trailed off.

Vern Cockrell nodded, as if that was the answer he expected.

TJ hesitated, gathered his thoughts, then spoke again. "There was no way to make any of them understand. How my adventures have made me stronger, braver, more confident. And of course, I couldn't tell anyone about the green book."

"No, you can't really explain what happened to you last night. I don't fully understand all of it myself. I'm still in a bit of shock that you were able to do what you did, fight those men and come through unscathed. It's remarkable." His dad looked at him with a parent's pride.

"I'm not a hero. It just...happened. They were in the house. And I took action. If I hadn't touched your green book, I know I wouldn't be alive now. For sure, I couldn't have defended our home the way I did, if I hadn't first had my frontier adventure. You know, being with the Robertsons, facing the Hansen Gang, and all that."

He sat down in the opposite love seat.

There was one question that was still bothering him. TJ had to ask. "Why was the desk drawer unlocked when I went into your bedroom yesterday?"

His father sat there. He studied his son for the

longest time, trying to decide how much to tell TJ. Finally, he answered. "Tege, I got a call from your mother the night before last."

Vern sighed and lowered his head a little. "She's already started dating again. In fact, she's met someone else she claims she's serious about. Frankly, I...I..."

His eyes filled with bitter tears. He looked up at his son. "I was--I still am--very distraught. That was most unwelcome news, to say the least. I had hoped there was still a possibility of reconciliation. I now know that was a highly unrealistic expectation, on my part. I haven't so much as thought about or even looked at another woman. And here your mother is practically engaged," he said, ruefully.

"Listen, I know the family breakup has been tough on you and Natalie. You've had your own suffering to deal with. So, I hid it from you that I was so incredibly upset the other night."

He explained, "I had, uhhh, opened the drawer to look at the clippings. To torment myself for the hundredth time. To blame myself, once again, that it was my sudden fame that probably destroyed what chance there was of salvaging our marriage. It seemed the more I achieved in my profession, the worse our relationship became."

He choked up badly. "I truly loved your mother, TJ. Still do. I believe she truly loved me, too, in the beginning. But through the years, our differences drove us further and further apart. She found habits, personality traits, and tiny things within me that she came to loathe. Some of the traits were the same ones she had perceived as being cute when we were dating."

He took a deep breath and slowly exhaled, corralling his emotions. "We did our best not to fight in front of you kids. Mostly, we just stopped talking to one another when you were around, so you wouldn't see the growing animosity. So, I don't think even you, as the oldest, knew how bad it had really gotten between us."

He suddenly stopped and eyed his son sharply. "Well, did you? Did you know?"

TJ gave his Dad a solemn look. "Actually, Dad, Nat and I knew all along you and Mom were having problems. We knew years ago, in fact. Natalie was the first to pick up on it, and she was just four years old at the time. We used to talk constantly about the possibility of our parents getting a divorce, and what we would do if it happened."

TJ wet his bottom lip with his tongue and focused, intensely yet unseeing, on the wall above his dad's head. His father didn't say anything, but waited patiently for him to continue. After a full minute, TJ brought his gaze back down to his father's face. Tears were leaking down his cheeks. "It still didn't make it any easier to handle when you guys finally did split up. It tore up both of us. Me, much worse than Nat."

Vern Cockrell stared at TJ. He shook his head in surprise. "Wow. Kids. You actually do perceive more than we give you credit for. I'm terribly sorry it's been so hard on you and Natalie. With all my heart, I wish your mother and I could have worked things out."

He weakly smiled at his son. "Anyway, let's just say that over the years, my love for her became a prisoner of my increasing resentment at the way she began to treat me. Oh, I still loved her, of course, but I wasn't able to show it because I was always getting my feelings hurt. And then I started to withdraw into my shell. That really got under her skin. As you know, she likes to use logic and argue things out. She loves to debate, loves to battle. On the other hand, I want to go and hide. She hated that.

"It was a losing proposition. It seemed the more money and accolades I received, the more I retreated into academics to escape the unhappiness and hostility at home. Instead of working on fixing our relationship, I ran away into my own cloistered world. I kept myself preoccupied at the office, in the classroom, and with my travels and papers. I could blame my desire to escape from reality on my somewhat withdrawn and reclusive personality," Vern laughed bitterly at himself. "But in my heart, I know better. I was a coward."

He looked squarely at TJ and repeated, "Yes, son, I was a coward. I didn't take responsibility for facing the problems. I didn't work on changing myself or on improving our marriage. I simply retreated. And I paid the ultimate price. If I had had the courage and fortitude to work on my own flaws, perhaps we could have made it." Tears trickled down his cheek as he stared at his son.

"Unfortunately, the substantial increase in my income gave your mother the financial edge she needed to bail out of the marriage when she couldn't take the unhappiness anymore. Frankly, she had stayed prior to that, solely because not having two incomes would have resulted in a dramatic drop in the lifestyle and kind of house we could provide for you and Nat.

"My huge pay raises meant she could leave me, with financial dignity and on her own terms, when she was ready to go. Even after splitting our assets, I could still afford to provide for you and give her a generous settlement.

"She is so strong willed. It's one of the reasons I fell in love with her in the first place. In many ways, she is the exact opposite of me. But you know your mother. Once she made up her mind she wanted a divorce, there was no changing her, no going back."

He glanced away from TJ and closed his eyes. "I continued to love her after the divorce. I still love her."

He gazed off into the distance, as if seeing something far away. "That night, I was so upset when I went to bed that I simply forgot to lock up the desk."

There was silence in the room.

Vern looked at TJ again, his dark eyes now intense and focused. "Son, I want to tell you how I came to have that green book in my possession. It's time for you to know.

"I want to tell you *my* story."

Chapter Nineteen
THE GREEN BOOK

Vern Cockrell had never had a man-to-man talk with TJ such as this. His only other attempt at such serious conversation was when he haltingly explained sex to his oldest child some three years earlier. The talk had been a dismal failure. The professor had been noticeably self-conscious and embarrassed. To his chagrin, he discovered his eleven-year old son had almost as much street knowledge about the subject as he.

He decided to speak to TJ this time as if he were a professional colleague, ignoring the age gap and the fact he was his son. Vern tended to do well when he spoke in an academic setting. "For the last nine years--except for that time I got pink eye from Natalie a day before the conference--I've always attended the annual AHA meetings. That stands for American Historical Association. Anyway, five years ago, the conference was held in San Francisco. I was a lowly assistant professor then.

"Your mother had just gotten a big raise, and

she was making more money than me at that time. To make things worse, she began reminding me, rather frequently, that she earned more and she was now the main breadwinner in the family. Needless to say, I was discouraged." he continued. "Unhappy. Listless. My ego and my manhood were rock-bottom. About the lowest point I've ever experienced except for the divorce.

"By chance at that particular AHA conference, on the first day I happened to sit at the same lunch table next to Professor David L. McCarty, an elderly, highly distinguished scholar who had been chair of his department for seventeen years and only recently had stepped down with Emeritus status.

"Professor McCarty was well-known in the profession as a gifted writer with unusually keen insight into the minds and motives of major personages within his area and time period of study. Having read some of his publications, to me, it was almost as if he had been physically present at key events. Although, of course, that was impossible I had thought. His writings were so brilliantly specific, so incredibly detailed, it was like he had been able to converse with the innermost circle of people surrounding these celebrated leaders of the past.

"Professor McCarty beamed profusely at me as I sat next to him. I remember being taken aback by his friendliness. He said, 'I'm pleased to meet you. I'm David McCarty. And you are?' Understandably, as a virtually unknown junior historian, I was intimidated to be in front of the great man. I remember stuttering, 'I'm, I'm Vern Cockrell,' and we shook hands."

For some reason, the older historian had taken an immediate liking to his younger colleague. He had subsequently shepherded Professor Cockrell around during the remainder of the conference. Even though they were attending different sessions at the conference, David McCarty had continued joining Vern Cockrell for dinner and in-between meetings, when possible.

Vern was immensely flattered. He couldn't think of a reason why the distinguished historian was being so kind to him.

He recalled, "I would see what I thought were grimaces of pain or discomfort in the professor's face. But then Professor McCarty would catch me looking at him, and he would instantly compose his face into a big, convincing smile." Whatever was bothering him, Professor McCarty seemed determined to keep hidden.

After the last session ended late in the morning of the last day, Professor McCarty had made a point of specifically contacting Vern Cockrell in his hotel room. "Professor Cockrell? This is Professor David McCarty. Sorry to disturb you. However, I have a favor to ask. Do you think you could possibly arrange to meet with me next week? At my office, on campus?"

The elder professor had stressed it was a matter

of strictest confidentiality and urgency. In particular, he emphasized the need to maintain secrecy about the subject of their meeting. "I'll tell you what it's all about when you get here," Professor McCarty had cryptically said.

Surprised by the strange request, but pleased nonetheless, Vern had worked it out with his department. An associate would take over his classes for the day. He had booked an early morning flight to Madison, Wisconsin.

Arriving on campus, he met Professor at his office late in the morning. "Good to see you again, Vern."

"And it's very nice to see you again, too, sir." They shared an early lunch. Then, Professor McCarty drove Vern to his palatial home.

Once there, he took Vern Cockrell into his spacious, well-appointed library-study. Vern sat in the plush high-back facing chair as the professor sat behind his huge mahogany desk. He gave a quaint smile, and began to talk. "Professor Cockrell, I'm an old man, and I'm in bad health."

He waved down the younger Professor's expressions of sympathy.

"I've been diagnosed with pancreatic cancer. They've given me three, four, maybe six months to live, at best. The various doctors I've seen are not hopeful at all. The disease may be spreading to other organs now."

Professor McCarty stopped and stared out of his

office window. Coughing slightly, he turned to Vern with a forced smile. "I finally started taking strong medication for the pain in the last few weeks. Most of the time, I can hide the severity of my discomfort from my colleagues. I haven't discussed the specifics of my situation with anyone else but Wilcox, my successor as the department chair.

"But lately, despite all the *wonder* drugs I'm taking, the pain has become rather intense." At precisely that moment a spasm seized his body. Despite his cast-iron will, the professor shifted uncomfortably in his chair and winced. At once he apologized. "I regret my lapse. I did not mean to display my illness in front of you."

Vern felt helpless and speechless at the sight. He gulped, but made no reply. What could he possibly say or do to relieve the man's suffering? There was nothing.

A little angry with himself now, the professor stilled his body and regained control. He fixed his piercing blue, watery eyes at the younger historian sitting across from him and continued. "My wife died two and a half years ago, and I'm afraid I wasn't very attentive to the signs that something was seriously wrong with me. Perhaps I didn't want to prevent it from happening. Perhaps I wanted to join Elizabeth," Professor McCarty said with a resigned look.

"No matter now. At my age and physical condition, surgery is no longer a viable option, and I refuse to do chemo treatment. I'll probably have to go into the hospital or hospice within the next 4-6 weeks. I'll soon be reunited with my darling bride again."

Vern sat across from the professor, stunned. "I'm so sorry." But really, words were insufficient.

Professor McCarty waved his hand to indicate brief acknowledgment. "My son and daughter are in different professions than history. My son, who is the youngest, is an optometrist. My middle child, a daughter, is a semi-retired pharmacist, now a stay-at-home mother with my new grandson. My oldest, also a daughter, died in a car accident sixteen years ago at age thirty-one."

He reached into his desk drawer and pulled out a green book. He laid it on the desk in front of Vern, carefully watching the younger man's puzzled expression. "This, Professor Cockrell, is the secret to my success."

He told Vern his story. "I was given it nearly twenty-seven years ago by the distinguished Edward E. Manchester. He was a noted expert on late 18th century European politics. Like I am now, he was an old man in the twilight of his career. He took a liking to me, for whatever reasons. He passed on the legacy of the green book to me. He died five years later as one of the most revered historians of pre-twentieth century Europe. Professor Manchester explained to me precisely how the book works. I am now going to explain it to you," he said.

Professor McCarty described to Vern how he was

transported back in time, and how the book allowed him to interact with persons of long ago, yet without possibility of actual physical injury between parties. He used it to go back to various places and events of the 19th century, a chaotic century marked by the fall of ancient empires around the world, by the rise of new modern empires, and by major transitions in science, government, politics, and religion.

He elaborated, "I absolutely cannot change the broad course of history. I cannot meet any deceased relatives or personages from recent past who might actually recognize me."

He discovered on his many visits that he could not seriously harm people, or be physically harmed in any way himself. In all other aspects, though, he could communicate, interact, and touch or be touched, both physically and emotionally. Apparently, the individuals he met retained no remembrance of him afterwards. "For them, it was as if I had never entered their world. For me, thankfully, I was able to retain the memory and knowledge of everything, even the smallest details, from my ventures."

The green book knew just where to place him in each adventure, where his presence would be non-intrusive, where he would be accepted without undue questioning, where he could observe and communicate without interference. It also imparted trivial information that was specific to the region, people and time period-- bits of knowledge that even the esteemed professor didn't know beforehand.

"I learned that the book, and not I, determined the exact instant I would come back from each trip. It was always an adventure, not knowing when I would return," he recalled.

He had used the book on numerous occasions to go back into time, but solely for historical research. "I must stress that my focus was never for personal profit or gain." The professor sternly cautioned Vern, "I doubt very much the power of the book will perform or activate for someone whose main motive is making money. I believe, in any case, that the book will simply not work if the individual is not worthy.

While he admitted that the unexplained higher quality of his later publications led to promotions and achievements, he had never deliberately sought after rewards or fame. He said, "My primary purpose in activating the book was always that of advancing our historical knowledge, which should be your intent, as well. Naturally, having the green book made me a much better historian in every possible way."

Professor McCarty conceded that use of the book could change the user's own circumstances: witness the critical acclaim subsequently achieved by Professor Manchester and himself. But it could not be used to revise history itself, that sequence of long ago, or even more recent events already cast in stone.

Above all, he advised Vern to use the book judiciously and sparingly. "Each adventure into history takes a little bit out you," he noted. "I have found that over time some tangible, albeit tiny, amount of myself is expended during each foray into antiquity." He waved his hand. "Energy, life force, soul, whatever you want to call it."

He leaned forward to make his point. "You must be wise. You must be very careful," admonished the old professor. "Keep your motives pure and your heart honest."

Vern Cockrell paused in his recollection to his son of how he became the latest keeper of the green book.

He then told of his own two uses of the book.

During the first occurrence he was transported to the front Confederate lines at Gettysburg, a day and a half before the battle began in earnest. He was placed within General Pickett's infantry command, wearing the slightly ragged uniform of a junior lieutenant.

"As a professional historian, I took the opportunity to query as many common soldiers and officers as I could throughout that night and the next day, without arousing suspicion. I actually bivouacked the first night with the other men in my unit and went into battle the following day.

"I became attached to Major Hornsby's unit as part of the brigade under the command of Brig. Gen. James Kemper." His voice became flush with sudden emotion as he remembered everything. "John Hornsby was a gallant man. He got hit twice by musket fire during the great charge. One in the thigh and one in the right lung, which proved fatal."

Emotion caught in his throat. He continued, "I lingered for a full minute by his side, but there was nothing I or anyone could do. I rushed on with the rest of the men into the fray."

As TJ listened with open-mouthed fascination, his father described how he participated in the futile charge up Cemetery Ridge. His father had witnessed, firsthand, the gore, bloodshed, and bravery of troops on both sides of the line.

Vern's vision vanished into the past, and his face became lost in the memory of the awesome event. "Under the protection of the green book, I was among the few men who reached the Union line atop the crest of the ridge. The battle scenes were exhilarating. And terrible! We must never, ever, forget the horrible price of war.

"Since I could not be physically harmed or detained, I was able to make my way back to General Lee's headquarters just as the demoralized Confederate Army began its hasty retreat south. I continued my historical research without pause or hindrance for many hours more, until the green book brought me home."

His next venture found him placed as part of the Confederate attackers at the Hornet's Nest in the bloody battle of Shiloh, Tennessee.

Again, he saw the savage brutality of hand-to-hand combat. He said, "I spoke to many a soldier and officer, before and after the conflict, gathering as much historical detail as possible. I learned a great deal about the mindset, the feelings, the training, the pain, the resolve, and the daily routines. I was able to probe the very fears, weaknesses, and strengths of the surrounding Confederate troops. For a professional historian, it was incredibly rewarding and demanding."

His thirst for history combined with his eyewitness experiences produced his two blockbuster books.

He had not sought after personal fame or fortune. "In my heart and mind, I was simply and honestly fulfilling my responsibility as a trained historian," he reminded his son.

Professor Edward E. Manchester. Professor David L. McCarty. Professor Vernon Cockrell. And now Thomas James Cockrell. All were recipients of the awesome force of the green book.

TJ sat, deep in thought. He had been equally stunned and fascinated by his dad's narration. Hearing about the lineage of previous users added to his appreciation of the worth of the green book.

His father smiled and said, "TJ, I know you must have some special qualities inside of you that I don't have. My use of the book didn't improve me as a person. Not one whit. It only made me a better historian. But you, on the other hand, it really seems to have had some tremendous after-effects. It's certainly brought out the best in you," he beamed with pride at his son. "You're more resourceful, braver, and much more mature as a young man. I can see it in you."

Yes, TJ knew he had been positively transformed in many ways by his Tennessee frontier adventure. He knew something else of importance, as well.

He now had a passion for history.

Chapter Twenty
THE PAST AS PRESENT

There were just three weeks left until the spring break. To his dismay, TJ found his celebrity didn't fade away quickly. After all, he had single-handedly fought off two armed burglars: men much bigger, stronger, and older than he.

More importantly to the many eyewitnesses present, he had beaten Brent Hasselbunt in front of dozens of students, who spread the news of his victory throughout the school. But he remained very uncomfortable with the continuing high fives and forced greetings, particularly from students who never had anything to do with him previously.

"TJ! TJ!" Ed Kirby raced to catch up with him in the hallway. "Hey, a bunch of us are playing touch football this Sunday afternoon at Wilson Park. We play almost every weekend between four and six. You wanna come?" he asked hopefully.

Ed looked over at Robert standing next to Tege.

"You've invited, too," he added, as an afterthought. "And David, tell him." He turned back to TJ.

"Maybe. I may have other plans. But I appreciate you asking me."

"You oughta come. It's a lot of fun," Ed enthused.

TJ knew several of the third and second stringers on the football team, plus a handful of the soccer, baseball and track athletes typically showed up. "Let me think about it. But, yeah, it's nice of you to invite me. To invite all of us."

He watched the boy stroll away. *I don't dig all this fake attention.* Like his Dad, he didn't care for notoriety at all. His father, too, had politely endured all of the events, publicity, flattery, and impositions of his personal space during his rise to academic fame and fortune.

At least Robert and David acted normal around him. *Well, as normal as they can be,* "Which isn't very normal at all," he finished out loud, chuckling and slapping Robert on the back as they both walked up the hall to Robert's locker.

"What's not very normal?" asked Robert, with a puzzled expression.

"Oh, nothing," TJ grinned at his friend.

The onslaught of wide-eyed groupies made TJ cling to his two true friends tighter than ever. Luckily, the basketball season would be over in another week. "Your last game is next Friday, right?"

"Yeah, we play Sunset at home. The game starts at 8:00pm."

"That's cool. That means the three of us can hang out together right after school," TJ said happily. "Say, how about the week after next, David and I come over to fly that awesome model helicopter you got for Christmas?" Robert's father was a flying toy enthusiast and had bought Robert a Silverlit scale model Black Hawk helicopter that featured incredible detail, a three-channel radio control, and a sophisticated gyro system.

"Sounds like a plan, Stan. Now, let's beat it to class."

TJ continued to achieve improved grades in every subject, including his old nemesis, history. He actually made an A on his history paper. Previously, he had never gotten above a C-plus on any history assignment. Mr. Smith, the teacher, was pleasantly surprised. TJ was elated. And his dad was quite pleased.

"I'm proud of you, son. Way to go. Keep this up and you'll be passing me by, some day."

His wild Tennessee frontier adventure had birthed in him a thirst for knowledge, for experience, for life itself. Each school night now, TJ worked harder than ever on studying and completing assigned projects. And not just history, but all his subjects.

In the evenings, for the first time ever, he and his father spent time together. *We're actually becoming friends,*

TJ mused. And after his experience with the green book, the two shared a top-secret bond.

During dinner and afterwards, they began sharing more details and impressions about their respective adventures. They also discussed various topics of history. Well, mostly, his father spoke, but TJ listened and paid close attention. He found himself interested in people and places of the past. He asked intelligent questions, learned fun facts, and let his dad's stories sink into his brain.

Despite his ordeal with the two thieves, and the trauma of having killed a human being in self-defense, TJ didn't suffer any lasting emotional or psychological problems from the event. The history episode and the green book together had strengthened him in ways he could not comprehend.

Recalling his dad's warning, he did find there were brief, scattered interludes when he felt a little strange, a little jagged, deep inside. *It's as if a tiny bit of me is missing, like there's a little dot of emptiness that wasn't there before.*

Whether the departed element was from his physical body or from his mind or elsewhere, he couldn't tell. TJ worried about it. Whenever such a thing happened, though, and the weird hollow feeling nestled within, TJ shook his head clear and encouraged himself. *I've just got to make myself focus on other things, stop thinking about it, and get busy doing stuff. Whatever this is, I know it'll go away in a few minutes.*

TJ's theory proved to be mostly right. The weirdness came and went at odd times, almost with a parasitic life of its own. But it seemed the busier he stayed, the less he felt it when it came and the quicker it went away. And so, he kept occupied all the time, especially with his newfound studying and learning.

But for those occasional sensations, the days leading up to spring break were decent for TJ, except for dealing with the unwanted fame. "It's nice to be finally treated like a human being at school," he said to his buddies, "although I still don't like all the attention."

His dad had called and awakened his mom the very same night of the intruder attack. His mom had at first wanted to catch a plane to Knoxville the next morning but upon hearing TJ was totally unhurt she finally decided against it. Her work schedule was very hectic this time of year. Vern allowed Tege to talk to Natalie once the grownups were through speaking.

"You know, I didn't get scared," he had confided in Natalie after mom had handed the phone to her. "Not even a little. I just knew I had to fight for myself, fight for our house, fight to protect Dad before he got home."

He had given his sister a blow-by-blow description of his brief battle with each burglar. Per Dad's instructions, he didn't tell Nat about his time travel adventure or about his non-wound.

"Tege, that's horrible! You could have been killed."

Natalie was generally cool, calm and collected, totally unruffled, but the news of TJ's ordeal frightened her. So much, that Natalie uncharacteristically began crying. Anne Cockrell rarely changed her mind, but in the aftermath of the violence involving her son, Anne altered her original vacation plans with her daughter and new boyfriend. She agreed instead to let Natalie spend the entire spring break with TJ and Dad.

Vern Cockrell was elated when he got the unexpected phone call from Anne several days after the burglary incident. "Tege," he said afterwards, "I've made reservations for the three of us to go to Disney World over break. We'll be staying four nights and five days!"

TJ leaped in the air when he heard. "Woo hoo, Dad!" He gushed, "That's great. Gosh, it's been several years since Natalie and I went on a vacation together."

The last family outing had been a five-day stay at a rustic resort off the Smoky Mountain leg of the Appalachian Trail. TJ was eleven and Nat six. During their visit, the Cockrells had attempted an all-day hike that turned disastrous. Tege had gotten severe poison ivy. Nat had gotten a bad bellyache from the mayo on the picnic sandwiches. And the mosquitos had been unbearable for everyone.

However, the latest holiday plans sounded wonderful. Equally sweet for TJ: auditions for the theater department's last school play would be held this coming Monday morning during his second period drama class.

When TJ showed up for tryouts, there was a new girl there who had recently transferred from the mountainous eastern part of the state. Her father was in retail management. He had gotten a well-deserved promotion, and the family had relocated to Knoxville, with barely two months left in the school semester.

TJ stared at her, astounded, during the initial tryouts. "I can't believe what I'm seeing." he said. "I can't believe it. I just can't believe it." He was stunned. Freaked-out was a better description. She resembled Sarah Robertson, *his* Sarah, in so many ways: her hair... her eyes...her face...her mannerisms...even her voice.

Mr. Mackey called out her name to audition for the desired role. Her name was Samantha. Samantha Robertson.

After tryouts, TJ hurried over to introduce himself. Three weeks ago, he would have paid no attention to her or any other female. He certainly would not have had the courage to engage in actual conversation with her. Rakishly, he grinned, *but I'm a changed man now.*

He announced himself with confidence. "Hi. My name is TJ, TJ Cockrell. You're new here, right?"

She turned from finishing a conversation with Mr. Mackey. She beamed a pretty smile when she saw him. "Yeah, that's right. My Dad got a promotion and we had to move here." She stuck out her hand and said, "Hi, I'm Samantha Robertson."

They shook hands and stood looking at each other. She smiled again.

Samantha broke the brief silence. "That's super nice of you to come up to me like this." She lifted her long, lovely, reddish-auburn locks out of her face. "I don't really have any friends here yet."

Wow. Her hair is exactly the same as Sarah's, too. TJ was amazed by what he was seeing. He began to choke up with memories of the past. He caught himself and forced his brain back to the present.

"You're great. In your acting, that is," he sincerely said. "I was watching you try out. You're very good. I just know you're going to get the part."

"That is so sweet of you." She continued to look at him with those enchanting Sarah eyes. She said, "If you're not doing anything, maybe we can have lunch together." Her lips curved with her bold invitation.

She likes to takes charge…just like Sarah, remembered TJ.

Samantha mistook his initial silence as possible rejection. "That is, if you're not too busy. Or you don't have other plans. Or whatever. But if you don't want to…"

TJ nodded his head in big approval. "Of course I want to have lunch with you. I'll meet you at the cafeteria entrance at noon, okay?" He continued, "Come on, I'll walk you to your next class."

Her smile of relief was disarmingly beautiful, so

similar to Sarah's that it took his breath away. TJ thought, *Robert and David are not going to be happy about this.* He decided he didn't care one bit.

At TJ's insistence, the trio gradually became an inseparable quartet over the coming weeks. "You'll like her. You'll see." he told his friends. David and Robert's friendship with TJ was strong enough that they allowed Samantha's presence into their circle without huge protest.

David was the better athlete and the better looking of TJ's two buddies. As a member of the basketball team, David had openly flirted with pretty cheerleader Renata Wellesley. Now that TJ had broken the opposite sex barrier, it only was a matter of time until David asked Renata out and had his first girlfriend, too.

Samantha had told TJ that her dad's first name was John. Out of sheer curiosity, TJ got on the computer late one night after finishing his studies. He used Google to find the ancestry of John M. Robertson. The further he went in his search, the more awestruck he became.

At the instant of the big discovery, his heart began racing. He got nervous tingles all over. Beads of perspiration actually broke out on his forehead. "Oh, my God. This is, this is beyond cool. This is unbelievable. What are the odds? One in a million? Ten million? A billion?" he whispered in an awestruck voice.

"Dad. Dad!" TJ yelled out from his own room to his father working at his bedroom desk. "Come here!

Come here, I want to show you something."

Seconds later, Vern stepped in, and this is what they both saw on the computer: Mr. John Robertson, father of Samantha L. Robertson, was a direct descendent in the bloodline of Mr. Thomas Henry Robertson, born March 17, 1789 in North Carolina. T. H. Robertson was the second son of Mr. Samuel P. Robertson.

Not too many years later, Samuel, also known as big Sam, Robertson and his family moved westward into what would soon become the state of Tennessee. They eventually settled in the County of Greene. Their farmstead was close to the Nolichucky River.

TJ knew he couldn't share his amazing find with Samantha. Perhaps she already knew her heritage. Or perhaps she would view him as some type of obsessive nerd--searching her ancestors like that when he barely knew her.

"Besides," he reasoned out loud, "you can't tell her about your history adventure. You've only known her a short time. From her point of view, why should you care about her family's ancient history? She'd think that's weird."

Except for telling his dad, he kept this exciting new fact to himself. But it made him like Samantha even more. A lot more.

Chapter Twenty One
JUST THE BEGINNING

TJ had felt a surge of joy shoot through his entire body at the unexpected revelation about Samantha's ancestry. *It's like I have a part of Sarah returned to me.*

In the busy week before spring break, he had exams, essays, or major projects due in all of his classes. Unlike his pre-frontier self, the new and improved TJ worked diligently on everything. Consequently, he did far better than before, surprising both himself and his father with his latest grades and results. But finally break arrived and school was out. "Now it's time to celebrate!" he crowed to all of his friends, both old and new.

Late Friday afternoon, David's dad dropped off David, Samantha, TJ, and Robert at the jam-packed, tony Crestwood mall.

"Bye, now," he said. "I'll pick you all up at the main entrance, right here, same place, at midnight sharp. That means everybody, Robert." He rolled down the passenger side window. "And don't be late!"

As planned, they were joined by Renata, now David's girlfriend, plus Blake Patterson, who played on the basketball team, Mike Foley, who also played basketball, and Candice Harper, another cheerleader and Renata's best friend.

The group spent the early part of the evening in and out of the many shops, the arcade, and last, Swenson's Ice Cream. "Oh, is strawberry your favorite flavor, too?" Samantha asked TJ.

"I love it. Once, you know, I almost made myself sick, I ate so many strawberries. My family went to a strawberry field, and we got to pick as many as we wanted, by hand. And I just kept on eating. And eating. And eating!" She laughed just like Sarah.

After ice cream, they all went to a 7:45 p.m. movie. Afterwards they went to the Cheesecake Factory to eat. TJ and Samantha constantly held hands. They had snuck a hesitant kiss or two in the darkness of the theater while everyone else actually watched the screen. The whole night was pure magic for them. Before and after the movie, they talked in conspiratorial voices, oblivious to the rest of the gang. Once their group got seated at the restaurant, Samantha snuggled close to TJ in the booth.

She squeezed his arm and giggled. "One time, when we were at my grandparents' house, when my little brother Billy was a baby, we were sitting at the dinner table. And Pa-Paw was coming back to the table from the bathroom. And he saw something on the carpet in the living room. They have a big door between the formal dining and living and so we could see him from the table. Well, we all figured out what it was immediately, but he didn't know. He knelt down and looked at it. Then he picked it up. Then he smelled it.

"Meanwhile, everybody at the table was cracking up. I never heard my dad and uncle laugh so hard in my life. My dad was almost crying, he was laughing so hard. My uncle couldn't breathe. I snorted a piece of okra up my nose, I was laughing so much. We were all watching Pa-Paw from the table before he finally figured out it was a little ball of poo-poo that had fallen out of Billy's diaper!"

TJ broke out laughing along with the rest of them, and then caught himself as other Cheesecake Factory patrons at the nearby tables begin staring at all of them. Robert's outburst was so loud that a waitress almost dropped her nestled platter of drinks and food as she passed by.

Samantha's family had the same southern warmth, same playful ability to give and take, and same easy naturalness of big Sam Robertson's brood. They both were so full of life, just the opposite of the Cockrells. Her presence warmed him.

As the night ended and everyone was heading back to the main entrance, TJ and Samantha slowed down to let the others move ahead. Taking advantage of the onrushing crowd of people and unnoticed by the other kids, they daringly stepped behind the large directory display to steal several long, passionate goodnight kisses. Then Tege and Sam raced to the west entrance to join the gang amidst cries of, "Where were you guys?"

TJ was supremely happy, happier than he had ever been.

The next morning, TJ and his Dad left for the airport to pick up Nat who would be coming in from Atlanta at the 11:55 a.m. Saturday arrival. The three of them would leave early Monday for their fun-filled, five-day Disney World vacation. TJ had routinely shared all of his secrets and problems with his sister, especially as she got older. He desperately wanted to tell Natalie about the green book and about the time travel escapades he and Dad had.

All week long, TJ pestered his father for permission to reveal their respective tales to Natalie. "Dad, you know, of everybody in our family, Nat is the *only* one who can absolutely, positively, keep a secret. Please, Dad. Please, please, *please*! I promise she won't tell anyone."

Finally, on the way to the airport, Vern Cockrell capitulated. He sternly commanded his son, "TJ, you can tell Natalie everything, on one condition. She has to promise to hold the information in the strictest confidence. No one except the three of us can ever know about the green book. Is that clearly understood?"

He added sadly, "Professor McCarty died a few months after bequeathing the book to me, so we will be the only people in the whole world who have knowledge of it."

TJ assured Dad that Nat had never once told anyone of his and her private conversations, of which there were many, over the previous five years. He knew firsthand Natalie could be trusted.

Coming home from the airport, Nat listened with her quiet, adult-like demeanor as her father, then her brother, spoke in turn. Her emerald-green eyes switched from one speaker to the other. She said not a word during their recollections.

She sat in the back seat with TJ, her pretty brow creased in concentration. When she spoke, her opening question took both TJ and his father by surprise. "So, Tege, you liked Sarah Robertson an awful lot, didn't you?"

"Well, yeah, I did," he said.

He considered the question in more depth. "A whole lot, actually. I didn't even know I was ready for a girlfriend. But then again, I never met one like Sarah."

He looked over at his sister. "I have an incredible history adventure. I meet Sarah. Then I return to the present. And I meet Samantha. And then her great, great, great-whatever, grandfather turns out to be Thomas. Nat, it's totally...unreal. Sometimes, I wonder if I'm going to wake up and find it's all a dream."

He continued, "But yeah, Sarah was special. Really special. She was a very beautiful person inside and out."

TJ became silent, lost in the memory of her sweet presence. He'd had slightly more than two full days with her; yet, emotionally, it was as if he'd known her for years. "I hope she had a great life." His voice choked up, husky with his feelings. "You know. A nice husband who loved her and was good to her. Great kids. Lots of happiness. I know from my Google search that she lived to be eighty-four years old. She had six grandchildren and ten great-grandchildren."

He blinked and laughed at himself. "I almost sound like a grownup and I'm still a kid! But yeah, I do hope she had a happy life. She deserved it.

"I miss her so much," his voice was almost a whisper now. His eyes welled up with tears.

Surprised, Vern Cockrell glanced up in the rearview mirror to view TJ's face. The father was shocked at his son's display of such feelings toward a female. In his mind, he still viewed TJ as mostly a child.

TJ exhaled slowly to gain control of his sudden feelings then turned to smile weakly at Nat. "It's okay, sis. I'm okay."

His face brightened. "But hey, Samantha is terrific. She makes me laugh a lot. She has a great sense of humor and personality. Even better than Sarah's! And she's very pretty. Who would have thought a month ago, that a month later, I would have two beautiful girlfriends, Sarah and Samantha, right after each other?"

Natalie's next question also caught Vern and TJ off guard. "So, when are you two going on another history adventure?"

Father and son looked at each other. Mr. Cockrell replied, "Natalie, honey, it's not the same as the fictional time travel that's portrayed in Hollywood movies. You can't really control it to come and go whenever you want. You can't command it. Or turn it on at any precise moment. It doesn't operate like a car ignition or a light switch."

Vern peered up in the rearview window to catch his daughter's eye. It was important that she understood. "For one thing, there's no guarantee it will ever work again for either of us. For another thing, it's the green book, and not the individual, that decides if the person is worthy, willing, and ready to go on a trip. And last of all, it controls when you go and when you come back. Frankly, Natalie, there is so much about it that we don't know."

She pondered on her dad's lengthy reply. "Well, I believe both of you deserve it. And I believe you're both ready to do it again!" she answered with conviction.

Mr. Cockrell and TJ glanced at each other again. With that, the conversation turned to other normal topics.

The three of them went out to dinner that night. Later, Natalie came to TJ's room. They sat on the opposite ends of the bed, facing each other. Brother and sister began to confide among themselves, as they had done so many times before the divorce and family break-up.

Nat said, "Can you believe it? Mom and I have started going to church now. It's what they call a non-denominational Bible fellowship. It's pretty interesting, kinda cool. I like the music a lot. It's a really big place with loads of people."

Nat told him she thought Mom had done it mostly to meet eligible, single men. "That's where Mom met Paul," she confided. However, Natalie didn't mind too much going there. She had already made some new friends at the church.

"So, what's this Paul guy like?" queried TJ. He thought about Dad, and how broken up he was over the fact Mom was seriously dating again. It was hard for TJ to accept, too.

"Aw, he's all right," Nat sniffed.

She frowned a little. "He's pretty boring, actually. He's an accountant like Mom, some hot shot in another CPA firm. He's ten years older than Mom." Natalie winkled her nose. "He tries to suck up to me. It's funny sometimes. As long as Mom's happy, it's okay, I guess..." her voice trailed off.

It was obvious to TJ that Natalie greatly missed

having Dad around. Her lukewarm comments about Paul got him thinking. In his mind, having dinner didn't really count as a family outing, and she hadn't seen their father or him for many months. The three of them were going on a vacation together, but he felt they should take advantage of every available moment.

He watched his sister as she continued to share about her new life in Atlanta, but his mind strayed. When she finished, TJ sat there, his brow furrowed. Finally, he asked her, "Hey, would you like to go see a movie? You, me, and dad? You pick the show?"

Her face brightened. "That's a good idea. I haven't been to the theater once since we moved to Atlanta."

"Me neither." He shrugged and said, "I don't really care what we see. Just spending more time with you and Dad is all I want. You pick the movie and where you want us to go."

Nat nodded in agreement. She always tried to please her big brother.

"Come on. Let's go ask Dad," TJ motioned to his sister.

For the first time in years, Vern Cockrell went to see a show with his kids. It was the Sunday matinee, and Natalie loved everything: the picture, the popcorn, the Pepsi, and the presence of her beloved brother and dad made the afternoon perfect. The last movie Vern had gone to see with them was Shrek 2. TJ was seven and Nat was four.

Afterwards, TJ and Nat spent a boisterous, but very happy hour discussing the movie's plot and the actors. The film, a YA flick, featured several big stars and had been well reviewed.

The departure day for their Disney World vacation, Monday, arrived sunny and without a cloud in the sparkling blue March sky. Their flight left at 11:05 a.m. from Knoxville to Orlando. Dad was in his usual first-class accommodations. Nat and TJ were perfectly content to be seated together in coach, where they could converse and cut-up without the listening ears of their father.

The airplane ride turned out to be highly eventful for Vern. The flight attendant in first-class and Vern clicked almost the moment he sat down. Helen was home-based in Knoxville. She was the daughter of a Baptist minister. She had been married for sixteen years to a pilot from the same airline company. "My husband was an athlete in college and he really kept in good shape for his age," she confided.

Yet, despite his outward fitness, he had died unexpectedly of a massive heart attack not quite ten months ago. Helen had been left with a daughter aged fourteen and a half, and a son aged twelve about to turn thirteen.

Vern Cockrell was anything except a ladies' man. Before meeting Anne, he had tended to be reserved and a bit shy around women. But the compatibility and chemistry between him and Helen was undeniably strong, almost palpable, at first sight. The many casual, innocent, and unintended touches and body brushes between passenger and flight attendant during the multi-hour trip ignited a flame in each that neither one had experienced for quite some time.

Helen kept finding opportunities to come back to Vern's immediate area and wait on him and the elderly lady sitting next to his window.

"Vern, sir," she smiled as she put her hand on his shoulder and leaned closer in, "would you like a refill on your drink?" Whatever perfume she was wearing, the professor thought she smelled wonderful and she looked utterly ravishing to his eyes. Helen had a slender well-toned body, an ample bosom, lovely black hair, a delightful sense of humor, and a wonderful personality. Everything about her intrigued him.

"And ma'am, how about you? Do you want another club soda?" she politely asked the older woman who was watching the frequent exchanges between the two younger people with keen interest and a sharp eye.

Throughout the flight, Vern and Helen continued a running conversation, each time learning more about the other's situation, family, and background.

"Although I did date and marry an athlete right out of college, I've always admired brainy men," she winked at him. "Did you know that high intelligence is normally associated with a high level of sensitivity, passion, communication, and personality?" She smiled playfully.

At the end of the flight, they exchanged cell phone numbers and personal emails. "I'll call you as soon as I get back from vacation with my kids," he promised Helen as she took his last empty drink glass near the end of the flight.

"Please do, Vern." She gripped his hand with intense meaning. "I look forward to seeing you again." There was a world of sweetness concentrated in her goodbye.

She waved to him then turned to answer another passenger's question about flight connections to Miami.

Back in coach TJ and Nat had been having a grand time during the flight: talking, whispering, laughing, plotting, planning, enjoying their snacks and drinks, and playing card games and puzzles. It had been over a month since TJ had last seen his sister. They had a lot of catching up to do.

As the plane began its descent, TJ obediently locked his tray and put his seat in the upright position. He sat up straight and folded his arms. He turned and grinned with mounting excitement at Nat as the plane's wheels hit the ground. "I can barely wait!" he exclaimed.

"Neither can I!" replied his sister.

"What ride do you want to start with?"

"I don't care. You decide."

"How about Space Mountain?" he said. The first time they'd gone to Disney World, Natalie had just turned one. She wasn't old enough at the time to know anything. So, whatever rides and attractions Nat wanted to do on this trip was fine with him.

TJ's mind filled with happy thoughts about Samantha, Natalie, Disney World, his dad, and visions of future exploits. So many positive changes had occurred as a result of his amazing trip into the past. He had a newfound confidence and ability to face the most difficult challenges and even tougher foes. He never would have survived the Al-Qaida Robbers in his Knoxville home if he hadn't first faced the Hansen Gang on the trail and in the woods. For the first time, he was not afraid to go to school. Beating Brent in front of so many had solved his bully problem, once and for all. Also for the first time, he had a real desire to study, learn, and apply himself. His grades were the best he'd ever earned. Like his Dad, he now had a real appreciation for history.

And Nat and he were together for spring break. Mom would never have let Natalie join him and Dad on vacation if it weren't for his fight with the two robbers. Normally cool and composed, his Mother had been petrified at the news. She had planned a big ski trip to Colorado with her new boyfriend and her daughter, but when she heard the story of TJ's battle, she put aside her anger with her ex-husband to allow Natalie to go to Disney World instead.

He'd had his first true romance with Sarah Robertson. And, in a very real and tangible way, he and Sarah were together again, in the beautiful person of Samantha. Yet he wouldn't have had the confidence to approach Sam had it not been for his adventure.

Yes, so many good things had happened to him that TJ just knew he would be going on another quest. He didn't know exactly when or where he would be traveling next, but he did know that his wild frontier adventure was only the first of many.

His mind fantasized about all the dangerous and exotic times and places he had learned about in history. The more he thought about it, the more his anticipation grew.

He promised himself. *This is just the beginning. Green book, I'm ready to go again whenever you are.*

TJ smiled.

~The End~

ABOUT THE AUTHOR

Born in Tennessee to a military family, Jack King crisscrossed the country multiple times growing up. After obtaining graduate degrees in both business and history, he began a successful career in sales and marketing working for Fortune 500, mid-sized, and start-up firms along the way. Mr. King is currently at work on the 2nd volume in the "Time Rider" series, "Time Rider - Red Attack", as well as a sequel to his historical fiction novel, "Quest for the Middle Kingdom - Tribulation".

CPSIA information can be obtained
at www.ICGtesting.com
Printed in the USA
FSOW01n1523090415
6240FS